The
Burning
Son

TH LEATHERMAN

The Burning Son by TH Leatherman

Copyright © 2016 by TH Leatherman

This is a work of fiction. Names, characters, businesses, places, events and incidents are either the products of the author's imagination or used in a fictitious manner. Any resemblance to actual persons, living or dead, or actual events is purely coincidental.

Published by Fivefold Publishing LLC, PO Box 586, Firestone, CO 80520.

Cover Artwork: Licarto

ISBN: 0-9983002-2-5
ISBN-13: 978-0-9983002-2-1

ACKNOWLEDGMENTS

There are so many people who helped me complete this book, it would be impossible to list them all here. That said, I'd like to thank my wife and boys. Your support made all the difference. Sue, Mark, Chad, Matthew, Bob, Jen, and the other members of TCCG, thank you for listening as much as you taught. Jess, thanks for editing services second to none. The fine volunteers of RMFW, thanks for your years of support and being the best motley group of writers a guy could hope to know.

CONTENTS

There is no avoiding war; it can only be postponed to the advantage of others.

-Niccolo Machiavelli

CHAPTER 1: OVER YALE

Flying over office buildings and cube farms, I wondered if fasteel and plasticrete construction was mandatory or just cost-effective. Downtown had spires, buttresses, curves, and anti-gravity sculptures. Every building a piece of art. This section was less inspired. Every building was the same three to seven story rectangle.

I gritted my teeth as I checked the chrono. We were late. If we didn't make the rendezvous on time, they might leave with the cargo. The sun had yet to come up over Yale's horizon, but I could see the soft, blue-green light. The nights in this part of the planet lasted only six hours during this part of the year. The city was in a blackout, so I was flying my YT60 light transport by instruments. Like many of the craft made on Yale, it was poetry in motion. Stubbed nose with short wings, it looked more like an unearthly sparrow than a cargo hauler.

A code of a dozen musical notes played over the comm. Translated it meant that the Erethizon were hitting the shield above my area. I touched the side of my flight goggles and my heads-up display flipped back to night vision. Everything turned soft green. Decreasing my altitude, I flew down the dark street. My breath quickened as flagpoles and signposts seemed to reach out to grab me. The AI created my surroundings as fast as it could. A floating walkway appeared. I tapped the controls to dive under it, missing it by centimeters. I could tell where the buildings were, but I was a little less clear on trees and lampposts. Brushing one while going 200 kph would end my day and everyone's around me in a spectacular way. It was dangerous flying, but being spotted by Porcu-bears was worse.

The map I'd reviewed before takeoff showed this district to be laid out in a grid pattern. Mostly. Global positioning showed me coming up on our destination, so I eased up on the throttle. A hovering red arrow showed our destination. "Twenty seconds to LZ."

Behind me, the marines shuffled into position. I brought us to a hover where we needed to be and breathed a sigh of relief. Our contacts were still there.

Eight meters. Five meters. Two. The transport settled to the ground with a bump. I put the systems in ready standby and checked the music coming across the military status channel. The tone and pitch told me all was well. Unlatching my harness, I went aft and entered the cargo bay.

Captain Ted Voorhees got up from the jump seat. The burly, no-nonsense marine grinned at me. "No bumps? No bruises? Mark, you're going to make my men soft. Where do you get off flying like this is some slugging luxury aircar?"

"Sorry, sir. Next time I'll spin us like a top before we set down."

He gave me a hearty 'haw, haw, haw!' "We'll turn you into a box jockey yet!"

I shuddered. "I hope not. I miss my starfighter. Are we ready to do this?"

He grunted in response. "Better be. We slugging need these weapons."

I looked at him out of the corner of my eye as the cargo door opened. The marines clambered out and set up a perimeter, their gauss rifles whining as they cycled. My cargo master, Adrian, followed them out in his heavy-duty exoskeleton. Captain Voorhees started after them, but I put a hand on his shoulder. "Is it that bad, sir?"

He showed his teeth like he was going to growl at me.

I held up my hand. "Sorry Captain. Above my pay grade and none of my business."

His shoulders slumped forward. "No, frag it, you need to know. Other than your candy-ass flying, you're a good officer. Don't say anything in front of the major." He stood up straighter.

"The sluggin' Erethizon blockade is hitting us harder than we let people know. We have plenty of food and machines, but the parts for some of the advanced weapons come from off-planet. We just aren't set up to make it on Yale. We rely on blockade runners like Captain Houston over there. They charge us like a ballroom call girl, but we gotta pay to dance."

He jumped through the cargo door yelling, "Eyes out, marine. It would be just like those sluggin' hedgehogs to sneak up on us while we're dealing." I followed. A blast of ozone and magnapple-scented air greeted me. I loved that smell. The trees grew along the edges of the space we'd landed in. The fruit was a bit tart for my taste, but the flowers smelled like freshly baked apple pie.

The parking lot we'd landed in had the green and red leaved trees on three sides. The large white and pink flowers were easy to pick out even in the half-light of the starlit sky. Captain Houston's ship wasn't there. Instead, she was accompanied by a ground transport. The planetary shield might protect us from orbital bombardment, fighters, and missiles, but it wouldn't keep us from being seen by satellites or drones. Both of our ships in the same place could attract attention. I sniffed. A military transport in a parking lot still looked suspicious.

I admired the lines of my ship for this run. The YT60 light transport was eight meters long and three meters tall. With sleek lines, it handled like a dream and was tougher than a rock ox. It didn't have speed like my starfighter and was limited to planet-side operations, but it made up for it in maneuverability. Fully loaded, she could thread a needle and turn on a credit.

Lightning flashed from a cloudless sky as the Erethizon battered against the planet's shield 120 kilometers above us. No sound, and the light show had gotten boring over the last three years. If they hit it hard enough in one place, they could sneak in a troop transport, missiles, or starfighters. So we'd send up our own fighters, and they could only hit the shield in random spots.

My hand strayed to my pocket and I stroked the coin there. My fingers traced the raised designs on both sides. I could see it in my mind's eye: a blazing sun on one side and my great-grandfather's head on the other. "Please, don't let me screw up, Grandpa."

Ted checked the positions of his marines as he spoke to me. "Where would that pirate, Houston, stash her ship?"

I shrugged. "The mountains west of here have deep valleys. She'd be able to hide a ship easily unless a drone was right overhead, sir."

He grunted and went forward to greet the smugglers as I hung back next to the ship. Captain Voorhees and someone who must've been Houston shook hands. This was my first time on a mission like this. The freighter captain had come down earlier than anticipated. On any other day, this would be Lieutenant Fox's duty, but Fred hadn't been on base and it had fallen to me. While I'm rated to fly almost everything in the Yale arsenal, navigators don't usually have much work to do during a blockade. Flying is a kick though, and there's nothing that says war has to be all death and dying.

Voorhees and Houston spoke before moving to the trailer she'd brought along. The smuggler wore a faded and worn Federation officer's jacket with captain's pips on the shoulders. A couple of the blockade runner's men showed off the merchandise. One wore a tattered flight suit from a military unit I hadn't seen before. The marine in the powered armor was pulling double duty as a cargo handler. His armor had seen better days, but the gently whirring servos sounded well maintained. They were pitched an octave lower than Adrian's, and the two sets of armor hummed pleasantly as they worked together.

Ted approved the shipment and passed a pouch to Houston. She opened it and smiled broadly.

Just then, the tempo of the music from the transport radio changed. Ted looked me in the eyes and jerked his head sideways. I scurried through the transport's door as Voorhees signaled Adrian to start loading the cargo.

I reached the cockpit and heard an old Terra tune, Mozart's "Requiem." My stomach fell through the deck and I broke out in a cold sweat.

A soft boom sounded in the distance. Two more were close enough to shake the ground. The marines took cover in the trees and I yelled out the hatch, "Requiem!"

Voorhees pointed to Adrian. "You heard the man, get your ass moving." Turning to Houston, "Jenna, get out of here. The planet shield just failed.

CHAPTER 2: FLYING THE UNFRIENDLY SKIES

On my monitor, my cargo master carried the last crate through the door. I willed him to go faster. At any moment an Erethizon fighter could spot us. On the ground, we'd die before we knew what happened. Our base would have its own shields. Since Aurora was the capital city of Yale, the sky would soon be crawling with Porcu-bears.

Adrian had just finished locking down the last crate when a screech came from overhead. Over the steady whine of my own engines, I heard Houston's ground transport start. Ted came up behind me.

"That was not one of ours, sir," I told him.

"Punch it, Mark."

I revved the turbines. We lifted off as alarms filled the cockpit. Shoving the throttle, I felt the ship lurch forward. A wave of fire and pavement engulfed us. We rode the shock wave. I fought for control and altitude. Treetops spun as I struggled to keep us flying. Loud whistling filled my ears. Damage readouts confirmed a hull breach aft but my instruments still responded. I put buildings between us and the fighter, offices. This late, no one should get hurt.

The AI identified the fighter as an Erethizon ESF32 and projected it into my heads-up display. Smaller than my craft, and boxier. It was a ship was built for space, so it was a lot faster than mine, but couldn't turn worth crap. I could turn on a credit, but I didn't have any weapons.

Weapons. Hull breach...

I called over the internal comm, "Sir, how are we looking back there?"

"Drafty as hell. We're carrying a sluggin' piece of parking lot. No one hurt."

The ESF32 lined up for another pass at us. I wove a little right and then a lot left. Trees and pavement exploded to my right as the starfighter opened up with its gauss cannon. He passed overhead and I fought for control through the air wake. "How big a hole, sir?"

"About a meter wide and half a meter tall, starboard aft."

Squats! My maneuvering might rip us apart. "Any anti-vehicle weapons back there?"

A marine to the core, Ted must have seen where I was going with this. "Oorah! Can your candy-ass keep us alive?"

"Yale will stop spinning before a Porcu-bear outflies me."

Ted gave the orders. "Lee, unpack that crate. Roddy, clear the deck over here. Move it!"

I saw the ESF32 lining up with us again.

"Evasive maneuvers in thirty ticks."

"Roger."

The starfighter began its attack run. I waited it out, then spun left and up. The fighter must have guessed my direction, but not how far I'd turn. Dirt and grass exploded to my right again.

"Still alive?"

"Bruises," Ted answered. "Call it combat camo. Keep us level for a few ticks?"

"You got it." I sped down a street just off the deck. The ESF32 would have to maneuver to maintain the attack angle.

Something didn't look right. "Aw, squats," I muttered. The ESF32 was gaining altitude, setting up a dive. I needed a way to buy time.

He dove. Again he waited for the best shot. I pulled up and right and the pavement to the left exploded as the gauss cannon ate the street we'd been on. The world became flame. Alarms screamed. Then we were through, my canopy shattered on the left, the smell of burnt circuit boards filling the cabin. My helmet had protected me from most of the flash, but everything looked blue.

Ted yelled, "What the hell?"

"He got tired of playing and fired a missile. We're out of time, sir."

"Five count."

The threat monitor kept cutting in and out. The ESF32 was lining up again.

"Three. Two. One."

I swung the tail of the transport right so that we were perpendicular to where I thought the starfighter should be. The display was dead. Flame and smoke poured into the cockpit.

CHAPTER 3: BACK TO BASE-ICS

"Ted?!"

"Sorry, Mark. Backwash from the IMPAS."

I gave the transport some lift and we rose out of the cloud. A fireball the size of an ESF32 fell to the ground. "Great shot!"

Without the immediate threat of death by gauss cannon, I turned northwest. William Sheppard was that way, our base. We used dead reckoning. The instruments were on their last legs, ready for recycling. Night vision was gone, but the sun was coming up and I'd grown up near here. For some reason, I'd been assigned close to home. My father might have had something to do with that...

***

Earlier

"Lt. Martin, sir?"

The boy in olive green stood at attention and saluted. His cadet uniform was a little too big for him, and that along with his peach fuzz mustache made him look absurdly young. I gave him a smile. "Yes, Mr. Bergman?"

He looked down at the standard issue tablet in his hands. "I know you're on your way to the flight line sir, but there's a call for you on SC1."

"Thanks, cadet. Dismissed."

Twenty-six standard years isn't old, but the cadets seemed younger every year. It's not the days, it's the light years. I turned left and made my way through the gray passages.

I entered the comm center. A harried ensign was hunching over the main board, listening to something and typing every couple of seconds. Five holo-screens and a half dozen communication consoles surrounded him on three sides. Letters and pictures danced in the air as he moved them. "Yes, sir. Yes, sir. Yes, sir." He noticed me and pointed to a secure booth across the room. Taking an image in one hand he turned it to face me. I studied the musical notes.

At the booth, I whistled to enter and put on the headset. "Hey, Dad. Love you, but I need to be wheels up in fifteen minutes. What do you need?"

A bass laugh answered me. "How did you know it was me?"

I imagined him shaking from a full body guffaw. "I'm a junior officer. If I get a call on Command Line One, it's got to be you."

"Greg wouldn't give you a call?" he asked with mock indignation.

"Admiral Barnes wouldn't use it for personal business."

"Ha! I suppose not. Have you spoken to your sister? I've tried calling her, but the hospital says she's in surgery. I can't leave a message. She wouldn't get it until tomorrow. I need you two to drop by my house as soon as you can."

I pinched the bridge of my nose. "The Porcu-bears are really active above the shield, Dad. The whole base is on lockdown, probably will be for the next couple days."

"Oh, I know," he said, like you might say 'the sun's out.' "I've cleared it with Greg. Come over after your mission."

My dad, Senator Martin, pulling strings to see me? "Right... I'll be over as soon as I'm free. About 0400."

"Four in the morning. Got it. I'll send Avery to pick up Sophie."

Why would he send his chief of staff to pick up my sister? "Okay, Dad. I'll see you soon."

***

I kept our speed down to lower the stress on the airframe. The fact that we were still flying was a minor miracle. The radio still worked, so I pinged the base. No response. They must have been keeping radio silence. The emergency channel was static. The night sky was punctuated with booms, flashes, and fireballs, but they weren't close, so I concentrated on flying.

Forty minutes later we made our approach to the base. It should have been in blackout, but there were lights scattered everywhere. Call me slow, but it took a minute before the sinking feeling set in.

CHAPTER 4: IT FALLS APART

"Sir, you better get up here."

Voorhees bounded up the ladder behind me as I brought us to a hover. "What have you got for me, Mark?"

I pointed out the cracked viewport. He grasped the situation faster than I. There was nothing left of the William Sheppard. It had been obliterated from orbit. Nothing remained but the small fires flickering on the edge of the crater.

Voorhees' shoulders sagged. To his credit, he recovered fast.

"Next nearest base," he growled.

"Susan Brown, sir," I answered. "Three hours at top speed, which we can't muster."

"Does the sluggin' radio work?"

"Yes, sir. Nothing on command channels."

The emergency channel crackled to life when I flipped through them for his benefit. Maurice Ravel, "Concerto in G."

Ted shook his head. "Well, that's it."

Numb with grief before, now I didn't know what to feel. In an hour we'd gone from stalemate to total defeat. What were we going to do now? Hole up in the mountains, go guerilla?

"How?" I asked.

"If it were me, I'd have found a way to sabotage the shield and bomb the bases from orbit at the same time." He sighed heavily. "How about a small town in the mountains? Something with a mine nearby?"

It took me a few seconds. "Titan, sir. Sixty klicks. Its titanium deposits played out twenty years ago. It's a ghost town."

"Take us there. At least we'll have plenty of party favors."

I swung the transport west and Ted shared the bad news.

Surveying the systems, I saw navigation, radar, and lidar were all out. The radio worked at least, and the engines were running but the controls were spongy when turning right. We still had two-thirds of a tank of fuel. Hydraulic pressure, which had been creeping steadily upwards, showed no signs of dropping. Checking it now, I closed my eyes and shook my head. We couldn't catch a break.

"Sir, we may not be able to make the mountains."

Voorhees climbed up behind me. "Battle damage?"

"Yes, sir. See that?" I pointed to the hydraulic pressure gauge.

"Yeah."

"It should read about sixty."

He scratched his chin. "How bad is 130?"

A whine in the port engine built in volume. "Bad, sir. Better strap in."

Voorhees jumped down and I took in the landmarks. We'd made it about halfway from the base to the mountains and were now just above one of the nicer sections of town. My sister lived nearby.

The whine built in pitch until it hurt my ears. I glanced at the gauge in time to see it peg in the red. The whine stopped with a loud "thunk." The pressure dropped to twenty and something red and oily splashed against the armored glass on the left side of the canopy.

The YT60 yawed to port. A supermarket. Three blocks away. It was as good a landing pad as any.

I fought to keep the craft in the air. Not working. Losing altitude. The landing gear—was there enough pressure to get it down? The left side didn't extend. The transport swung to port as the starboard engine overpowered its busted partner. I applied lift, trying to keep us upright. Toggling the landing gear didn't work. The parking lot came into view.

Fighting my efforts to keep us level, the YT60 kept tilting. In my head, I could see the transport flip over and crush everyone on board. The market came into view and people scattered, but some were wide-eyed and frozen in place. "Move, you idiots!" I screamed as if they could hear me. We were about to fall out of the sky and squash half a dozen people..

CHAPTER 5: SOPHIE

Something must have clicked, because they scattered like someone fired a shot. I reduced the power, but all the lights went out and the engines seized. There was a fraction of a second of quiet. "Oh, squaaaaaats!" We fell the last two meters and landed with a sickening crunch, settling at an angle.

I unbuckled and went aft. Adrian climbed over the crates in his exoskeleton, shooing away the marines fighting to open the hatch. The cargo master didn't so much open the door as tear it off its hinges.

Outside, two of the marines were yelling at the top of their lungs. Ted hadn't been kidding: there really was a half meter section of asphalt lodged in the tail. Adrian gave me a salute and a goofy grin.

I returned it. "Thanks, Chief."

A large group of people gaped at us, armfuls of groceries forgotten. They didn't linger long, but scurried to aircars and groundcars alike. Quite a crowd for the middle of the night. Clearly the bad news about the planet shield had reached them.

I surveyed what was left of the YT60. Every surface was scorched. Dents and holes covered the armor. The large gash in the tail looked like someone had thrown a rock through tissue paper. The canopy was shattered, but the engine on the near side looked okay. "Any landing you can walk away from..."

Voorhees clapped me on the shoulder. "Thanks for saving our bacon."

"You asked for the best. What's the plan, sir?"

The marine looked around. "I'm going to commandeer a tractor and get this sluggin' load up the mountain."

I bit my lower lip. "Sir, my sister and dad live nearby."

His brows furrowed like he wanted to argue with me, then relaxed. "And you want to make sure they're ok, right?" I nodded. "Go on. We're not flying anywhere. If you think you can get them to join us, then by all means."

"Dad will come. Not so sure about Sophie. She lives about a klick from here. I'll be able to borrow her aircar."

The edges of his lips twitched. "Then we won't wait for you. See you in Titan, your Highness."

It had been the big joke on base. Two generations ago my grandfather had been the king. Back before Yale had become a republic. I ignored the jibe and gave him a crisp salute. "I'll meet you there."

***

It was a brisk jog to my sister's house and dumb luck that the transport had fallen apart where it did.

The sky lightened to a pale purple. The lawns I passed were perfectly manicured and speckled with small orange flowers. Magnapple trees lined the streets. I'd better enjoy them. They didn't grow in Titan.

Sophie was smart. Really smart. Like me, she cherished our family's long heritage of public service and she had a big heart, so it didn't surprise any of us that she chose to become a doctor. She'd completed her surgery residency last year and was hired on at Aurora General soon after.

With the invasion underway, she must've already been called to the hospital. I hoped I could catch her before she left. Erethizon occupation tactics were simple: destroy the military, appoint a governor, and use existing leaders to form a new government, one that would serve the church above all else. Imprisoning families to keep the politicians in line was common.

It took twenty minutes to jog to Sophie's. The sky lit up several times in the direction of downtown. The capital. Sometimes the flashes were accompanied by far-off booms.

Running up the driveway, I circled around back and knocked on the kitchen door.

A yelp came from inside. Sophie pulled the shade aside. Smiling, I waved. She glared at me and opened the door.

"Marky, you scared the hell out of me. What are you doing here?"

"We gotta go, Soph. The shield's fallen."

She motioned me inside. "I know. The hospital called. They need everyone. Thirty seconds and you would have missed me."

I shook my head. "You can't go to the hospital."

"The hell I can't! People are dying!"

"Sophie, they're going to find Dad and use you and me to get to him. We need to be gone before that happens. There's a squad of marines waiting for us in Titan."

"I'm a doctor. I'm going to the hospital."

"You go there, and you might as well be walking into a prison cell. They expect you to be at the hospital. Going there won't help anyone."

Sophie's cheeks reddened as she glared at me. I clenched my jaw so tight my teeth ached. She had to realize I was right.

Her eyes softened at last. "Okay. How did you get here?"

"Crash landed about a kilometer from here."

Her eyes widened as she looked me over. "Are you hurt?"

"I'm fine, Soph. The other guy isn't. Can we use your car? I want to get to Dad before they do."

She walked toward the dining room. "I'll run upstairs and get a few things together. Check to see if anything in the guestroom closet will fit you."

I followed her. "We don't have time to..."

"You need a change of clothes, something that doesn't scream 'fighter pilot.'" She started up the stairs. "My ex left some things behind in the guestroom. You're about the same size as him. See if any of it will fit you."

She was right. I pulled on a fresh pair of slacks and a button-down shirt. The shoes were too small though, so my flight boots would have to do. In five minutes, I was ready to go. I decided to keep my flight jacket. It was smart clothing, so I instructed it to remove my insignia and change from blue to brown.

Sophie was waiting for me with a medkit and a backpack slung over one shoulder. "Times a'wasting. Let's go get Dad. Do you have the coin?"

"Yes. It's in my pocket."

The Lunis 400XE was in the garage. Shiny and black with elegant lines, the aircar was the very picture of power and grace. Its AI recognized me and opened automatically as I approached. The aircar started with a touch and purred quietly. Edging out of the garage, I alerted the traffic control system that we were driving manually. Soon we accelerated up and away.

As we headed south to Dad's, Sophie used the car's comm to call him. An automated response came back: "We are sorry. All lines are busy at this time."

Soph bit her lower lip, her eyes shiny.

"Try a text," I suggested.

That seemed to go through and we rode the rest of the way in silence, waiting for a response. Well, not silence, exactly. The flight control AI kept warning me that I was driving too fast.

From that altitude, we could see more of the fighting going on around the city. There were pockets of resistance here and there. Strangely, most of the people in groundcars and aircars were following the traffic rules. They were letting the AIs do the driving. Only a few were speeding outside the traffic pattern, though not as many as I would have expected.

When we got close I merged with the local traffic. Circling the block, my dad's mansion came into view.

The front yard was lit up, an Erethizon troop transport sitting on the lawn. Four squads of aircar-sized spiky bears patrolled the estate, plasma rifles at the ready. Lights glinted off their shiny black plasticene armor.

CHAPTER 6: MAN DOWN

A Porcu-bear trooper looked right at me as we passed over the street. Sweat trickled down the small of my back. Over the low wall, I could see that his face shield was up, revealing his dark black eyes. He shifted the grip on his rifle and his lips pulled back in a silent snarl. I held my breath. His gaze was unflinching. Just before we finished our pass he turned back to his patrol of the grounds.

Releasing the breath I'd been holding, I brought us around for another pass. This time our aircar didn't attract attention. Sophie gasped as our father was escorted out of the house. He was surrounded by towering Erethizon guards, his head bowed and his hands behind his back. The guards shoved him into the transport as we turned the corner.

Sophie gripped my arm. Her voice was firm. "We save him."

"We can't."

She gritted her teeth. "What do you mean we can't? That's our father. I heard about survival training. Are you saying a few Hedgehogs will stop you when a dozen instructors couldn't?"

How had she heard about that? "Sophie, that's twenty-four Porcu-bear shock troops. They're expecting trouble. It's not the same thing."

The troop transport rose above the trees. It didn't linger, but headed south.

"Marky. They're getting away."

I punched the dash and she jumped in her seat.

Turning the aircar, I followed at a discreet distance. It didn't take long to figure out where they were going. Ten minutes later, I brought the aircar to a hover. The troop transport kept going.

Beside me, Sophie's jaw dropped. I didn't blame her. Floating over the capital building was a long, warty grey block the size of three skyscrapers. Gun emplacements bristled from everywhere. It was easily as big as seven city blocks. We watched as the transport disappeared inside.

"By Astra's song, what is that?"

"An Erethizon battleship. Still think we can take them?"

She shook her head.

"We're not giving up, Soph. We're waiting for the right time. They'll send him to a re-education camp somewhere, probably off-planet. We'll find out where he's being held and rescue him."

I turned northwest. Sophie glared daggers at the vessel until it was out of sight. Turning off the aircar's running lights, I exited city traffic. This valley would take us to Titan. I could just make out the unlit strip of road by moonlight, a creek running alongside it glinting in the light. The aircar's short-range radar kept us from flying into a mountain despite the darkness.

"Squats."

Sophie chewed her lip. "What?"

"The fuel light just came on. Car, where is the nearest fuel station?"

The aircar AI's pleasant female voice responded, "The nearest fuel station is five kilometers from your present location." A map appeared on the center screen.

When we rounded the bend the lights for a twenty-seven hour automated fuel station came into view. A tractor-trailer was parked a little off to the side. Not unusual; truckers often stopped at fuel stations for the night.

Landing, I started the hydrogen pump. I'd just thumbed the authorization when an ashen-faced woman ran up to us, her hands dripped with blood.

Reaching for my sidearm, I realized it was two meters away in the aircar.

She speared me with her gaze. "The nearest hospital, where is it?"

It struck me then. I had seen her before. "Captain Houston? Is one of your men injured?"

She paused and eyed me suspiciously. "Don't reckon I know

you, son."

"Lieutenant Martin, ma'am. I piloted Voorhees' transport."

Relief flooded her face. "Is it here? My third mate ain't good. Shrapnel from that hedgehog missile. I thought we could get him to the *Leo*, but I don't think he'll make it."

I glanced behind me. Sophie grabbed her kit. "I don't have a hospital, but how about a doctor?"

She saw the medical case. "Thank God. Right this way, doc."

She sprinted to the tractor. The man in the flight suit from our meeting earlier that night was unconscious on the ground, the marine next to him.

Sophie knelt and checked him out. "What's his name?"

"Dan," said the wide-eyed marine by his side. The armored soldier's hands were shaking. His breath came in quick gasps.

Sophie put a monitor on Dan's left arm. He didn't stir so much as an eyelid. "Well Dan, I see you need to learn how to duck. Not to worry though. I'll put you back together and you'll have plenty more chances to learn." Her eyes and hands were in constant motion, assessing the wounds and checking his vital signs.

She looked at the marine across from her. "What's your name, soldier?"

"Jay, ma'am."

"Jay, Dan has a nicked carotid artery in his neck. His brain has been starved for blood. Can you get me some water? We need to reconstitute some plasma from my kit before he suffers brain damage." Her voice was calm and confident.

His breath slowed. "Yes, ma'am," he said as he stood and ran to the tractor.

I pulled Captain Houston out of the way. She moved reluctantly, her eyes fixed on Dan.

She finally turned her attention to me. "Ted?"

"Voorhees and his men are fine," I assured her.

"No weapons on your transport. What'd ya do? Throw rocks?"

"A good thing we picked up a few things that go boom."

She knitted her brows. "No kidding?"

"Ted got the IMPAS unpacked and we shot it down through a breach in our hull."

Captain Houston shook her head in disbelief. "You took out a hedgehog starfighter with an unarmed light transport."

"I dodged. Ted's marines shot it down."

Sophie approached us. "Captain, what's your blood type?"

"A positive."

She shook her head. "Then I've got good news, and bad news." She didn't wait, but pressed on, "The good news is that I've stopped the bleeding. The bad news is that he's lost a lot of blood. I've given him all the artificial blood I have with me, but no one here has a compatible blood type. He needs a medical facility and he won't make it back to town."

Houston stared up the valley and grimaced. After a moment, she returned her attention to Sophie. "He's also my ship's navigator. I need him to get out of here. If we can get him to a facility, can we get him back on his feet?"

My sister shook her head. "He'll be out for a few days at the very least."

"I reckon I can do what needs doin' in a pinch. My ship is twenty klicks from here. It has a medical bay, but no doctor."

"Captain," I said, "I can help with the calculations."

Sophie nodded. "First things first. My car will get us there faster. How attached are you to that tractor?"

"Borrowed. Is your car rated to carry five?"

Sophie turned to me with a questioning look.

I nodded at the Captain. "It's got power and then some. What it doesn't have is space. Soph, you, your patient, and this guy are in the back. Captain, you're in front with me. You can give me directions. Let's move!"

Houston and I made a seat with our arms and carried Dan to the aircar. Blood soaked into my shirt and pants. My sister opened the door and we eased him in, the tan leather of the aircar's interior staining red. Sophie slid in and held his head in her lap. Dan looked drawn about the eyes and mouth, and more than a little gray. Jay stowed his powered armor in the trunk—he wouldn't fit in the back seat with it on.

I wasted no time getting us into the air and called over my shoulder, "Soph..."

"I'm not leaving my patient. Nothing you say will make me."

I said a silent prayer for Ted and his marines. He didn't need a pilot for the kind of raids he'd be conducting, but I needed to find some way to send him a message. At best this would be a delay in meeting him. At worst?

I pushed that out of my mind. Concentrate on what's in front of me. First save Dan's life. Find a way to save Dad later.

Houston was as good as her word, and in a little over eighteen kilometers we arrived in a secluded valley off of what passed for the main road.

It wasn't a big ship for a star freighter. Matte black, about eighty meters long and twenty meters wide, it looked like a light in-system ship with a lot of extra equipment tacked on.

I flew over it to get a better entry into the docking bay. On the screen, my altitude jumped from forty meters above ground to 2000 meters above ground. "What the..."

Houston chuckled. "Radiation absorbing paint over radiation shielding."

She spoke into the comm and the docking bay doors opened. I lined us up and eased us in, bringing us down gently right next to a pair of older model Galvin 439 light fighters. Three people in powered armor with assault rifles and an officer in first mate tabs stood nearby. The rank insignia resembled Terran Confederacy rank, but wasn't the same. Probably system defense of some member planet. All of the armor had welded patches in mismatched colors. Houston jumped out the passenger door and a marine opened the rear door.

"Welcome back, ma'am," the young officer said.

"Thanks, Sara." The captain turned to one of the people with rifles. "Bev, help Jay get Dan to the infirmary. This is Doctor Martin. Give her whatever she needs." She caught my eyes with hers. "You and I need to talk. Follow me."

I didn't argue and followed her out of the docking bay, up a ladder, then forward to her small office. Sitting behind the desk, she motioned for me to take a seat. Behind her, a 3D holographic image of the ship rotated slowly.

She was an attractive middle-aged woman with piercing blue eyes. Her laugh lines crinkled as she studied me. We sized each other up for a couple of moments before she spoke.

"What were you doing when you happened across us?"

I shrugged. "Hiding out. The Porcu-bears got our bases from orbit. Voorhees and I were going to a mine to set up a guerrilla base."

She gestured at my clothing. "Why not just blend in?"

How much should I share? She was a smuggler. Where did her loyalties lie? "Playing possum doesn't sit well with me. If we can't have a stand-up fight, I'll settle for hiding and hitting soft targets."

"Have you always been a box jockey?" she asked.

I glanced down at my hands. "I'm a navigator. With the war on, they need more pilots. Flying cargo is a side gig."

Her eyes narrowed. "Anything wrong with cargo?"

"No." I shrugged, "If it floats, flies, or hovers, I've got the skills to make the kills. I'm not too proud to play support. Being a navigator was a great way to see the galaxy until the Porcu-bears took away the sky."

She sighed and nodded. "The Erethizon are taking out the independent planets like Yale one at a time. Now that it's fallen, that leaves Aspen, Sagitta, Freya, and Norma. Once those are gobbled up they'll stop and build up their forces to take on the Terran Confederation itself, or else the Muscat Empire."

That didn't sound right. "What happened to New Cancun and Butcher's World?"

"Sabotage on Butcher's World. The sneaky hedgehogs landed a dozen assault groups and took out the shield nodes. As a resort world, New Cancun was lightly populated and had nothing of military value. The Erethizon made an ultimatum. It was refused. So they opened a hole and dropped in enough XB20 to sterilize the planet for a millennium."

"Biological weapons. Dear God." My stomach turned over and I swallowed hard at the thought of millions of people dying as the virus ate them from the inside out. Plants would have turned to sludge. A millennium was being generous.

"How could the Theocracy justify that? The Erethizon want to convert the galaxy, not kill it."

Houston shrugged, "'*Groupa tan hounga.*' Join or die. Make an example of the little guy to keep the others in line. The high priests don't care about lives, only power."

"There have to be resistance cells. We're talking trillions of sentient beings."

She nodded sagely. "State-run news networks and media. Inside the Theocracy, every planet embraces the one true light. The hedgehogs land and overthrow the corrupt governments." Waving her hands with a flourish, "The people rejoice to be free to follow the path. Or so their story goes. If there is resistance, we'll never know about it."

It sickened me to hear it, but she was right.

She looked at me with an expression I couldn't read. "The question is, what do you want to do about it?"

Anger boiled behind my eyes and in my heart. "I want to hit them where it hurts."

She waved her hand dismissively. "They're the strongest military in known space. The Terrans are building up, but they won't have enough tonnage before it's their turn to fall. The Muscat? Better weapons and armor, but it's a numbers game. There aren't enough of them. The Dru?" she snorted, "Spies and information brokers. No military. Telepathy kept their world at peace for five thousand years. Armed conflict was completely unknown to them until recently."

I spread my hands and indicated the ship. "So where does that leave you? Smuggling weapons?"

"Not always," she admitted. "Medical supplies, food, intelligence. We aren't picky. We're not the tip of the sword, but we keep the others sharp."

Ted's comments about how much we had to pay came back to me. "And turning a profit."

The captain nodded. "We take risks and we get paid for it. I'm not going to apologize for that. If we get caught, we'll be lucky if they kill us. We don't start wars or supply weapons to both sides."

Biting my lip, "Now you're thinking that having a replacement navigator and a doctor on board will help."

Houston smirked. "It occurs to me that we have an opportunity to help each other. You need a place to lie low while you make life difficult for the hedgehogs. I happen to have a temporary need for a navigator and a doctor."

Ted and I had served together for a long time. Leaving him behind didn't feel right. He could also use a doctor. That said, Sophie was a high-value target. Just being there would put all of them at risk. The point was moot, though. She wouldn't leave Dan until he was stable.

Regarding Houston levelly, I responded. "I'm interested, but I need to speak with my sister and find a way to send a message to my unit."

The Captain nodded her understanding. "I expected as much." She held out a personal AI. It was a forearm clip-on.

"That's an expensive piece of hardware," I said. Staring at the device in her hand, I had to wonder if she was serious.

She gave me a one-shouldered shrug. "Call it a gesture of goodwill. It's loaded with guest access codes," she said, handing me the cuff. "It doesn't have secure access, but it will help you get around. Pin this badge to your collar. The crew will know you're a guest. I don't want to rush you, but the dizzy dancin' out there won't last long. You need to go ashore or claim a bunk inside of an hour." She continued as I took the hardware, "You can use the AI to message me and use its map to keep from getting lost. I'll be on the bridge getting us ready to go. I'll scare up a message drone, but how you'll get it to Ted is up to you."

Clipping the badge to my collar, "Thank you, Captain. I'll let you know as soon as I can."

She reached across to me. "You're either going to be one of my officers or the guy that saved Dan's life. Either way, call me Jenna."

I took her hand in mine. "I'm Mark. Good to meet you Jenna."

She gave me a tight smile as I left the cabin.

I put on the cuff. "Show me the ship's schematic," I told it. A holographic image of the freighter popped into being in front of me. I saw the ship's name at the top, the *Leonard Fox*.

"Show me how to get to medical." The image showed a blinking yellow path through the ship.

Everyone I passed on the way to medical wore something different. Some wore ship suits, others wore shirts and pants. Most of them were clean, so there must be a laundry unit on board somewhere. I almost tripped over a pack of maintenance rats. The genetically engineered creatures were widely used to clean ship passages and the crew's head. Judging from the state of the deck, the batch living aboard the ship needed some adjustment.

The medical suite was well-lit. A bay window looked into the surgical suite. Sophie was in a bloody blue smock hunched over her patient, Jay assisting.

Her eyebrows knitted together in concentration. There were dark circles under her eyes. During the war I'd learned a little emergency medicine. From what I could see on the monitors, it didn't look good for Dan. I watched in fascination as Sophie cut with a laser scalpel, injected a bright orange tube of medi-nano, and pulled a long shard of shrapnel from his chest. Tubes from the table pumped artificial blood to replace what he'd lost.

"Come on Dan," I said, "you can pull through. You've got the best doctor on the planet putting you back together."

"She seems competent."

I turned to find the first mate standing behind me. Her nametag read 'Chew.' I remembered her as the young officer with the first mate's insignia from the docking bay.

Holding out my hand, "I'm Mark."

She looked at my hand like it was diseased, and didn't take it. "Sara Chew, First Mate."

Cold. I chalked it up to concern for her crew and turned back to the window. The surgical suite was stocked with the kind of state-of-the-art medical equipment you'd expect to see in a planet-side clinic. "Your medical bay is well stocked," I commented.

Sara nodded. "Our work is dangerous. It pays to be prepared. Our last doctor was poached by the *Horatio*. They offered him another share and a trained nurse."

Pay. I hadn't thought about that. If we stayed, we'd have to work that out with the captain. Standard contract for an officer on a merchant freighter was a modest salary plus a double share of the profits.

Bev walked into the medical suite and handed me a metal ball about the size of a cup of coffee. "Captain's compliments, sir. I'm to wait here while you compose your message."

"Thanks." I spent a couple of minutes providing the drone with Ted's description and his likely route to Titan. I decided to tell him that we'd secured transport off-planet. Given the situation, I didn't expect Sophie to argue with me. This would keep us out of Erethizon hands and allow us to mount a rescue operation when feasible. I would conclude with a promise of intelligence and resources.

Message composed in my head, I translated it into song and whistled it to the drone.

Bev raised her eyebrows at me in an unspoken question.

"Genetic quirk of Yale. Almost everyone can sing and hear in perfect pitch. We used it to create a code the Porcu-bears have almost no chance of breaking."

I handed her the message drone.

"Neat trick," she said, and left the medical bay.

My sister was wrapping it up, closing holes and putting away her instruments. It was a grisly mess, but Sara didn't flinch. Her eyes stayed locked on Dan. Sophie shrugged off the smock and pulled off her gloves before stepping through the sterilization field.

Her mouth was a hard line as she spoke. "I've stabilized him. He's going to need an artificial kidney. I'll fabricate one later. His pulse is thready and his BP is lower than I'd like. He's close to renal failure and toxemia is a concern. The medi-nano is repairing the organ damage and the table is filtering blood and keeping it oxygenated. I want to do more, but we need to give his body time to heal."

Sara looked concerned. "What do you mean?"

Sophie gave a worried sigh. "He lost a lot of blood and we had to inject a thrombolytic near the hippocampus. We can keep his body going and repair the nerves and ganglia. After that, his brain should remember how to keep him going. But his memories, experience..." Sophie shook her head. "I won't know until he's awake."

Sara gave no outward sign of her feelings. Her voice was monotone. "Thank you, doctor." She turned and left the room.

In the other room, Jay checked Dan's condition. I spoke over my shoulder to Sophie. "How's your assistant?"

Sophie wagged her head side to side. "Jay is the medical corpsman for the marines on board. He's good with emergency medicine, so he'll do as a nurse in a pinch." She paused. "We can't stay on Yale until Dan's better, can we?"

It was more of a statement than a question. I nodded. "Houston has offered us positions on her ship."

"Good. I don't want to leave Dan. Does she know about Dad?"

I smile slightly. "No. She needs us and we need to not be in prison. Not being where they expect us..." I shrugged.

Sophie frowned, deep in thought. "Well, can't get more unexpected than hooking up with pirates. Then what?"

"We make a plan, come back, and save Dad."

She raised her eyebrows. "Ambitious. I like this strategy. What's the first move?"

I held out my arm to show her the AI cuff. "Take ten minutes to finish installing this AI on my arm. I want it to be able to track my vitals and connect to my thoughts."

She shook her head. "No way."

I gave her a sidelong glance. "Why not?"

"'Cause I want one too, dork."

My sister might be an insufferable smarty-pants, but she's also a crack surgeon. She had the cuff wired to me in no time. Sitting down, I took a few minutes to get to know my new imaginary friend. I heard a ping and some text scrolled past my vision on the holographic display. The words stopped and a prompt appeared, asking which language to use. After I indicated common Terran, it walked me through the set-up.

It took a few moments to go through what the AI could do for me. I stopped after ten minutes. There would be plenty of time to explore the skills later.

Captain Houston was on the bridge, talking into the intercom. "Rowdy, how are we looking?"

An odd growly voice responded, "We can be ready ten minutes from when you give us the word, Captain."

I approached her and waited.

"Mr. Martin, what have you decided?"

"Ma'am, Dr. Martin and I will be happy to join your crew, if the terms are acceptable."

She handed me a tablet with a contract on it. I glanced through it. It didn't have anything devious in the sub-clauses. I made a couple of adjustments in regards to pay and handed it back. She thumbed the contract and handed it back to me to do the same.

"No haggling?" I cocked my head in her direction.

"No." She nodded toward the forward consoles. "Welcome aboard. Please go to the navigation station and familiarize yourself with the controls. Mr. Walashek, please introduce Mr. Martin to the *Leo*."

The helmsman gave me a hairy eyeball. "Are you replacing Dan?"

I lowered my eyes and shook my head. "I can't replace him."

"Well then, we can be friends." He swept his arm over the console. "Let me introduce you to the *Leo*."

We went over the systems. He pointed to the navigation and helm controls. "Do you recognize the system?"

"Yes. It looks like the one I used on a cruiser before the war." Hard to believe that was only three years ago. It felt like several lifetimes.

"Good." He nodded. "Thrusters, here. Navigation, here. Ship's systems, here and here. Let's pull up the drives. I may need to go to the little pirate's room. You'll need to know the basics."

Shaking my head, I said, "This looks odd here. Main engine and thruster controls? You have more than one propulsion system?"

The side of his mouth went up. "Good eye. These are your reaction thrusters. They're for small adjustments and docking. In a star system and on-planet, we use an ion drive."

My eyebrows crawled up my head. "Nice. Fuel isn't a concern then. As long as the reactors are going, so are we."

"You didn't just fall off the magnapple cart, did you? All right, let's see if we can stump you." He pulled up a menu on the last set of drives. "What are you looking at?"

Reviewing the interface, it took me a few minutes to grasp what I was seeing. "Flight controls, but where do we adjust direction. Does the AI do it for us? And this gauge, what does it measure?"

There was a twinkle in his eye. "I'll give you a hint. The pirate alphabet begins with 'aye.'"

"Ha ha. And ends with 'Arrr.'" Then my brain caught up with the conversation. "No way."

He gave me a knowing look, and nodded enthusiastically.

I gaped at him. "You're telling me we have an R-drive?"

"Pretty stellar, huh?"

I'd wondered how the *Leo* had slipped past the Porcu-bear blockade, a dozen ships guarding the warp gate. The answer: it hadn't.

Warp gates allowed near instant travel to anywhere within the network. Almost every system in human-occupied space had a gate.

The *Leo* could use them, but it didn't have to. Fifty GS years ago, a physicist named Jean Claude Ricou found a way to wrap a ship in a gravity bubble. In this pocket universe, the ship could travel faster than light, but not almost instantly like a warp gate. R-drives were rare in human-occupied space, but common in Muscat space.

It all fell into place. The major limitations of an R-drive were time, gravity, and straight-line movement. Any mass in local space would deform the precise gravity field needed.

Wally gave me the rundown on the R-drive and then showed me the interface for the ship's AI.

The captain came over. "What do you think?"

"He knows his stuff, ma'am," Wally answered.

The captain favored me with an amused expression. "Mr. Martin, you seem to have impressed Mr. Walashek. Impress me. Calculate a launch window forty minutes from now. Three in-system jumps and a jump to a set of Galactic Reference System coordinates. They're in the computer under designation TC3. Have you programmed an R-drive jump using GRS numbers?"

"No ma'am, but I understand the concepts. With a little help from the *Leo*'s AI, I can get it done."

The captain's lips twitched. "Good. Have it to me in thirty minutes."

"Where will I find the ship's mass figures? Are the jumps to confuse pursuit?"

She pointed to a folder over my shoulder. "You'll need to add in the mass of you, your sister, and the aircar. The jumps are to hide our trail. Some ships around here might take an unhealthy interest in us."

Twenty-eight minutes later, I had the calculations. The captain reviewed them over my shoulder. "Good, Mr. Martin." She turned to her right. "Ms. Chew, please sound navigation stations. Rig for silent running."

The sound of a bell filled the bridge.

After a couple of moments, Sara reported, "Ma'am, all stations report ready for sail."

"Good. Mr. Walashek, do you have Mr. Martin's numbers?"

Wally grinned from the helm console. "Aye ma'am. They look good."

The Captain gave a slight smile. "Noted. Mr. Walashek, please take us out. Ms. Chew, engage stealth."

"Aye, ma'am!" They said in unison.

I felt a weight in the pit of my stomach as the ship started to lift. It only lasted a moment before the inertial compensator kicked in. I watched on the ship's monitors as the *Leo* rose about two hundred meters straight up.

A wave of nostalgia hit me as the mountain valley shrank below us. We were leaving my home planet. It might be years before I'd be able to rescue my dad. Who knew how long it would take before I   could   come   back?

My reverie was cut short as a sudden impact threw me from my seat.

.

CHAPTER 7: DUE NORTH

Belatedly, the collision alarm sounded.

The captain turned to the tactical station. "Ms. Chew, report!"

"Fighter ma'am! Slammed into us. Engineering reports no serious damage, but stealth is ruined."

The captain swore under her breath. "Mr. Martin, we're going to have to be more creative with our exit. Set a course to follow the terrain and exit at the polar cap."

I heard myself say, "Aye, aye," as I pulled up a map of the planet. I refined for gravitational and magnetic anomalies in which we could hide. It might not be enough, but every trick helped. Entering the new course, I nodded to Wally. He wasted no time in igniting the thrusters. The ship adjusted to the new vector.

The course would take us over a mountain range and through magnetic north. It was the area least likely to have patrols, and it would make us damn hard to spot due to the magnetic interference. I prayed for a minor miracle.

The seconds stretched on. We waited, expecting to be discovered and captured at any second, or perhaps simply death by orbital impacter. At least it would be over before we knew what happened.

The seconds became minutes.

Ten. Fifteen. Twenty.

Cruisers and destroyers crisscrossed the skies. Several times we hid in a valley or hugged a mountain until a Porcu-bear ship passed out of range.

31

Wally followed the course, straight and true, and we were soon over the pole. This was our moment of truth. I'd experienced firsthand that the ship was hard to detect on radar or lidar. Unfortunately, we would be more visible to gravity sensors the further away from the planet we got. Once in open space, we'd be nearly home free.

It might have worked, if there hadn't been two ESF32s in our path.

"We're being hailed." The *Leo*'s AI cut into the tense silence on the bridge.

Captain Houston pursed her lips. Her expression and voice were calm, but her knuckles had turned white with strain. "Where are they, Ms. Chew?"

"Five hundred kilometers to starboard, ma'am."

Captain Houston quirked an eyebrow. "We must have damn near run them over."

"Two fighters, ma'am. We're leaving them in the dust, but not for long. They're powering up." Sara didn't look up. Her gaze was intent on the screens. "They were drifting, powered down. Sneaky of them."

"Wally, give it all she's got." The captain ordered. "Ms. Chew, shields if you please."

"Aye, aye," they answered.

The relative speed indicators jumped as the ion drives engaged. We were picking up speed faster than I'd expected a freighter could. These were fighters though, and they would be on us soon enough.

Sara regarded the captain from the tactical station. "Do you think running will work, ma'am?"

She shrugged. "It might. They've got a lot going on down there. What's one freighter among a planet of resources?"

"I hope you're right, ma'am." She said, shaking her head. After a moment Sara sighed, "They're closing now."

"They're hailing us," the AI announced. "They've ordered us to heave to and prepare to be boarded."

The captain regarded the main system's console. A steady red light gave us something to focus on when addressing the AI. "Did they use their own language?"

"Yes, ma'am."

"Then we didn't hear it."

After a few minutes, the *Leo*'s voice spoke again. "They've asked in common Terran this time. Translation. 'Transport, not known. Stop, there are boards.'"

"If they weren't about to blow us to bits, I'd be half tempted to ask them if there are nails in the boards," the captain mused with a worried half smile. "Let's see how badly they want us. No response, *Leo*. Wally, steady as she goes."

After a few tense minutes, the *Leo* spoke again. "Ma'am, I've intercepted a signal back to the fleet. They're asking for permission to fire on us."

"Thanks, *Leo*. No changes yet. We don't want them to know that we can read their mail."

Turning to the captain, I lifted an eyebrow in question.

She shrugged. "We bought the latest codes."

Whistling softly, I returned my attention to the displays.

"Ma'am, they just..." The AI was interrupted by a klaxon. The ship shuddered.

"Thanks, *Leo*. I got the message. Sara, shields?"

"Down a bit, but holding, ma'am," she answered.

Two more jolts followed. Then the first officer shouted, "Missile separation!"

.

8 CHAPTER NAME

"Those trigger happy sons of farthogs!" The captain swore. "Point defense, Sara."

"Active," she responded. "Tracking. Missile destroyed."

The captain's lips formed a tight line. "Let's try negotiating, but let's be ready for Plan C. Wally, have the R-drive ready to go."

The helmsman frowned. "Ma'am? We're too close to the planet."

"Do it." The captain swiveled left. "*Leo*, open a channel."

"Aye, aye. Channel open," it responded.

"Attention honored escorts," Houston spoke into the mic on the arm of her chair. "We apologize for our rude behavior. Our cargo is fragile and due in Saggita. We thought only of our employers when we lifted off without your permission. Will you accept our deepest regrets?"

A moment later the AI responded. "They're speaking in their own language. It translates as they accept your apology and request we heave-to again."

"Thank you, respectful Erethizon warriors. We beseech your pardon and fear the Great Urson. May we offer you a gift to appease your anger?"

There was no response.

The captain continued. "We're carrying several canisters of Sildian nectar. It is a popular sweetener on Saggita. It's legal there, but not in Erethizon space. We could leave..."

An explosion rocked the ship.

"Slug it!" Houston cursed, "So much for bribery." It was a worthy attempt. Nectar was a potent euphoric to Porcu-bears.

"Weapons free ma'am?" asked Sara from the back of the bridge.

"No." There was a harsh edge in her voice. "Don't piss them off any more than they already are." There was another jolt as the fighters hit us again.

"They're targeting engines," Sara said, stress evident in every word. "Aft shields down to 50 percent. 30 percent."

"Wally, flip us end for end," ordered the captain.

"No good, sir," Sara cursed. "They've got the angle. They're flanking us. 15 percent."

The captain hit the comm panel on the arm of her chair. "Rowdy, they're about to punch through to the engines. Get your repair crews ready."

"Aye, aye," replied the growly voice.

"Shields down," exclaimed the first officer. "Taking damage."

There was another hard jerk to starboard, and then, "Thruster nozzles damaged. Engines offline." Sara reported with resignation.

The captain sighed. "That's it then. *Leo*, signal our surrender."

The AI's voice calmly replied. "Aye, aye, ma'am. Signal received and acknowledged."

Houston looked over her shoulder. "Sara?"

The first officer monitored her screens. "The fighters are positioning themselves to fire grappling lines. They're on our keel and above us amidships, ma'am."

The captain met my eyes.

I felt I should say something. If I'd stayed on-planet with Ted, I wouldn't have delivered myself and Sophie into Erethizon hands. Worse, us on board would make things worse for the crew of the *Leo*. I should have told Captain Houston more of the truth earlier. "Thanks for trying, ma'am." I gave her a half smile.

"Have a little faith, Mr. Martin," she replied.

Faith? They had us. They would be firing tow lines and moving us to the destroyer. It would board us, and then it would only be a matter of time. My sister and I would be the Porcu-bears' guests at a prison planet somewhere—pawns to force my dad into compliance.

"Grappling lines fired. They're arresting our spin," Sara said from the tactical station. "Spin arrested. The fighters are reeling us in. 150 meters. 120 meters. 100 meters."

"Wally, fire the R-drive."

I heard the captain's words, but didn't register what they meant.

"Drive online," responded Wally. "Negative energy shell forming."

Something didn't make sense. You couldn't use an R-drive this close to a planet. The nearby mass... It struck me then.

The bubble started to form and stars winked out as the light was pulled away from us and into the envelope. The planet below went from blue to purple.

"They know something's up, ma'am," Sara said. "They've released the lines."

"Too little, too late," Houston replied.

I watched the display in fascination. The fighters attempted to escape only to be dragged back and crushed in the hand of an invisible god. We couldn't create a field precise enough to make a pocket universe, but the tidal force produced by the negative energy shell was inescapable at this distance.

"Rowdy?" the captain called over the comm.

"Twenty minutes, ma'am. I'll have temporary nozzles installed, but I'll need a few hours to fabricate a set at full strength," came the response.

"Sara?" Houston called over her shoulder.

"The destroyer is picking up speed."

The *Leo* cut in, "Ma'am. The Erethizon battle cruiser *Quills of God* has sent you a message. The destroyer bearing down on us is from his battle group."

"Thanks, *Leo*. Please put it through."

"Terran freighter *Leonard Fox*. This is Commander Grova. Please heave to and prepare to be boarded. In addition to causing the involuntary martyrdom of two of our faithful, you are known to be in possession of property that belongs to the Theocracy. If you continue to resist, many of your crew will die. We are prepared to destroy your vessel rather than let the property leave the system."

"Sara, did we take on any cargo in Yale?"

"No, ma'am. We didn't have time."

"I wonder what cargo they think we have?" Captain Houston scratched her chin and then shrugged. "The commander won't come to see us himself? I can be grateful for small favors. Mr. Martin," the captain addressed me, "We need to stay ahead of that destroyer. See what the repairs do to our exit."

I punched up the repair estimates and our relative position. "We'll stay ahead of them, ma'am, for a time. They're a hair faster. They'll catch us just short of the system's sun. About eight hours."

"Can we jump?"

Shaking my head, "No ma'am, too much orbital real estate. We could get free faster by getting off the ecliptic, but..."

The captain answered the unspoken objection, "But we'll decrease intercept time."

I nodded glumly.

Captain Houston thought about it for a few minutes. "*Leo*, please sound the all clear. We won't be in their missile envelope for a few hours. Mr. Martin, I'll want you, Ms. Chew, and Ms. Gudka in my cabin for a strategy session. First, put on something a little less red. See Mr. Boldrini for some new clothes. First section has the watch."

The *Leo* answered, "First section has the watch. Aye. All departments notified."

I looked down and realized I was still wearing the clothes I'd been wearing at the filling station.

Calling up the ship's roster, Mr. Boldrini was listed as Cook/Quartermaster. His duty station was in the galley. I'd run by there after checking on my sister.

***

I didn't make it to medical. Sophie mugged me in the passage outside of the mess hall. Sophie grabbed my shoulders. Her eyes were as wide as saucers. "What hit us?!"

I blinked. "Uh, a gauss cannon."

She scowled at me. "No way a gauss cannon jerked us around like that."

It clicked then, from what seemed a lifetime ago. "Oh that! Sorry, that was a fighter."

"Come again?"

"A fighter slammed into us as we were lifting off. We had to get tricky with our exit." I looked her over. "You didn't get hurt did you?"

She stamped her foot with exasperation. "No, but it gave poor Dan a concussion."

Glancing over her shoulder, "Is he all right?"

"He isn't any worse, but it didn't do him any favors."

"Sorry. We killed two starfighters," I grimaced.

"We're on our way out of the system?" Mixed emotions played out across her face.

"A destroyer is chasing us down. We'll be forced to deal with it before we can get away."

"Mark..."

I rolled my shoulders and smiled. "We'll come up with something."

She didn't look convinced. "Mark, this is a freighter. Correct me if I'm wrong, but couldn't a destroyer—I don't know—destroy us?"

"It has more weapons and it's a hair faster," I explained, "but we're not trying to fight them. With a little luck, they won't even get close."

It wasn't true, but Sophie needed hope, not reality. There were going to be at least two hours in which they were going to be able to take pot shots at us. If we survived that, and if we could somehow trick the destroyer, we might be able to get away.

There were a lot of ifs and maybes, and a lot of things that could go wrong.

I gave her a grin and entered the mess hall. A man was making Bev a sandwich from behind the serving line. He was rugged, with dark hair and the shadow of a beard. He also had an infectious smile.

He held out his hand. "You must be Mark. I'm Boldrini. The captain messaged me. Can I get you something to eat?"

I shook the offered hand. "A pleasure to meet you. I'm not hungry yet. You're the cook and quartermaster?"

"'Fraid so. But I have help. You'll meet my assistant Rafe later. Let's see what we can get for you."

He led me through the kitchen to a storeroom. The ten by ten meter room was filled with overflowing shelves. He pointed to a section piled with clothes. "Help yourself. Just leave the dirties by the door. I'll run them through the laundry and have them back to you before you know it."

It didn't take long to find what I needed. What at first seemed like an unorganized mess was in reality sorted by size. There was even some smart clothing that would size itself when I put it on. I chose brown pants, a smart T-shirt that would change colors, and a sturdy looking leather flight jacket.

***

Aasha Gudka was one of the senior staff I hadn't yet met. A tough-looking, blue-eyed blonde with more than a few cybernetic parts, her smile was surprisingly friendly. One eye, an arm, and a leg were shiny chrome. It was a little unnerving with the eye. She shot me an appraising look as I entered the wardroom at the back of the bridge. The captain and first mate were already there.

The captain brought the meeting to order. "Please be seated. Rowdy is still unavailable. Aasha, have you met Mark Martin?"

"No, ma'am. It's a pleasure to meet you, Mark." She leaned in and offered to shake with her mechanical hand.

I shook it without hesitation. "The pleasure is mine."

Her eyes widened with surprise. "You didn't flinch. Good man. Have you known many augments?"

"Yale has been at war with the Porcu-bears for three years." I shrugged, "We've had casualties."

The captain rapped her knuckles on the desk. "Okay people, we've got five hours to come up with the best plan possible to leave the Hedgehogs in the dust. Let's hear some ideas."

Ms. Chew started, "We can shoot our own missiles, but all it'll do is annoy them."

I nodded. "They've got more than enough countermeasures for anything we throw at them, but that brings up an interesting point. Do we have any countermeasures of our own?"

The captain shook her head. "Not much. We rely on not being seen."

39

"So, why can they see us now?" Aasha shrugged in confusion.

"A fighter slammed into us," replied Sara, "took off some paint. Rowdy has more, but not enough to cover the damaged area."

Aasha whistled softly. "Ouch. What's the marine complement of an Erethizon destroyer?"

The Captain looked at me. "It's fifty, isn't it?"

"Sixty-four," I responded. "How many do we have on board?"

Aasha's expression soured. "Twenty. One to one, my people will take 'em out. Draw them in, force them to battle on our ship, we could take on another ten. But twice that many..." she shook her head.

The captain waved it off. "I wasn't keen on letting those flea-bitten carcasses on my ship anyway. Back to countermeasures. I don't think we have the materials to make mines, but how about decoys or flechette?"

Sara eyed the ceiling as if she'd find the answer there. "No, we can't make reliable mines. Decoys, I'm not sure. Rowdy might be able to cobble something together, but time will be an issue. Flechette should be easy. We could whip up a cloud of hull bits in no time."

"Why isn't Rowdy here?" I asked.

"Busy with repairs," said Houston.

"What if we didn't manufacture the mines?" asked Sara, "We have a few missiles, right? Is there some way we can rig them to act like mines?"

The captain tilted her head. "That will work. We did something similar last time we were at Butcher's World. It was before you came aboard. Racy can reprogram them, and it wouldn't take long."

"And Rowdy could use some of our camouflage paint to make them harder to see," added Aasha.

"Great. On a different note, why can't we use the same trick with the R-drive with the missiles?" I asked

"Because the same tidal forces created by our negative energy shell will accelerate the kinetic energy and hard radiation generated by the missile." The captain shook her head, "We'd jump from fryin' pan into Dante's own inferno."

I rubbed the coin in my pocket, thinking about the physics involved, and realized the captain was right. "Let's not do that."

"Okay," said the captain, "we've got a flechette cloud and makeshift mines. What else?"

Aasha shrugged. "Is there anything we can do to slow them down? Throw something in their path that will trip them up?"

"They use a magnetic drive," I said. "In theory, a stronger magnetic field would disrupt it but I've never heard of anyone actually doing it."

"It would be easy to drop a bunch of magnets in their path," Houston said.

Sara shook her head. "No, Even if we could find some way to disperse them, the bow would pull them in before they reached the stern. We might blind their magnetic sensors, but mass sensors, radar, and lidar would still function. It'd be a minor annoyance at best."

"That's an idea," said Aasha. "Can we blind them altogether? Force them to stop?"

"The missiles do that when they explode. The effect is short-lived though," said Sara. "We'd have to make a miniature sun to be effective enough to help."

"It must be possible," I mused, "but you'd have to re-engineer the missile. I don't know if the engineer would be up to that."

The three women spoke as one. "Rowdy can do it."

The captain continued after a moment. "If it's possible, Rowdy could do it, but we're back to the same problem. We don't have the time."

"We've got gauss cannon," said Aasha. "Just like with the engagement, we can use them to take out missiles. What we use is a little light to do any serious damage to a destroyer, though. They're supposed to be for fending off other pirates and fighters. How many can they throw at us?"

"Two bow tubes, eight broadside port and starboard," I answered, "They're light, but one is enough to blow a hole in us big enough to fly an aircar through."

The captain frowned in concentration. "We've got shields, but not enough to stop a warhead." She waved at a screen on the wall, and an image of our projected course appeared. A red triangle represented the destroyer chasing us. "These are all great ideas, but will only slow them down. They're the hare to our tortoise. How do we turn them into hasenpfeffer?"

It took me a moment to realize that she'd used an AI implant to command the screen. I located the controls on my wrist AI. "Captain, if I may?"

She shrugged.

I pulled the screen back so that it showed the sun as well. "We took this route because there's less planetary mass on the other side of the star. Also, the units blockading the warp gate will be further away. We're going to be traveling really close to the star. Can we use that?"

"Well," said Aasha, "we can always hope and pray that a solar flare cooks their balls off."

There was a round of chuckles.

"Hold that thought." I pointed at the sun. "What would a missile do to that?"

The captain rolled her eyes. "You'd cause a minor disturbance in the corona, the surface area of the star. Not enough to create a flare."

I tilted my head sideways. "What if we used the R-drive?"

"Mr. Martin, are you drunk, high, or suicidal?" There wasn't a hint of humor in the captain's voice. "You'd get your flare, sure has Hades, and incinerate us in the process."

"Not if we're quick." I stood up next to the screen. "We'll be moving at, what? 80,000 mps?"

Sara quirked an eyebrow. "Something like that."

"So, we break the surface tension with a couple of missiles." I poked at the image of the sun. "We turn on the R-drive for three seconds as we pass over it. The flare starts, but we pass before it fries the area of space we just left."

The captain steepled her fingers. "We leave the drive on too long, or goose it too late..." She mimed an explosion with her hands.

Sara added her two cents. "We'll also have been shooting at each other for an hour or so by then. Even at the outer edge of a solar flare, we'll need at least half our shields."

"We'll refine the timing with the *Leo*'s AI. He may even be able to detect a wave or something that will help us out." I knew it was a crazy idea, but I couldn't think of a better one.

"Let's table that," said the captain. "I'm not going to say no, but it's a lot of risk."

Aasha chimed in, "What if we jettison the cargo pods?"

In the end, despite another half hour of brainstorming, the flare idea won out. It was risky and it just might kill us, but it was the best idea we had.

CHAPTER 9: DESTROYERS DESTROY

The captain called battle stations. In half an hour, we would be in the destroyer's missile range. The holo-tank showed the ship approaching astern. The AI imposed a red globe around the *Leo* at a range of 33,400 kilometers.

"You were right, captain," I said, "They didn't try for the ballistic hit."

"Nah, missiles are expensive. The Hedgehog captain won't want to fire on us when we can just do-see-do around 'em. He'll wait until we're in his missiles' powered envelope."

"True, but we'd have to move. Even if the warhead didn't arm, it would have been accelerating for twenty minutes. A two-ton missile moving at 100,000 kph packs a serious punch."

"Ma'am," said Sara, "They're in scan range. They have more tubes than we expected. Two bow, two stern, twelve on a side."

"Oh, crap." I turned to the captain. "Sorry ma'am, I had no idea they could shoot that many."

She waved it off. "They think we have something they want. We shouldn't have to deal with a broadside. Though it would be a mixed blessing. They'd have to stop accelerating to do it, but it would be a mess o' Jotunn wasps to deal with. As it is, each time they fire bow tubes it will slow them down. If they slow down too much, all the radiation from the sun will mud their eyes. They won't be able to see us."

The Erethizon destroyer crossed the edge of the bubble. Sara barked, "Missile separation. Two incoming." She was cool and collected. "Aasha reports gauss cannons unlocked and set for computer control." She was on the auxiliary bridge near engineering, where the controls for the belly cannons were located. Sara was at the tactical station on the bridge, manning the controls for the dorsal cannons.

In the holo-tank, flashing red dots traveled along a dotted line: the missiles and their expected route to our ship.

On the screen, the missiles didn't look fast.

No one so much as breathed.

When the missiles were close enough to target effectively, the gauss cannons opened up. Metal streamed out. The AI superimposed a blue line indicating where the shots were headed. It bobbed and wove like a snake as it sought out the targets.

The snake caught the missiles, and there was an audible, collective breath.

The captain nodded. "Good. Now he'll wait a spell and fire again. The missiles didn't have enough fuel left to avoid our cannons."

It didn't take long before they fired again. "That was quick," I commented.

The missiles closed on us and again the gauss cannons let loose a stream of steel. It took longer this time, but we got them. Everyone concentrated on the holo-tank, watching for their next move.

The minutes crept by and the enemy hadn't fired again. However, they were gaining on us.

The captain looked over her shoulder. "Ms. Chew?"

"No reaction. They're pouring on the speed."

The captain turned to me. "Mr. Martin?"

I reviewed my screens. "We've gained twenty minutes. Not enough for the radiation to hide us, or close enough cause a solar flare."

Sara cut in. "Maneuvering!"

We all watched the holo-tank. The destroyer cut its sub-light drives and turned its side to us. This was the moment. The good news was that they were no longer accelerating; we would gain the time we needed to reach the star's corona. The bad news was the devastating broadside coming.

The captain looked over her shoulder at Sara. "They aren't playing nice anymore. Ms. Chew, give them two fish and two ducks. Something to think about while they're sending us their best."

"The fish are away, ma'am." A couple of moments later: "The ducks are in the water."

The "fish," our missiles, would keep them honest and force them to maneuver. Not a real threat to a warship. But the "ducks" were the missiles programmed to wait until the destroyer got close.

The destroyer completed its maneuver and spat twelve missiles out at us. It then rolled and shot another twelve missiles from its port side broadside.

"Fornicating farthogs," exclaimed the captain, "Twenty-four is a death sentence. They want us bad. Against that..."

Sara yelled, "Missiles!"

We all looked at her like she was crazy.

She continued. "Their missiles will be close together because we're a small target. We can fire our missiles at theirs."

The captain shook her head. "Sara, our missiles aren't designed to do that. We have to program the ranges in advance. It will be like throwing a pea and then shooting it out of the air, even with the AI helping you."

"You don't want to try, ma'am?"

Her expression clearly said what she thought of our chances, but she shrugged. "Do it. It's better than waiting to become charred whiptail."

The aft missile launcher fired five volleys of two. I watched the screen as our missiles reached out to meet the coming carnage. The first volley missed and exploded after the barrage. The second pair closed in. It was closer, but still detonated too late. The third blew up in their path but not close enough.

Sara glared. "Come on, you bastards."

The fourth caught a piece of the outside. Only one.

I gulped a lungful of air, remembering to breathe. Our fate was down to the last two cylinders of atomic death. They drew steadily closer to the incoming missiles.

Contact! Right on the money and spectacular. Every sensor was blinded. When the interference cleared, there were eight missiles still bearing down on us.

The captain let out a loud breath. "Okay, we're back to our plan for dealing with the volley. Helm, cut the ion drive and swing us around. Ms. Chew, you and Ms. Gudka are on point defense. Work outside to in. Mr. Martin, see if the flechette can lead some sheep astray."

Sara went to work and I did my best to line up metal clouds with the incoming missiles. Sara and Aasha managed to pick off four of them. I got three.

"Oh, squats!" I screwed my eyes shut.

A boom more felt than heard wracked the ship.

"What are we looking at, Sara?" barked the captain.

"Nothing yet, ma'am. Rowdy is getting the details."

My displays showed engine status. "At least we're still getting drive data."

"Got it! Port shields are down, minor damage aft, a breach in cargo bay three. Repair crews en route." She gave the captain a brief, tight smile. "We're here, ma'am, but..."

Houston turned her attention back to the holo-tank. "For the moment. Bridge to Engineering. Rowdy, we need that port shield."

No response.

"Row..."

"Sorry, Captain," he growled, "The node is fried. It will take five hours."

There was absolute silence on the bridge for several heartbeats.

Sara was the first to break it. "Ma'am."

"I know, XO." The captain closed her eyes.

It wouldn't work. The port shield was down. In even our most optimistic simulations, we needed at least 20 percent. The flare idea was a bust.

"Wally, roll us."

We could keep the starboard side of the ship toward the sun. It would be fine for normal movement, but nothing fancy.

It wasn't enough. We'd gained time, but it would only delay the inevitable. We weren't close enough to hide in the sun's radiation. At some point in the next thirty-six minutes, it would all be over.

CHAPTER 10: ESCAPE THE SYSTEM

We poured on the speed, delaying the inevitable. The Erethizon destroyer was gaining ground, the Porcu-bear captain closing. He wanted the most effective broadside to finish us off.

Death inched closer and closer astern.

"She's maneuvering!" Sara called out from the back of the bridge.

This was it: the end of the ride. The destroyer would launch a final volley and there would be nothing for us to do about it. We were on the opposite side of the sun from the planet by then. If we had been closer to Yale, I thought, at least I would have been able to see my home one last time before a missile ended everything.

But it didn't come. The destroyer kept turning.

The captain spoke first. "What's he doing?"

Sara squinted in confusion. "They can't be doing that on purpose."

The destroyer was angled oddly. Tactically, its position was awful. None of its remaining missiles would have a straight shot. Their position only made sense if they were trying to maximize thrust to break solar orbit, and while they had plenty of momentum, a star creates a huge gravity well. We were pretty close to the sun. The AI projected its course as continuing around the sun.

"Where's their thrust?" asked the captain.

I projected an anticipated course on the screen. "The AI says it looks more like an oval. Not enough to break free." Were they letting us go?

The captain tilted her head. "Ms. Chew, please magnify the aft section of the destroyer."

A close up of the tail end of the destroyer appeared on the screen. It was a mess. It looked as if some huge beast had taken a bite out of it, three-quarters of the aft section exposed to open space.

"They've only got one main thruster left," I noted. "Half power, if I'm any judge."

"This close to the sun, sending anyone there..." Sara shook her head. "It will be a death sentence."

They were going to fall into the star. There wasn't a thing anyone could do to stop it.

"Back up the vid, Ms. Chew. What happened?"

Sara put a recording of our battle up on the left monitor and rewound the feed. A few minutes after their missiles and our missiles annihilated each other there was an explosion in the aft section of the destroyer. We hadn't seen it because we'd been too preoccupied with the remaining missiles. Further review showed that our "ducks" had waited for the ship to pass by as intended. When it did, they had performed better than expected, streaking into the tail of the ship to give it a one-two punch, first taking out the shields, then the engines.

We were still inside the destroyer's range. They could still fire on us, but they had bigger things to worry about now—like staying alive.

The *Leo*'s AI spoke up. "The Erethizon destroyer is calling for help." A few seconds later, "Commander Grova has responded that there are no ships close enough to render assistance. There has been unexpected resistance on the southern continent of Yale. All other ships are involved in pacifying the planet."

"Give 'em hell boys."

Leo continued, "The destroyer has acknowledged. They are going to try to rig missiles to provide thrust." There was a pause. "Incoming hail from Commander Grova."

"On screen," replied the captain.

"Crew of the *Leonard Fox*. You have damaged a ship and stolen a required artifact. The Theocracy has issued a kill or capture decree for your ship and crew. You will find our claws have a long reach. Wherever you flee, the Erethizon will be waiting. Grova out."

"Ma'am," asked Sara, "How many K.O.C.'s is that for us?"

"Three, but every other time they haven't gotten a good look at us. Perhaps Rowdy can change the *Leo*'s appearance and we can get a new transponder." She shrugged, "Something to think about."

We would live to fight again.

The captain relaxed back into her chair. "Mr. Walashek, please make all speed to our jump point and make sure we give that star a wide berth. It's a killer. Mr. Martin, please update our course to get us to open space as soon as possible. Ms. Chew, tell Rowdy he has about a day and a half to make repairs before we can jump."

"Aye, aye, sir," we said in near unison.

CHAPTER 11: FIRST IMPRESSIONS

Sara showed me my quarters and over the next two days, the most sleep I got was a series of catnaps between watches. We made three small jumps around the system to confuse anyone who might be following us. Each jump required me to come to the bridge to make last-minute course adjustments. During those early days, Sara and the captain each stood a six-hour watch with me. I was also checking on Sophie and Dan as much as I could, so when the time came for the big jump I was only staying awake through a liberal application of coffee.

"You want to go where?" I was a bit confused by the numbers in front of me, but then again it might have just been due to my over-caffeinated, under-rested brain.

"It's the notation in the astrogation computer for TC3." I recognize Houston's tone as the same one my first grade art teacher used when I'd drawn my version of a dinosaur. The assignment had been to draw a magnapple tree.

"I see it, but there's nothing there. It's a point above the galactic ecliptic. There are no charted stars or rocks for light years in any direction."

"There's somethin' there, Mr. Martin. It's a space station called *Ocelot*." I'd never heard of it. I was a bit nervous about plugging in the coordinates.

I ran the plot, knowing that I was essentially throwing a dart at a target billions of kilometers away. An R-drive will only move you along straight lines, so the navigation has to be done with care.

Celestial bodies do not sit still in space like they do on maps. They spin with the galaxy and every other thing nearby pulls and tugs at everything else.

Checking the numbers, once, twice, and even a third time, I sent them to the captain. She glanced at them before handing them off. "Wally, bring us about if you please. Starboard seventeen degrees, up sixty and change."

"Aye, aye. Starboard seventeen and up sixty."

The ship moved to the new heading, overcorrected, and then moved on the beam.

"We are on course and on target, ma'am."

The captain pressed the comm on her armrest. "Rowdy, how are we lookin'?"

The growly voice responded. "Ready to wrap and roll when you give the word, Captain."

The captain surveyed the bridge. "The bears have crashed the dance, my friends. Let's be somewhere else. Hit it."

Stars winked out, but Yale's sun was still the closest one. It was a brighter yellowish pinprick among the other lights from this far outside the system, though. It changed colors from yellow to green to blue before disappearing completely. We were in a bubble of negative energy. In a way, we were the only things in existence, surrounded by impenetrable blackness: our own pocket universe.

There was no sense of movement, even though I knew that our speed relative to the reality we just left was somewhere just north of a light year a day. The course we set had us arriving in twenty-eight days. Wherever we were going was 30.7 light years distant.

"Mark?"

I regarded the captain over my shoulder. "Ma'am?"

"We've been running around like horny toads on an anthill. Get some sleep. I'll take the first watch, Ms. Chew will take second, and you can relieve her in twelve hours."

With an, "aye, aye" in my wake, I left the bridge for my cabin.

***

Sleep claimed me for ten hours. I woke hungry, thirsty, and with an intense desire to find the head. I walked into the mess hall and found a few crew eating. Sophie was sitting at a table with Mr. Boldrini, the ship's cook. He stood up as I came in.

"Mr. Martin, glad to see you made it down. Rafe is out delivering meals right now. What can I get you to eat?"

We ambled over to the buffet line. "What have you got?"

"Well, the special of the day is a grilled Lir tilapia and orange sauce. It goes well with the vegetable leek. I've also got some steamed broliform and cannon carrots."

"It smells wonderful. Is it always like this, or is this a special occasion?"

He gave me a broad smile. "Just because the crew can't go anywhere else doesn't mean they should suffer. I want to them to look forward to eating."

I took his advice and went with the tilapia and veggies. I grabbed a glass of water and sat with Sophie. Boldrini joined us.

"How are you adjusting, Sophie?" I took a bite of the tilapia. It was wonderful.

She finished chewing before speaking, munching with delight. "Getting there. I'm happy to be alive but worried about Dad."

"Me too. Where did they put you?"

She waggled her head side to side. "I have a small apartment next to the medical bay. It's like being on call all the time. At least I'm close if they need me."

"Speaking of the medical bay, how's Dan?"

Sophie frowned. "I'm going to keep him unconscious for a couple more days. He needs rest. I'm healing the trauma where I can, but I'll need to wake him soon. He can't tell me where it hurts while asleep." She cocked her head to the side. "The first officer keeps coming down to check on me. It seems a bit obsessive, but I guess it's better than being ignored."

Boldrini closed his eyes and inclined his head. "It isn't you that she's concerned about, doctor. Dan and Sara are a couple."

Sophie put her hand to her mouth in mild shock. "I'm so sorry. I didn't know. She's never gone into his room."

He nodded. "Sara is from Shoshing. They don't express emotions in public. It's considered impolite. Don't let her fool you though. She's passionate underneath it all."

Ms. Chew entered the mess and Boldrini went to take care of her. When she was served, she sat with a couple of marines in the corner of the room. Her eyes rested on me for a moment, but I didn't know how to read her bland expression. It might have been disgust or pity and it lasted only a moment before she turned her attention to her food.

Sophie put her hand on my arm. "When do you go on duty?"

"2000 hours. Eight o'clock ship's time. I want to wander around and get a look at the ship and meet some more of the crew." I went to grab another bite of the tilapia, but there wasn't any left on my plate. I must have been hungrier than I thought.

Sophie got a mischievous smile on her face. "Will that include engineering?"

"Uh, yeah. Given its location, it will be last on my list, but I want to see the drives." I raised an eyebrow at her. "What's in engineering?"

She stood up and took her plates. "Do me a favor. Please tell Rowdy that I need him to take a physical. Ship's records say he's overdue."

***

I wandered down to crew berthing and met some of the crew and marines on board. The deck crew members were polite. The marines had already heard that I was a fighter pilot and, predictably, had a chip on their collective shoulder. They viewed drive jocks as elitist, and most pilots thought of them as rock-wolvers: vicious, but not too bright.

The exception was the platoon leader. "Hey, flyboy. Come to mix it up with us grunts for a while?" Aasha punched me on the shoulder a bit harder than I'd consider playful.

I smiled at her. "Well, I don't know about mixing it up, but I'll buy them a round next time we're planet-side. The captain told me about the drop these guys made at New Tuscany. Did they really hold off three squads of Porcu-bears long enough for their contacts to get away?"

Her smile broadened. "Yes, they did." Her face fell then. "We lost Remy, though."

"Outnumbered and outgunned, you only lost one man. The fact that you got away at all is a testament to your leadership and training."

She looked me straight in the eyes. She didn't need to blink, so the effect was a little unsettling. "Thank you, sir. We were more than a little lucky." Her good eye traveled up and down my body. "You have a sidearm, Mark?"

54

I grinned. "I brought an AP12 with me."

She pretended to look impressed and failed. "Small, concealable, accurate, and a dozen shots."

"You don't need more if you hit your target, grunt."

She gave me a shrewd look. "Okay flyboy, care for a wager?"

"What have you got in mind?"

"Rowdy will set up a firing range in one of the empty cargo holds in a few days. Rubber pellet shot. If you can outshoot me, I'll give you unfettered access to the range. If I win, you pay my first night's bar tab when we get to port."

I thought about it a minute. "We both use my weapon, ten shots, any stance, and if I lose, I'm only paying for your drinks, *not* anyone else you decide to buy drinks for that night."

She snorted. "Smarter than the average star head. Okay." We shook on it.

The two marines I'd seen eating with the first mate walked into the berthing area. They were horsing around and fighting over a football.

"Hey Aasha, can you tell me where..."

I found myself against the bulkhead, nursing the back of my head.

"You should watch where you're standing, sir." The marine said "sir" like it meant "pissant."

I held out my hand for him to help me up, but he ignored it. Pushing myself to my feet, I dusted myself off. "What's your name, marine?"

"Warren, sir."

Turning to the other one, "And yours?"

The other marine, still holding the football, answered, "Jones, sir." The challenge in his voice was evident.

I smiled like I didn't have a care in the world. Aasha didn't say anything, just shook her head sadly. That told me all I needed to know.

"Gentlemen, thanks for your advice. Mr. Warren and Mr. Jones." I nodded, then turned to Aasha. "Thanks for your time. I'll be in touch soon so I can kick your ass on the firing line."

I left crew quarters and headed down the spine to engineering. It was high past time I met our engineer and got a look at the machinery that kept us flying.

***

At the top of the ladder, I surveyed the engineering bay. It was hot in there.

I could see two fusion plants, gravity generators, and environmental, electrical, and water runs. There were a few maintenance drones zipping about with tools and equipment, but no one was about. On a modern ship, it wasn't uncommon for the routine chores to be performed by robots, but there were usually a half dozen engineers riding herd on them. I descended the ladder. Standing next to a console, I called out. "Rowdy?"

No response. "Rowdy?"

A red and black furry mass sprang from behind the gravity generator and sprinted at me faster than a runaway aircar. My arms went up and I stepped back. "Whoa!"

In front of me, on the console, three centimeters from my face stood a Muscat. They were the first alien race we Terrans had come across as we'd spread out among the stars. Their homeworld was covered in dense jungle, so they preferred temperatures a bit hotter than Terran norms.

None of my pre-war missions had near their territory, but he looked like any picture I'd ever seen of his species. Standing at about a meter tall, he had large, pointed ears, a bushy tail, and a long snout. Muscats resemble the Terran fox, if a fox could stand upright and have almost human arms and legs. Like most of his race, he wore a harness instead of clothes, and several engineering tools hung off of it.

I tried to recall everything I'd learned about Muscats in high school. As a race, they were hyperkinetic, intensely curious, and had little regard for personal space. There was also something odd about their social structure, but it wasn't coming to me... maybe because one was standing nose to nose with me.

"Uh, hi."

He twisted his head a little. "I don't know you. What are you doing in my engine room?" His tone wasn't hostile, just questioning.

How did you greet a Muscat? I couldn't remember. "Um, I'm Mark Martin. Are you Rowdy?"

He backed up a little bit, much to my relief, and tilted his head in the other direction. "I'm Raw'noriede, but yes, feel free to call me Rowdy. Everybody else does. What are you doing in my engine room?"

It came back to me then. The traditional greeting was two audible sniffs, which I then performed before answering his question. "I was touring the ship and meeting new shipmates. I wanted to say thank you for your speedy repairs."

He sniffed me back and jumped down to the floor. Right next to my leg, he looked up at me. I mentally reminded myself not to back up, but it was hard since his face was ten centimeters from my crotch.

He held his hand in the air for me to shake. I did so, noticing that the hand had black fur up to the forearm, but black skin on the palms. And while the fingers did have long nails, I wouldn't call them claws.

Just then, I remembered what was odd about the Muscat social structure. But I hadn't seen another Muscat on board. "It's a pleasure to meet you Rowdy. I'm surprised, though. I thought your race usually travels as a family."

Rowdy smiled. His smile reminded me of a greyhound I had when I was a kid. "I did bring my family with me."

With a sweep of his hand, he drew my attention to two more Muscat on the far side of the room. They looked similar to Rowdy, but with tufts of white fur on their chests. "Meet my son and daughter. This is Raw'nadi and Raw'scadi. Please call them Randy and Racy."

At the introductions, they raced forward and suddenly I found myself encircled by little, furry people. I did my best to sniff them both, but it was difficult—they couldn't seem to hold still. For their part, they stuck their hands out to shake.

"I'm pleased to meet you, Randy and Racy. What do you do aboard the ship?"

Randy hopped up on the console so he could get right next to my face. "I run the environmental systems. Air, hot, cold, water, and waste. I make sure we all stay breathing."

"Thank you. You're doing good work."

He beamed at me, that same greyhound smile. "You're welcome!"

Racy did a couple of spins around my legs then ran up the ladder so her face was level with mine. "I handle the systems and software. If the computer breaks or needs updates, I take care of it."

"Impressive, Racy. I'd heard Muscat are good with machines."
Then a thought struck me. "Racy, I lost my music. I had to leave
Yale in a hurry. Does the ship's library have any?"

She regarded me, wide-eyed. "There isn't any in the ship's
library. I have some on my tablet, but it's from my home world and
most Terrans don't like it. Ms. Chew, Ms. Romanov, and Mr.
Sanchez all have extensive collections on their tablets, though."

Rowdy looked at his daughter curiously. "Racy, did they tell you
they had music, or did you just... find out?"

Racy's ears folded back and she ducked her head at her dad.

Rowdy gave her a stern look. "Terrans have a different
understanding of privacy, shisha. Please be respectful of that."

"Yes, doma."

I smiled at Racy. "Your father is right, but I promise I won't
tell. It will be our secret."

She gave me a small smile.

"Rowdy, do you have any reactor cleaner I could use?"

He reached under the console and pulled out a tube of the stuff.
"Here, but be careful with that stuff. Don't get any on your skin. It
burns and itches, and water only makes it worse."

I grinned knowingly. "Oh, I know. When I was a midshipman,
one of my chores was to clean the reactor casing. I accidentally got
some on me then. Not something you forget easily."

One of his ears twitched. "Are you going to use it to remove
scoring on one of the fighters in the launch bay?"

"No, I have something else in mind." I turned and started up
the ladder. "I'm going on watch soon, but it was a pleasure. I look
forward to spending more time with all of you."

***

Stopping by medical on my way to the bridge, I favored my
sister with a half-hearted glare. She just burst out laughing.

"You didn't warn me about them."

She got her giggles under control. "Not a chance! Seriously
though, how did it go?"

"They're good people. I liked them. Their... intensity will take
some getting used to though."

Sophie bit her lip, mirth barely under control. "I bet."

CHAPTER 12: WAKE UP CALL

A couple of days later I walked into medical to find Mr. Warren and Mr. Jones. I nodded in their direction. "What's up with them?"

"A couple of crybabies," answered Sophie. "They got into something that made them itch all over. They claim someone put it in their bunks, but I'm not sure I believe them."

"I wouldn't," I said. "If they're so itchy, why are they sleeping?"

"I couldn't stand their whining."

The captain and first mate entered just then. "What happened to War 'n Pace?" asked the captain.

Sophie gave the captain a questioning look. "War and Pace?"

She shook her head. "Dave Warren and Pace Jones. Trouble on four feet. Their collective nickname is War 'n Pace. Those two get into more trouble together than any ten other crew members."

"They got into something sticky and itchy," Sophie repeated for her benefit.

"Did they?" The captain arched an eyebrow in my direction.

I made a show of not noticing. "Is Dan ready?"

We entered his room and Sophie administered the drugs that would wake him up. For a while nothing happened, then his eyes opened and he tried to sit up.

"Easy there," Sophie said as she helped him to sit up. "You've been out of it for a while. You're going to be a bit weak until you can get some exercise."

He seemed to focus on her for the first time. "Thanks. Who are you?"

"I'm your doctor, Sophia Martin. My brother and I brought you here. Do you know where you are?"

Dan looked around. "Yes. I'm in the medical bay of the *Leo*."

Sophie smiled. "Very good. What's your name and rank?"

"I'm Daniel Piez, second officer of the *Leo*."

Sophie nodded encouragingly. "That's great, Dan. We're going to ask you some questions and see how your memory is doing. Would that be all right?"

He blinked rapidly and nodded. "Yeah, that'd be fine."

The captain started. "Hey, Danny boy."

"Hey, Captain."

"Where did you grow up?"

He answered immediately. "Mars colony, the town of Armstrong's Step."

"Good," she said. "Which academy did you attend?"

He hesitated before responding. "Phoebos. I attended the academy on Phoebos."

"And where did we meet?"

He smirked. "You tell everyone that you hired me from a pool of candidates on Siren, but we actually met the night before in a bar brawl."

She barked out a laugh. "True enough. Your turn, Mark."

"Hey, Dan," I said, "I've been filling in for you on the bridge. I'm going to ask you some questions on basic astrogation and give you some simple exercises."

He nodded and I continued, "What's one AU?"

"Astronomical Unit. It's the distance from Old Terra to its sun."

"What about a light year?"

He raised his eyebrows. "Seriously?"

"Humor me," I said.

"Fine. It's 9.46 meters times 10 to the 12th power."

"And coordinates?"

He didn't answer right away. He had to think about it. "Um, coordinates are expressed in X, Y, and, and... Z. They are given in relation to... to um... wherever you are in the galaxy."

"Good, Dan." I nodded encouragingly. "Now, assume we're at Alpha Centauri, and we want to get to Wolf 1061. What steps would you take to plot a course?"

"Um." He was silent for several seconds. "We need the eff... the eff..." There were a few more seconds of silence.

"The ephemerals. Our navigation points. Go on, Dan."

"Then the az... the az... damn it. It's right there." He had a look of intense concentration on his face.

"The azimuth..." I prompted, but he cut me off.

"I know, damn it! Give me a minute." Dan was silent for several moments, but it soon became obvious he couldn't dredge up the information. His eyes widened with fear and confusion. He knew he should have the answers, but they weren't there.

"It's okay," said Sara, "we'll come back to it. I want you to think back to our first date. Do you remember that?"

"Um. I remember something about New Cancun. It's an ocean world, right?"

"That's right, Dan."

He continued. "There was. There was a hut, or something. On the beach. No. Yes."

"It was over the water," coached Sara. "What else do you remember?"

"There was something about going to see a holo-vid. And some sort of feast on a beach."

"That's good." Her eyes sparkled a bit, but she didn't burst into tears. "The holo-vid was three months later, but I'm glad you remembered. What do you know about your family?"

"I have a mother and father back on Mars."

Sara waited for a moment longer. "Any other family?"

"No," he shook his head. "I guess I'm an only child."

"You have a brother and a sister," she prodded.

"I do?"

"We'll come back to that," she said encouragingly. "Tell me about your friends on board."

"Oh, yeah." He grinned broadly. "Dave and Pace. Are they here?"

"In the next room." Sara slid her hand in Dan's.

He looked at Sara's hand in his. "We... we used to date?"

Sara smiled. "Yes. Yes, we did."

Dan looked into her face. "How did I feel about you?"

Sara blinked. "We were planning a future together."

Dan glanced around at each of us. "I'm sorry. I don't...

remember that."

The edges of her lips twitched up. "That's okay. We can start over."

The lost expression stayed, but he answered. "Yeah. I guess so."

The color drained out of Sara's face. "Um, we'll talk about it. Everything will come back."

Sophie stepped in. "Sara, it may just be temporary."

The first mate nodded, but her expression said she wasn't sure.

Dan bit his lip.

CHAPTER 13: SAWTOOTH SARA

"What are you reading, sir?" Wally cut into the silence in which we'd been traveling. It was toward the end of the watch three days after we woke Dan. Since then, Captain Houston and I had been splitting Sara's watches. She insisted she was ready to work again, and I was certainly ready to stop working twelve hours at a stretch.

It took me a minute to register that Wally had spoken to me. "Oh. I'm sorry, Wally. I'm studying the ship. We survived the Porcu-bears with strategy and a lot of luck. If it's all the same, let's rely less on luck."

He grinned at me. "Good thinking, sir."

"What about you?"

He looked back down at his console. "I'm studying astrogation. Watching you work was exciting. Dan never let me watch. It's math, but fun math." He paused as he thought about what he'd said. "That's not right."

"Sounds fair to me. Thanks, Wally. That means a lot." I cocked my head to the left and regarded the other helmsman on the bridge. She wasn't on watch but had chosen to hang out with us while she studied. "What about you Ms. Romanov? Picking up some Erethizon?"

Natalia gave a short laugh. "No, sir. Muscat."

I was a little surprised at that. "Muscat? Most of them speak Terran. Why the interest?"

Her face reddened and she rubbed the back of her neck. "Well sir, Gina—I mean Ms. Ortega—speaks Erethizon. Lavesh speaks

Dru." She shrugged. "It seems like we could use someone on the bridge that speaks it since the Muscat on board work in engineering. Racy programmed a tutorial for me."

"The Dru have a spoken language?"

She nodded. "Yes, sir. Dru telepathy is limited to fifty meters. They have a spoken language for distance communications. Their written language is hopeless."

"Impressive. Do you think Racy would mind if you shared the program with me? With Rowdy, Randy, and Racy on board, it would be worth it to learn a few words and phrases. Especially since I might be around a while." The rumor mill was already circulating that Dan had lost some skills.

She thought about it for a moment. "I don't think she'd mind, sir. I'll ask, but you can have it now."

My wrist computer trilled and a mail icon appeared in my field of vision. I thought clicked it and the file loaded. "Thanks, Natalia."

It was shift change, and Ms. Chew climbed up the ladder to the bridge. I stood as Sara approached the watch station. "Ms. Chew, the ship is on course. No incidents or actions to report. You have the watch."

She eyed me like I was a smear of grease on the deck. "Thank you, Mr. Martin. I have the watch." Just hearing her voice chilled the temperature on the bridge by ten degrees Celsius. I knew she was still adjusting to the situation with Dan... and that he felt nothing for her.

Wally glanced at me, then raised an eyebrow in her direction as we left the bridge. I just shrugged.

It was lunch mess, so I made my way to the galley. Sophie had just sat down, so I hurried to the serving line. Lunch was gumbo, and Boldrini had set up two kettles: one with okra and one without. I took a bowl with the unusual veggie and sat down across from my sister.

She inhaled the aroma as she ate. "I have to admit, I'm surprised by the food."

I shrugged. "What were you expecting?"

"I don't know, something like a hospital cafeteria. This is like a nice bistro." She stared into space. "The way Boldrini mixes spices and textures... I don't know, it's like art."

"He's probably a trained chef. On a freighter like this, you want to distract the crew from remembering they're in a metal can for months at a time. I bet Captain Houston views Boldrini as an investment in morale."

Sophie watched Boldrini laugh and joke with the crew as he and Rafe served them.

I heard a clatter coming from the door. I turned to find Rowdy and his family converging on the serving line. Food in hand, they headed straight for us.

"Hi," I said.

"Hi!" They responded in a chorus and swarmed over us. Rowdy sat right next to Sophie, and by that, I mean he practically sat in her lap. Randy and Racy set their plates on either side of me. Before I knew it, Randy was in my lap with his nose almost in my food.

He took a deep sniff and regarded me over his shoulder. "Gumbo. I like the way Boldrini seasons it, but he should use fewer vegetables and more sun lizard."

I laughed. "I can appreciate that. Mind if I finish it?"

He turned around in my lap and looked innocently into my eyes. "No," he said, then sat right next to me. Several of the crew around us were not quite laughing. Between bites, I asked Racy about the language program.

"Oh! Yes," she said with enthusiasm. "Natalia said you wanted it. You can use it. Let one of us know if you need help with pronunciation. Muscat is a tonal language and some Terrans have trouble with it."

"I can sing and play the guitar. Shouldn't be a problem."

She stood, her nose almost touching mine. "You can sing? Can I hear?"

Pulling my head back so there was one Racy in my sightline instead of two, I answered, "Not right now, but I'll be happy to later."

She sat back down. "Okay, I'll come by your cabin in a couple of hours. Will that work?"

"Fine."

Sophie couldn't quite suppress the giggles. "Are you going to be okay, Mark? I need to get back to medical."

"I'll be fine."

"Really?"

It must have shown on my face. "New friends. Sad Dad can't be here."

Sophie smiled sweetly and put her hand on my shoulder. Then she smacked me on the back of the head.

Getting off watch a week later, I heard someone descend the ladder to the mess deck as I walked from the bridge. My cabin was right next to the ladder and the door wasn't shut. Pushing it open, I found my room trashed. Pillow fluff everywhere, my uniforms on the floor, the sheets shredded, and all of it smeared with something smelly.

The captain, ambling down the passage from her cabin, stopped at my door. "Hmmm," was all she said.

"Hi, Captain."

"It's just you and me, son, and we're not on the bridge," she said. "Call me Jenna."

"Thanks, Jenna. Any advice on earning the crew's respect?"

"You seem to be doin' just fine," she observed.

I waved an arm to take in the room.

She shrugged noncommittally. "War 'n Pace are the bratty younger brothers of our crew family. I could talk to them if you like."

"No. It's better if I take care of it myself." Taking in my room, I started thinking about an appropriate response.

The captain continued, "I'm more concerned about you and Sara. How's that coming?"

I snorted. "She hates me."

"How're you going to reckon with that?"

"I don't know," I admitted. "She's the XO and can make my life difficult. Tread carefully, I guess. Maybe an opportunity will present itself."

"And War 'n Pace?" she prompted.

A slow smile crept across my face. "Dirty tricks? I can handle that."

"Dare I ask?" she asked, her eyes twinkling.

"I'd rather give you plausible deniability."

She barked a laugh. "Now that we've established I'm ignorant of this mess, perhaps you can fill me in on the details I didn't know."

"Very wise," I said. "It would be a shame if you revealed them by accident. I'm going to change the settings on their wrist AIs."

Her eyes widened. "It won't take them long to change 'em back."

"Not if I change their passcodes. I bet those two rock heads have never changed the defaults." I pondered it for a few moments more, the plan coming together in my head. "While they're in the shower. With prep work, it shouldn't take more than five minutes."

"In that case, I'll leave you to your scheming." The captain waved and continued down the passage.

***

A couple of days later I met Racy on my way to medical.

"*Ump'tau grita wonoo.*"

Racy's head tilted a little. "I'm pretty sure you meant to ask me if I'd meet you for lunch later. Do you want to eat a rope?"

"Ugh." I scrubbed my face with my hands. "What's the correct tone?"

"*Wonoo* goes up at the end for food. Going down is the word for rope." She smiled. "Rowdy, Randy, and I will be happy to join you and your sister for lunch again."

"Great, see you in an hour."

"And after that let's grab a conference room." She continued down the passage, "Your pronunciation needs help."

I groaned and entered the medical bay. I waved at my sister. She waved back but didn't look up, absorbed in her view screen.

Knocking on Dan's doorframe, I got the impression I'd interrupted something. Sara's glare could've liquefied nitrogen.

"If you're busy, I can come back later." I offered.

Dan smiled without feeling. "It's okay, Mark. I could use a break."

Sara stood stiffly. "Yes. A break sounds good." She shouldered her way from the room without a backward glance.

We stared after her as she exited the medical bay.

"Seriously," I said, "need a moment? We can do this after lunch."

"I need the distraction, Mark."

"Trouble in paradise?" I suggested.

"I know there's supposed to be something there, but it isn't. It's like I'm reading from a tablet. I know the facts, but the feelings are gone. Worse, it's not coming back." He sighed.

I couldn't imagine what that would be like. "Is it just her, or everyone?"

"No. I remember my mom and dad, and now my brother and sister. Everything I feel for them is still there. But everyone I've met in the past three years..." he ran his fingers through his hair, "not a trace. I know what happened. The order is a little screwy."

"Kinda like your math skills?" I guessed.

"Different, but similar," he acknowledged. "I seem to be able to relearn the math, even starting from scratch. It's still as fun as I remember. I can't seem to relearn how I used to feel."

The comment lay there for a bit before he continued, "It's going to take months to relearn this stuff."

I nodded.

"I've asked the captain to drop me off on *Ocelot*."

"I'd heard. How does that make you feel?"

He shrugged one shoulder. "It is what it is. I'm going back to Mars. I need to rediscover my past."

"Still want to do this?" I gestured to the screen on the wall of his room.

"Definitely. Lead on, Macduff."

We spent the next hour going over geometry and trigonometry. We were winding up the lesson when my sister knocked. "Take me to lunch, Marky. I'm hungry. Hungry doctors make bad decisions, like ordering an appendectomy to treat a rash."

"Right away, Doc Sophie." I saluted.

"Rafe will be down soon with your tray, Dan," she offered.

"How much longer are you keeping me down here, Doc?"

"Three days," she replied. "Then you'll have to serve yourself lunch, goldbricker."

"Can't wait."

We went to the mess hall and grabbed our trays. The lunch was near-cow casserole with lots of cheese and broliform.

I'd just sat down when I heard the voice of a little girl call loudly from across the cafeteria, "Can we play dress up now? You wear the pink dress."

I glanced over just in time to see Pace Jones cover his wrist. "Son of a slugging farthog!" There were a few laughs from the marines nearby.

Across from him, a loud fart sounded from Dave Warren. That was enough to set them off. Half the room was laughing at the rascals.

Sophie narrowed her eyes at me as I gave my best wide-eyed, innocent look. "Mark, you pulled the same trick on my boyfriend in high school, didn't you?"

"Oh look," I called, waving toward the hatch. "Rowdy, we're over here."

***

"You weren't kidding," said Aasha, "you *do* know which part of the pistol to point at the target."

"Ha ha. So that's what happens to unemployed comedians. They become marines." I opened the breach and popped out the clip.

"Ninety-two is a pretty good score," she said as she entered it on her tablet. At the other end of the range, the old target faded and a new image took its place.

We sat there for a few moments, with Aasha paying attention to her tablet and me standing there holding the pistol with the handle out for her to take.

Aasha didn't appear to notice and instead looked over her shoulder at the target.

"Are you ready?" I asked.

I barely caught her acknowledgment before the pistol leaped out of my hands. The clip slammed home and suddenly nine rounds were in the target, in the blink of an eye.

There was a full two-second pause and then a tenth bang.

"Oops," she said as the target image rematerialized before us, showing nine neat holes in the bullseye. "I missed the last shot. Ninety points. You win." She didn't hesitate, but ejected the spent clip and handed my pistol back to me, handle first.

I blinked stupidly for a handful of heartbeats before taking the pistol back.

She walked out of the range without a backward glance. "I'll let *Leo* know you're allowed down here. Make sure to schedule your time in advance."

***

I entered the bridge to relieve Sara's watch. Natalia and Wally were already there changing over their duties.

Sara almost sneered as she said, "The ship is on course. No incidents or actions to report. You may relieve the watch."

"Thank you, Ms. Chew. I have the watch," I answered formally.

She waved her hand. "Whatever."

I motioned for her to join me at the back of the bridge. She followed. Keeping my voice low, I put my back to the rest of the bridge. "Is there something I need be aware of, Ms. Chew?"

She grimaced like she'd bitten into something sour. "No, Mr. Martin. No problem."

"The hostility? What have I done to upset you?"

She gave me a measuring look before she continued. "It's you. You are the problem."

"Wha—"

She cut me off. "You think you can come in here and take Dan's place? You can't. You're not even half the astrogator or even a quarter of the officer. You waltz in here, with your doctor sister, having exactly the skills we need. I don't buy it. You were there when Dan was almost killed and then you just happen to show up on the way back." Sara shook her head. "You may have the captain fooled, but not me. Not for a second."

"My transport was blown out of the sky. I crashed in a parking lot."

She lifted an eyebrow. "Ha! You expect me to believe you shot a starfighter down in an unarmed transport? Sell those cowan droppings to someone else. And the way you're carrying on with Racy is just disgusting."

I had a hard time believing Sara was serious. The hard glare said she believed every word of it. "I didn't shoot down that fighter, the marines did that, and Racy is teaching me Muscat, nothing more."

Sara put her finger right under my nose. "I don't know what you're playing at, Mark Martin—if that is your name—but whatever it is, it won't work. I will not let you hurt anyone else I care about. You hear me?"

"They're my crew too now."

She set her jaw. I thought she was going to punch me, but the moment passed and she stormed off the bridge. Natalia eyed the hatch to the bridge warily but made no move to follow the first mate. Taking a few deep breaths, I sat in the OD station. Natalia and Wally waited as if expecting something to happen. I wondered if Sara might be a spy for the Porcu-bears. It would be a clever move to deflect suspicion by blaming me.

After a couple of moments, Wally spoke up. "Problems, sir?"

I shook my head. "No, Wally. Just a difference of opinion. Nothing to worry about."

Wally nodded. "Pardon me for saying so, sir, but the last engine man who upset her never came back from liberty."

"Thanks for the heads up. It won't come to that."

"If you say so, sir."

He stared suspiciously at me. I wasn't sure I believed it either.

CHAPTER 14: *OCELOT*

It took another week to reach our destination. I sat at my navigation station on the bridge with the three deck officers and Wally. Everyone focused their attention on the countdown timer as it made its way to zero.

Wally called out the final seconds. "Five... four... three... two... one... R-drive disengaged."

The view screen showed the universe outside as it went from black to star-speckled darkness.

The captain turned to me. "Get us a fix when you're able Mr. Martin."

It wasn't long. "Ma'am, we are within one AU of the target."

"Do better next time, Mr. Martin. What's here?"

She was twitting me. One AU, one distance from old Terra to Sol, was so close it didn't matter. Eighteen parsecs, 552 trillion kilometers, and we were within eight light minutes.

"Nothing in our immediate space. There's something a little less than half a light hour away." Using visual and gravity sensors, the ship's AI created an image on the forward display. "An odd collection of ships around three... no, four asteroids."

Jenna did smile then. "Good. Welcome to *Ocelot*, Mr. Martin. *Leo*, please hail them and ask for a slip. Mr. Martin, plot us a course and give them about twice the no wake zone you'd give a planet or space station. They get a might touchy here when someone comes rabbitin' in."

"Aye aye, ma'am." The calculations were easy. There were no

other celestial bodies to worry about, but because we had to accelerate and slow back down, it would take longer to get there. Four days. I routed the plot to the captain, who reviewed it carefully before forwarding the numbers to Wally.

"Mr. Walashek, steady as she goes."

Wally looked at the plot and made the corrections. "Aye aye, ma'am."

I gazed at the view screen. The space station appeared to be four asteroids lashed together somehow, one big rock and three smaller ones. It looked like the paw of some giant animal.

***

The course laid in, the captain called normal watch. I was on first watch, so I headed for the mess hall. With a little luck, I'd run into Aasha or Rowdy and find out a bit more about the space station.

Aasha was there, watching our approach on the big monitor. A smaller screen displayed a news channel. A pirate port with its own news station? Clearly, *Ocelot* was not what I expected.

She grinned as I came in. "Whadda ya think?"

I shrugged. "Don't know what to make of it yet. What is it?"

"A smugglers den. Officially, it doesn't exist. You won't find it on any charts. It's one of several places out here that work outside of interstellar law. We can get supplies and do business without some planetary or multisystem government getting in the way."

My eyebrows bounced off the overheads. "Any laws?"

She shook her head. "Not really. Old Anubis runs the place."

"Anubis?"

"That's not his real name. No one knows his real name, but he built the station. Took a few mined asteroids, moved them out here, added gravity plating, environmental, a few docks. He has enforcers to keep the peace, but the main rules are no fighting on the station and no cutting in on his business."

"His business?" I asked.

"Docking fees and ship supplies. The station is armed and armored, so the smugglers and pirates behave themselves."

I couldn't see any obvious weapons at this distance. "How well-armed?"

Aasha wrinkled her nose. "Any real military wouldn't break a sweat turning it into space dust."

The idea rattled around in my head for a minute. "I'm betting it wouldn't do them any good either. Blow it up or take the station and they'd just set up someplace else a month or two later."

She inclined her head in agreement. "Exactly. Mostly Terrans and Muscat on the station, but a few Hedgehogs and Dru as well. Everything is for sale, so try not to be shocked." She gave me an evil grin. "Also, don't go anywhere unarmed and travel in groups."

"Thanks, I'll tell Sophie."

Aasha grinned and looked over my shoulder.

"She's right behind me, isn't she?" I felt a smack on the back of my head. "Hey, Sophie."

The news channel caught my attention with a picture of the Terran Confederacy flag and the Dru shield in flames. I groaned. Just great: another diplomatic incident. I listened to the news story with interest. A Terran colony ship had arrived in a system to find the Dru already in possession of the habitable planet.

Sophie snorted. "No big surprise. A water world, and the Dru are aquatic."

"Yeah," I said, "and I just bet the Dru ambassador will claim he knew nothing about it." Sure enough, the report included video of the official denial. The next frame was a picture of the ambassador having lunch. In the background was the TC Colonization Authority in New York. His water collar and blue skin easily identified him among the human crowd.

Sophie scowled. "I thought that area of the city was restricted to Dru."

I nodded. "It is. Score another blow to galactic relations."

There was another newscast about a new technology. Envirotek had developed a way to speed up atmosphere processing on new colony worlds. A Muscat company had cried foul, saying that the tech infringed on several patents they held.

The next news feed had me riveted. It was an interview with the Erethizon ambassador to the Terran Confederacy. Celebrity news personality Charlotte McNulty sat across from the Porcu-bear. She seemed at ease with the 2.5 meter alien. She'd worn a stylish, bright red dress for the occasion and they'd brought in an oversized chair for her guest. I mentally cringed at what the four-centimeter quills that covered his body were doing to the leather upholstery.

Charlotte shook her blonde mane and smiled. "Thank you for

joining us, Ambassador Magnimus."

He patted her arm. "My pleasure, Charlotte." His bear-like mouth opened, showing his pointed teeth. Calling it a smile would be too charitable.

"Ambassador, my understanding is that hostilities have stopped on Yale."

He inclined his head. "Mostly. Forces loyal to the Theocracy are maintaining order in the cities. A lot of the outlying areas are still controlled by terrorists. Theocracy ships remain in the system, providing support for the Monarchy."

The interviewer's brows furrowed. "Monarchy? I thought the legitimate government was a Republic?"

He spread his paws. "As it turns out, the people of Yale voted to reinstate the Monarchy. The day before we broke through the insurgent lines they elected a new king. As you know, governments often request to join the One True Way. We strongly encourage them to keep their existing leadership. We only ask that the leaders respect church directives." A picture appeared on the screen of Mr. Spangle, head of the Minority Royalist Party carrying a crown on a velvet cushion.

Charlotte arched an eyebrow in his direction. "That seems very convenient, Ambassador."

The Erethizon took a deep breath and his quills stood out straight like a sea urchin before settling back down. "It came as a surprise to us as well, but we are a benevolent people. If this is what the people of Yale want. We will abide by their decision."

She nodded in understanding. "So what happens now?"

The Porcu-bear turned to face the camera. "The new monarch and some of his cabinet have expressed his desire to take a pilgrimage to the holy land. We have agreed to transport them. We've asked that they not stay too long. Their homeworld needs their guidance right now. New initiates often spend months enjoying the wonders of the Great Temple of Urson. Our garrison priests are quite capable of supporting the local peacekeepers until then."

"What a load of cowan," exclaimed Sophie.

I shook my head. "At least we know that the resistance is still strong."

"And that they put Mr. Spangle on the throne. Can you believe they brought back the monarchy?" My sister made a show of pulling her hair. "I guess it makes sense. A central authority. Fewer leaders to coerce and control."

"They sent the new King and the Senate leaders to a re-education camp," I said. "Safe bet that dad was one of the senators. We need to find out where they took them. We know it wasn't Arcadia. Wherever they've stashed their concentration colony, it isn't there."

She turned to me. "Where do we start? How do we start?"

"How about a smuggler's den?" I gestured to another screen showing our approach to *Ocelot*. "I bet we can price what it would cost to extract him as well. Provided we can find a mercenary unit that is honest and skilled enough for the job. Then we just need to know where to find him."

"Good luck," she sighed, "we'll need it."

***

Docking at the space station was a careful procedure. *Ocelot*'s traffic control AI took over as the ship made the final approach, and then we eased into the docking clamps.

I turned to the captain. "What do we do for customs inspection?"

She laughed. "Nothing's illegal here. What would they look for?"

I shrugged. She had a point.

The captain declared liberty for anyone not on duty. My section had the watch, which put Wally on lock duty as soon as we were settled in.

He had his hands full as a steady stream of people made their way off the ship. He logged everyone's mass as they exited and would add it back to the ship's total mass when they came back aboard. After the first rush, I went down to medical to see Sophie. She was reviewing what looked like a list of medical supplies.

"Hey sis, what's up?"

She smiled up at me. "Nothing, just checking the station net for medical supplies. We're running low on consumables like artificial blood, stimulants, and painkillers. I'm having to wade through a bunch of hallucinogenics and euphorics. Seems things illegal everywhere else are not necessarily illegal here."

"Run the suppliers by Boldrini. It's buyer beware out here."

Sophie shot me a knowing look. "Oh yeah. Way ahead of you. He's coming down after he gets his own order for stores in."

That was the Sophie I knew and loved, always one step ahead of her little brother. "I was wondering, have you spoken with Sara recently."

She shook her head. "No. I think she's avoiding me."

I gave her the gist of our conversation on the bridge. She nodded her head, deep in thought. "Makes sense."

"Clue me in?"

My sister gave me a patient smile. "For all practical purposes, her boyfriend died. Except he didn't and he's still here, which is much worse."

It was twisted, but I followed.

She continued. "So she's going through the grieving process. With a disease or something, there's no one to blame, but in this case, we showed up. We did everything we could to save him, and did, but in her eyes we failed. She's hurt, angry, and looking for someone to blame. Some part of her may realize she's wrong, but she's not going to accept that. It's too unfair."

It made sense. "She's the first mate. Her bad side is bad for us."

Sophie shrugged. "Talk to Jenna about it."

"She's the captain. It's an officer thing. You can't complain about someone in your chain of command to another member of your chain of command." I sighed. "Change of subject. You want to go shopping later? I need clothes, music, and a couple of beers. Join me?"

She gave me a curious look. "What are we going to use for money?"

"Check your wrist computer. We got paid when we docked."

Sophie got that faraway look I associated with checking a HUD, a heads up display. Her eyes registered surprise. If it was like mine, the salary was the agreed amount, but the profit shares were large. Apparently, smuggling was a lucrative business.

She paused a moment. "Um. Yeah. I'll meet you in the main lock in four hours."

As I was leaving medical, my wrist computer trilled. The captain wanted to see me.

CHAPTER 15: ROUGH AND TUMBLE

The captain's door was open. I knocked on the frame.

Jenna looked up at me. "Thanks for coming, Mark. Please come in and shut the door."

I shut the door and came to attention in front of her desk.

The captain laughed. "At ease, Mark. I haven't been a Confed captain for fifteen years. Have a seat. I wanted to let you know there are some hedgehog mercs on the station."

I nodded. "Ms. Gudka told me."

"The Theocracy are a bunch of fanatical zealots, but they ain't stupid. Watch your tongue."

"Okay, Jenna. I'll be on my guard. What are we dropping off?"

"Everything in Cargo Pod Four. Frozen food. They don't grow much on the station. No space. Food and water are always in demand."

"And what are we picking up?"

She waggled her eyebrows. "I don't know yet. I'll be working my contacts here to see what jobs are available. That will determine our next two or three runs. You should come with me on a couple."

***

I stopped by the squad bay. "Hey Aasha, can I borrow an escort?"

The edges of her lips turned down. "What? You can't take care of yourself ashore? I have to find some poor schmuck to babysit you?"

"Me and my sister. I want someone who knows the station. Extra eyes wouldn't hurt either."

She snorted as she walked into the berths. There was a loud clang as she hit the metal bunk with something. "Come on Jay, I just found your extra duty."

The bleary-eyed medic followed her out a moment later. He smiled when he saw me. "Hey, flyboy."

"Listen up," Aasha said. "The doc and her little brother want a tour of the town. You're their escort while they're here. Do that and we'll be good."

"Feeling generous, Sarge? That's not like you."

"For the rest of the stay, you're their beck and call boy," she clarified with an evil smile.

"No liberty? Sarge!" he protested.

"You're lucky I'm not puttin' your ass ashore."

"But Warren..."

She shook her head. "But Warren nothing. You're the one who got caught."

He glared at Aasha but spoke to me. "Mark, when are you thinking?

"Two hours."

"Okay, main lock. Check out that pea shooter of yours from the armory."

***

The docks of the asteroid were in bedlam. The walls were a mixture of dull gray rock marked with water, air, and electrical runs. A clear industrial sealant kept in the air and heat. Bright yellow cargo lifters raced in both directions along the concourse as spacers dressed in every color ship suit tried to stay out of the way. The most common ship suit was gray with blue piping; must be the station colors.

Then there was the smell: spices, electronics, and human sweat all rolled into one, plus the cinnamon scent I had come to associate with Muscat.

My AI logged into station net and I located a strip mall two levels up and an elevator just around the bend to our right.

As we walked along, Sophie asked, "Why did they take our weight when we left the ship?"

"Mass," Jay and I answered in unison.

"Mass what?"

Jay laughed. "Mass, Doc. You remember how the captain took down your weight when you signed the contract? They need to know the exact weight, the mass, of everything and everyone on board."

I gave Sophie a wry grin. "We use the total to make the calculations on how much power it takes to get the ship moving and how much field strength is needed for the drives." I cocked an eyebrow. "You didn't lie about your weight did you?"

Sophie punched me in the arm. "No."

We threaded our way through the hustle and bustle. I heard bits of conversations going on around us in a dozen different Terran and Muscat dialects. Those seemed to be the dominant races on the station. Considering where we were in the galaxy, it made a certain amount of sense.

My sister cocked her head in Jay's direction. "What did Aasha catch you for?"

He rolled his eyes. "Cooking grease. War 'n Pace and I coated the ladder into engineering. They must have heard Rowdy coming and left. I finished the top stair and turned into a snarl full of teeth."

"There's a ladder in engineering?"

Jay laughed. "Ship lingo, doc. We call stairs ladders."

We made it to the elevators without getting run over, and I punched the button for the main promenade.

Jay leaned over to Sophie. "Doc, you'll want to put that purse in one of your leg pockets."

Sophie had brought a small clutch. She looked a bit confused, but did as he suggested.

The lift doors opened up onto still more chaos, just without the cargo lifters. Here I could see a few blue-skinned Dru. A head taller than the Terrans, thinner, with no hair, ears, or noses, they looked like scattered blue balloons bobbing just above the crowd. The smell of seaweed now mixed in with the human sweat and cinnamon.

We were at the bottom of three levels. The main thoroughfare was twenty meters across. You could walk up through the middle to the other balconies. Beings from all walks of life could be seen leaning against the rails on the upper areas or walking between the shops. Lighting panels in the ceiling far above gave the illusion of sunlight.

Suddenly, three Terran kids raced through the crowd right past us. Reflexively, Jay reached out and grabbed one of them by the collar. He glared down at the girl, who couldn't have been more than eight years old.

"Hey! Let me go!"

He hoisted her off the deck in one hand and held his other hand out as if he expected her to give him something. "Give it back. Now!"

The girl glared back at him, but eventually handed him a small purse that looked like Sophie's. I realized with a start that it *was* Sophie's. Her eyes shot open wide as she checked her open leg pocket.

Jay set the girl back down and she disappeared into the throng. Jay gave a knowing look to Sophie. "That's why. Please secure the zipper this time."

"Thanks, I will!"

We made our way down the corridor, alternating between looking for pickpockets and store windows. Sophie found a dress shop staffed by a gray-nosed Muscat. The dresses were stylish, unique creations. Using a step ladder, the Muscat got all of her measurements. She picked out three dresses and the tailor said he'd have them delivered.

I found a men's shop run by a Dru named Augurga. The smell of seaweed hit me as I walked through the door. It seemed like every time I turned around he had exactly what I needed. Dru speech is at the lower end of human hearing, so I had to listen carefully. He had no trouble understanding me. His shop seemed empty considering the selection.

He answered my unspoken question. "Thank you. I'm glad you appreciate my work. Many races have an inflated view of our abilities. They are distrustful, suspicious, or afraid."

"You can read surface thoughts, right? Other race's thoughts are a bit confusing?"

He nodded. "It takes getting used to. Often it is feelings and impressions, not words. Some races are harder than others. Few of my people can understand a Muscat." He paused and turned to my sister. "No. The Erethizon are the easiest to read, Dr. Martin. Their thoughts are usually simple, straightforward."

I picked up two pairs of slacks, four shirts, shoes, and an assortment of socks. Undershirts and underwear rounded out my purchases.

I finished paying. Augurga offered me a last bit of advice. "There is an Erethizon chapel on 1L2 and an electronics store on the promenade called Werga Components. You and your sister should avoid them."

"Sound advice. Thanks."

He gave me a short bow from the waist. "You are welcome, Mark Martin."

Jay said he wanted to visit a weapons shop, so we followed him to a shop with several blades and pistols in the window. The name of the shop was Foxfire Arms. A grizzled old Muscat with an eye patch sat behind the counter. Jay asked the proprietor if he had some things in stock. He went to the back room to check. Browsing the display cases, I saw several weapons illegal on Yale. I also saw three Erethizon neural whips. Why any sane person would use such a weapon was beyond me.

The whips caused excruciating pain. They would incapacitate most people, but if you wanted to knock someone out there were plenty of better weapons to do the job. If your only intent was to cause pain though, I couldn't think of a better way to do it. To hear it described, it made you feel like you were being set on fire.

We ran into Aasha on the way out of the store. She seemed surprised to see us. "Hi guys. What's up?"

Jay jerked his thumb over his shoulder. "Just getting a look at the new MX70s."

Aasha's eyes lit up. "The one with the gyroscopic stabilizers and smart rounds?"

Jay nodded. "Oh yeah."

They continued to gush about guns as I checked out our surroundings. It was then that I noticed exactly where we were. Two doors down across from us on the promenade was Werga Components, the store the Dru had warned me about. Just as I was about to get my companions' attention, something else caught my eye. Sara was coming out of the store with a package under one arm. She was accompanied by War 'n Pace.

She hadn't seen us yet so I turned to my group. "Hey guys,

we're a little closer than I'd like to be to a shop I'd rather avoid. Can we move a bit further down the corridor?"

Jay looked around and caught sight of the storefront. "The Erethizon shop? Aren't you being just a bit paranoid? Not all of them are religious fanatics or spies." Then he noticed who was there. "Ugh. I'm a little miffed at those two though. What do you all think about lunch?"

***

Booty Bay was done up in a pirate theme from the days of wooden ships and sails. The walls, chairs, and tables were made to look like rough-hewn oak but was actually some sort of composite. It looked a little cheesy to me, but they had human waitstaff. They were dressed as sailors and wenches of course, but seemed friendly enough.

Jay had been spot on about the food. I had a Lir near-salmon in garlic herb sauce that was fantastic. It seemed that my three companions were enjoying their dishes as much as I was. The bill was more than I was expecting but then I remembered that everything had to be shipped to this remote rock.

Jay and Aasha kept us entertained with stories about places they'd been and cultures they'd seen. Jay's family was from Hephaestus, a mining and manufacturing world with a lot of tectonic activity. It was easy to see why he'd left. Aasha, meanwhile, had grown up on a space station on the edge of Muscat space. Almost all of her family still lived there and she sent them voicemail every chance she got.

One thing Aasha wouldn't talk about was the accident that caused her to replace half of her body with cybernetic parts. I got the feeling it was traumatic. I'd discussed it with Sophie a few times. Some people forced to replace body parts with machines often felt like there was less of them than before. They felt less than human. Carefully watching Aasha's "real" eye when she talked about it made me wonder if that was the case with her. The merry light in her eye was sometimes replaced by something else— "haunted" might be the right word for it.

We didn't dwell on it. The conversation moved on. Sophie told us about a male patient who had been stung by razor bees after covering sensitive parts of himself with honey. I told a story about a sailor who had passed out drunk. His buddies had left him at the zoo... in the land leech exhibit.

The conversation was light, but I couldn't help thinking about Sara coming out of the component shop. What had she been doing there? Was she there on ship's business? Personal? I couldn't put it out of my mind.

At one point a couple of men in light armor and dog's head patches on their shoulders passed by the hallway outside. Everyone gave them a wide berth. They had the swagger of bullies.

"Jay," I said, "I want to head back to the ship."

"Doc?" Asked Jay.

"I still need to visit the clinic on 2L3, to check the quality of nanites."

He shrugged at me.

"Just ask Aasha. I'm going straight back to the ship. Promise."

Jay eyed me for a moment, before getting that far away look people get when using their HUD. "Aasha says that's fine. Just don't go down any dark alleys."

I smiled. "Deal."

***

At the door, I stumbled over the less than successful pickpocket from earlier. After checking my pockets I gave her my best hairy eyeball. "Fancy meeting you here."

"It wasn't an accident," said the little waif, "I followed you here." She looked up at me with bright blue eyes. They were in stark contrast to the rest of her. There was enough dirt on her face and clothes to fill a small garden.

Her matter-of-fact tone struck my funny bone, and I barked a laugh. "Aren't you afraid I'll turn you in to security or something?"

"No," she said, as if she didn't have a care in the world, "Pythia said you wouldn't hurt me. She always tells the truth."

"Okay, so why are you following me?"

"Oh, yeah!" as if she remembered something. "Pithy wants to see you. She said it was important."

I waited. There had to be more. When the urchin continued to stare up at me, I prompted her, "Why should I see Pythia? Is she a shopkeeper? Does she have something for me?"

She rolled her eyes at me. "Duh, everyone wants to see Pithy.

84

She, like, knows everything about everyone."

My curiosity aroused, I motioned with one arm for her to lead the way. As soon as she turned I checked the pistol in my holster. I thought about telling Jay where I was going, but it was just a little girl. I couldn't possibly be in danger from her. At the lift, I saw War 'n Pace watching me from up the passage. They didn't do anything, so I shrugged it off.

She led me down four levels and we exited the stairs and turned left. There were fewer people down here and some of the lighting panels were out. I started to get a bad feeling. It got worse when I noticed three rough-looking guys trailing us down the passage.

I unclasped the holster and, in plain view of the ruffians, put my hand on the pistol. It didn't deter them. They started gaining ground. I was about to draw on them when they stopped and scrambled over each other to run the other way. Ahead there were two armed men standing on either side of an unmarked metal door. Dog's head patches on their shoulders identified them as station security.

My escort walked past them through the door. I paused and looked at both of them with my palms up. The one on the left looked me up and down before jerking his head sideways, indicating I should proceed.

Inside was a comfortable waiting room. Three people in nice clothes sat scattered around the room. They looked up with interest as I entered. But interest turned to annoyance as the waif led me into the next room, leaving them behind.

There, she fidgeted next to me, so I took a moment to take in the room.

It was well-lit. A large, red, overstuffed chair sat on a raised platform at the back of the room, four smaller plastic chairs placed in front of it. A heavily armed woman stood leaning against the wall next to the big chair. The only other person in the room was a little girl in the corner. She sat with her back to me as she presided over a tea party with two stuffed animals and a doll. Her shoulder-length blond hair was pulled back with a velvet band.

"Um, Pithy, I got him," the waif said.

The little girl at the tea party stood and put her hand up. The armed woman crossed to her and gingerly took her hand before leading her to the red chair.

It was when she sat down facing the room that I noticed her

eyes were milky white and completely lacking irises. "Thanks, Holly. There are some people I have to see after Mr. Martin, but do you want to play later?"

"Can we eat first?" The urchin, Holly, bit her lip and smiled shyly.

"Yeah. I'll have Mr. Bootzin pay me in meals for the rest of the week."

Holly exited the room, leaving me with Pythia and Ms. Guns-and-Knives. "Come here, Mr. Martin. I want to see your face."

"See my face?" I asked as I approached her.

"Feel your face, dummy," she huffed. "I'm blind, but everything else works fine, so don't talk slow or anything else annoying like that."

I sat on the platform and put her right hand on my face. I gasped as I felt little electric shocks wherever she touched me. She put her other on my face and I closed my eyes as she explored the dips and ridges of my cheeks and nose.

Satisfied, she smiled sadly. "It's not over. Bears have chased you from your home, but you've found a new home. It isn't safe, though."

She ran her fingers along the ridge above my eyes. "Soon the mother wolf will call for you. She will offer you three gifts. You'll want to turn them down, but you shouldn't. You'll need all three to survive what's coming."

Her fingers found the corners of my lips and pulled them down. "The Bear will chase you from her home, under the sea, and back here again. You'll need to learn something from that, but you may not understand right away."

Her thumb pulled one side of my lips up. "The rest is hazy, but I think you'll see me again." She pulled the other side up. "Yes, you'll see me again. Maybe things will be clearer then."

Pulling her hands back she sighed, "You have questions. Ask me."

"Who are you?" I asked.

"Pythia. And yes, I work with Reggie sometimes. Reggie is the guy most people know as Anubis, and..." Pythia covered her mouth and cocked her head in the direction of the guard. "Sandy was going to say it's rude of me to answer people's questions before they ask them. I'm so sorry, Mr. Martin."

"You're a telepath?" I asked.

"No. I see the future," she said. "Anything a few minutes from now is pretty clear, but further out it's more like dreams. The images mean something, but I don't know what."

"So, the mother wolf?"

"A mother wolf with three cubs and three boxes with bows." She shrugged. "And no, I don't know what it means. I only know you need to accept the gifts. If you don't then the bad bears catch you."

"Anubis?"

"You'll meet Reggie soon. Tell him I said 'hi.'"

"How can I repay you?"

She smiled broadly. "You can sing me a song! No, not the one about the magnapple tree. Can you sing the one about the pink elephants and purple sun cats?"

***

It was late by the ship's clock when I finally made it back to the *Leo*. I needed to catch a few hours sleep before I was back on duty. It felt like I'd just fallen asleep when there was a knock on my door. Rubbing my eyes, I climbed out of bed and pulled on a ship suit. The captain was at my door.

"Get your lazy ass down to the armory and suit up," she ordered, with more energy than my groggy brain was prepared for. "You, me, and Aasha have an appointment with the afterlife." I had no idea what she could possibly mean.

I stopped by the head on the way and splashed water on my face. Aasha met me in the armory.

"Put this on," she instructed.

"That's powered armor," I said, stating the obvious while the fogginess worked its way out of my head.

"That it is, pretty boy. You ever wear any?"

"Yeah," I said, yawning, "a couple times. Standard biometric interface?"

"You move, it moves," she confirmed. "Pinky fingers and voice commands for the menus, heads-up display for targeting. Ever use a TR45?"

She tossed me the rifle and I caught it. The weight knocked me back a couple of steps. "No, but I've fired a TR32."

"Similar. No manual safety. Kicks twice as much." She pointed to the selector switch. "More options for rounds, but we're going in for show, so we won't worry about that. If we have time before we lose our firing range, I'll give you a proper demonstration."

"For show?"

"You bet, cupcake." She slugged me hard on the arm. "We're negotiating contracts in the big dog's den. The captain can't afford to look weak. That means a show of force, but with people smart enough to follow her lead."

I nodded. "And the firing range?"

"We're set up in a cargo hold, flyboy. If all goes well, it'll be full this time tomorrow."

***

We followed the captain down passages on one of the lower levels. The station seemed to be set up with habitation at the top, shops in the middle, and services at the bottom. Since Anubis ran everything on these rocks, it made sense he'd be down there.

We stopped in front of a blood red door with gold filigree flanked by guards. The guard on the right handled the details. "Name?"

"Captain Jennifer Houston of the *Leonard Fox*. You know who I am, Brad."

"And you know the drill, Jenna. Just a sec." He spoke into a wrist comm.

A couple of moments later the hatch opened and we went inside. The waiting room was overdone in velvet, plush carpeting, and cushioned couches. Our escort asked us to sit. The captain sat, but Aasha and I stood. We kept an eye on our escort and the room.

"How long do you think, ma'am?" asked Aasha.

"A half hour at least. The big dog needs to feel important."

It was forty minutes.

A section of wall rose up and another guard motioned us forward. We walked down a long narrow corridor with another hatch at the end. Inside, a dark-skinned man was looking over the shoulder of a man with white hair who sat at the smaller of two desks. An armed guard stood in each corner of the room. Several shelves lined the walls, filled with seemingly random objects and piles of papers.

"Shut off the power and air on the number four slip," The

dark-skinned man said. "And lock them down. They'll pay or they'll pay."

"Persuasion, sir?" asked the man at the desk.

"Not yet. Let them sweat for a few days before we send Aziz to help them see the light."

"Trouble, Anubis?" asked the captain.

His hard, dark eyes swiveled in her direction. "Not at all. Just business." He crossed to a large rosewood desk and activated the terminal on it. "Is this a social call or are you looking for work?" His voice was all business.

The captain played it off as flirting. "Can't it be both?" she asked with a saucy wink.

"No." He snarled and turned to his terminal. "Captain Houston, *Leonard Fox*, 3,500 ton freight capacity Pike model T5621, lightly armed, R-drive, stealth ability." There followed a long silence punctuated by occasional stabs at the keyboard. "I've got a hundred units of STPs going from the Andri Belt to Delta Pavonis," he said finally.

"Pass," said the captain.

"It pays well."

"We don't do Terran trafficking. "

Anubis shrugged. "STPs: Simulated Terrans. Not sentient beings, more like cattle."

The captain couldn't quite keep the disgust out of her voice. "Not enough of a difference. Pass."

There was another pause followed by two more keystrokes. "Had your fill of Porcu-bears yet? Got a weapons shipment from Gra'nome to Aspen."

"Aspen? Good to see they're planning ahead."

He shook his head. "No. You'll be sneaking over the wall. The Erethizon left two detachments in Yale: two battlecruisers, a frigate, and three destroyers. They moved the main flotilla to Aspen."

The captain groaned. "What's it pay?"

"Double base plus ten for 3,000 tons. Early delivery bonus if you can get it there in three months. Interested?"

"We'll get the guns to Aspen. Send me the paperwork. Got anything going to Gra'nome?"

"Not a thing."

She grunted. "We'll find something to make the chicken

scratch."

Anubis studied the captain's face. "I'm sure your engineer will be happy to visit his home."

"I'm not so sure about that."

"Any other shipments you want to discuss?"

"No. We'll rustle up our own shipments for the gaps. Thanks, old dog."

His face didn't betray whether he liked or hated the nickname. I didn't want to play poker against this man, but I thought of something as we were ushered to another wall that became a passage. I turned back to him, "Pythia says hello."

"Thanks." One corner of his mouth twitched up.

CHAPTER 16: CAROUSING

I was sitting in the tiny space laughingly referred to as the ship's office when Jay came in to say hello.

"Hey, Mr. Martin," he said as he plopped himself down in the plastic chair on the other side of the desk. "What did you think of your first trip to *Ocelot*?"

I laughed. "I don't know what I was expecting, but whatever it was, that wasn't it." I thought about it a moment. "I didn't think about the pickpockets, but in hindsight, I should have. The security was a little shocking. The five-star quality food was a pleasant surprise."

Jay smiled. "Glad you liked it. It isn't profitable for everyone to get all punchy, so on *Ocelot* people behave themselves. Still, if you get dumped here or fall on hard times, people get desperate enough to cause mischief. If the pickpockets get caught, they'll be spending the next couple of months cleaning sludge out of the waste recycling system or patching micrometeorite holes—whatever unpleasant task no one else wants to do."

That made a lot of sense to me. It was often pretty hard to hire people to do those dirty or dangerous tasks.

Jay continued, "Anyway, a few of the guys are going to a bar tomorrow night, do you wanna come along?"

I thought about it for a few heartbeats. It would be an opportunity to bond with the crew. On a military ship, the officers wouldn't carouse with the enlisted, but I wasn't in the military anymore. The protocol among this smuggler crew was a bit looser than even among the merchant crews I'd seen. There was still the question of safety, but I'd be with my crew and no one in their right mind would challenge a pack of marines and sailors. It would also give Jay a chance at liberty, even if he had to spend it with me, which I suspected was the whole reason he'd made the invitation.

I nodded. "Yes, that sounds like fun. When and where?"

"Meet us in the lock at 2000 ship time."

"I'll be there."

He left the room and I returned my attention to the screen. I'd put out a request for bids for a rescue mission. The results weren't encouraging.

"Hey, little brother." Sophie was leaning on the doorjamb.

"Hey, sis."

"What's wrong?"

I gestured to the screen. "Mercenaries. Trying to hire someone to find and rescue dad."

She came around to my side of the desk. "And?"

"And no one will touch it. Plenty of people were interested at first. That changed when they learned that dad was held by the Porcu-bears. Offers vanished like water in a vacuum."

Sophie bit her lip. "Now what do we do?"

I sighed heavily. "We find a different rock to turn over. There's got to be someone willing to help."

***

We met at the appointed hour. Jay and Aasha were there, as well as Rafe, Rowdy, Gina, and Wally. We checked out of the ship and ended up at a bar on 2L3 called Rossum's Comet.

It was decorated with black walls speckled with pinprick lights and the occasional plastic asteroid or moon thrown in for good measure. The subdued lighting came from fixtures made to look like red, yellow, or white suns. The main bar was made to look like a comet with a long tail. Like the seafood restaurant, it was cheesy to the point of being comical. The floor felt gritty beneath my boot soles.

We pulled a couple of metal tables together in a corner and ordered the first round. Given the décor and distance from any civilized world, I was expecting watered down, stale beer, but it was pretty good: a nutty brown ale from a system I'd never been to, but it tasted great.

While it was noisy, I didn't yet have to yell to be heard. "Hey Jay, how do they end up with such good food and drink out here in the middle of nowhere?"

He leaned toward me and waggled his eyebrows. "Smuggling is big business. There's a lot of money floating around out there for people willing to take a risk. If you have enough credits, someone will find a way to get you what you want."

I caught a peek at the tab as Aasha paid for the first round. A bit more than you'd pay at a decent bar planet-side, but it wasn't extravagant.

The music started up. It wasn't a live band, but it was rock music. It was pretty good with heavy bass and an industrial feel to it.

Gina was discussing ship's gossip. Jay and Aasha were discussing the merits of various bars they'd visited. I looked around for Rowdy and found him striking up a conversation with a female Muscat a couple of tables away. War 'n Pace had shown up. They were chatting up a couple of girls with purple and green hair. I wasn't involved in any of the conversations, but it was nice to listen in and enjoy my beer.

I noticed a blonde girl in a red dress eyeing Wally from the bar. The dress was hugging her curves. As she caught his eye, she made her way across the room. Her hips swayed and those eyes had a hungry look to them that had nothing to do with food.

Everything about her screamed maneater. She sidled in next to him. "Hey spacer, I was feeling a little cold and lonely over there. Can you warm me up and keep me company?"

I was aware of a change in my friends' moods. Out of the corner of my eye, I saw Gina eye the girl and I saw Aasha tense up, although she was pretending not to pay attention.

"Hi, I'm Wally."

"I'm Violet."

He gave her a half smile. "It's a pleasure to meet you, Violet. What's a sweet flower like you doing in this out-of-the-way garden?"

She bit her bottom lip as she took in his eyes and mouth. "Looking for trouble."

"What kind of trouble?"

She looked him up and down. "The kind of trouble that gets

you into my flower bed."

"I'm not sure I'm the right gardener for you."

She gave him a sly look. "I'm worth it."

"Drinks first."

"My time ain't cheap honey."

His eyes widened, and I could see the light dawn. "Thank you, but no."

Indignation played across her face as Violet left the table. I saw her head in the direction of War 'n Pace. They each had an appreciative leer. The twins in purple and green weren't impressed.

I turned to Gina. "Anything's for sale here?"

"Oh, yeah. Wally handled it well enough."

The drinks kept flowing and the conversation moved from weaponry to speculation about our next cargo to people they knew on some of the ships in port. During a lull in the conversation, Aasha staggered up to me.

"Hey, flyboy. Watch this."

She weaved over to a table not far away. I didn't think anything of it until I saw Jay down his beer.

He gave a heavy sigh as he tugged on Wally's sleeve and pointed. Wally downed his beer and put a few credits on the table.

I looked from one to the other. "What's going on?"

Jay shook his head. "Evening's done. Drink up and be ready to grab Aasha."

I followed them over to where Aasha was chatting up a buff sailor. "All I'm saying is that I've seen piss with more backbone. Did you get special training, or do you naturally lick boots?"

He took a swing at her. She blocked it with her artificial arm and hit him with a left hook. The whole table surged toward Aasha and knocked her into the next table.

CHAPTER 17: TIME TO GO

Jay and I waded in. I kept it friendly until some farthog tried to stomp on my knee. I broke a mug on his face, then used it to catch blows. The broken glass kept anyone from getting too close. Jay and I pulled a few people off of Aasha. She swung wide and clocked me in the temple. I shook it off and caught sight of Wally and Gina. They edged around the outside of the brawl, heading for the door. War 'n Pace stood back to back. I saw Warren grab a punch and pull the guy into Pace's raised knee. Scoundrels they may be, but they knew how to fight.

I deflected a couple of swings and threw a guy past my hip. Jay blocked a punch and kicked a guy in the chest. We managed to each get an arm under a shoulder and practically dragged Aasha out from under five spacers. I took a punch to the kidney and half a beer to the face in the process, but she was still swinging. A foot caught her in the eye and it didn't even faze her.

Rowdy joined the fray with Muscat-sized shock sticks. He watched our backs and lashed out at anyone who came close. The little engineer was quick on his feet and managed to dodge most blows. He smashed a girl in leathers across the face and jabbed some guy in the jewels with his shock sticks.

We had managed to get Aasha to the door when someone hit me with a chair from behind. Using another guy as a ladder, Rowdy hit him three times in the head. I regained my feet only to trip Aasha. With only Jay to hold her back, she was trying—and almost succeeding—to get back into the bar. She still had a maniacal grin on her face. Five meters from the door she calmed down and pulled Jay and me in for a bear hug.

"I juz love youse guys!" she slurred.

I spoke over her head to Jay. "Does she do this often?"

He shook his head. "Often enough."

Aasha just laughed. "Five mo minnies. I would'a had 'em."

Boots thundered down the hall toward us. Aasha pushed me up against the wall and kissed me, hard and sloppy. Station security thugs rushed past us.

She finally came up for air after they were long gone. "Oh Ms. Gudka, you are a dangerous girl," I breathed.

"Flyboy, you have no idea." She licked her lips and gave me a salacious grin.

***

Back aboard the *Leo*, we went our separate ways. I hadn't gotten completely undressed before there was a knock on my cabin door.

Aasha stood there, her eyes steady with mine even though the rest of her was weaving. "I want more."

"This is a very bad idea."

She licked her lips. "I'm full'a bad ideas. Right now, all of them involve you."

I leaned against the door. "Tell me."

"Nuh uh." She shook her head. "Show ya."

She pushed me back into my cabin and into my bunk.

***

Aasha wasn't there when my alarm went off. My AI informed me I had an hour before I was due for my shift. A shower and a med patch had me feeling almost human again, and I headed for my watch.

"How's that eye, sailor?" the captain asked when I arrived in the ship's office.

"Fine, Cap. Looks worse than it is."

She shook her head. "Well, my doubts about you fitting in with the crew are gone. Anubis's goons reviewed the vid feeds. You're confined to ship for the rest of our stay."

I laughed and it made me wince. I'd been punched in the gut

and it was still tender. "No worries, Cap. I'm done with shore leave anyway."

"By the way, none of my business, but she's a love 'em and leave 'em type."

"It's just one night."

She shrugged. Houston came around the desk to look at my screen. "Orion News Service?"

"Yeah, I guess not being on Yale didn't affect my subscriptions. I was surprised that I could get some of them out here."

She shrugged. "Auto-downloads and uploads. Standard protocol for Terran ship AIs. Mail and news services. I think old dogface has three of them running the station. How many subscriptions do you have?"

"A dozen."

Houston blinked, "No kidding?"

I shrugged.

"Then I have an extra duty for you. You're our new intelligence officer. Collect information about systems along our route. I've got enough on my plate, and I could use the help."

"Aye, aye, ma'am."

***

A couple of days later, the captain called a preflight briefing for all the department heads. Sara had the seat to the captain's right, but everyone else sat wherever they felt comfortable. Boldrini and Sophie sat close to the captain. Aasha and Rowdy sat next to me at the other end of the table.

The captain started the conference without preamble. "We've got a legit job for our first leg. We're taking engine parts to Gra'nome. I don't need to tell any of you that the Muscat Queen has not taken sides in the Erethizon and Terran conflict. While we're picking up the weapons, we need to keep a low profile. Don't do anything that calls the buzzards to our feast, and that includes bar brawls." Several of us looked a little sheepish at that. Aasha smiled and gave me a wink.

She continued, "From there, we'll be picking up weaponry and smuggling it into Aspen. We'll get the shield codes when we arrive and make a stealth approach. The Erethizon will be in the system in force, so we can only hope that it goes better than the Yale operation did." There was a grumble of agreement.

"We'll be picking up water and frozen fish to bring back to *Ocelot*. Aspen is full of fisheries, so we've got high demand and low cost on each leg of our journey. I expect the shares to be lucrative."

A murmur of appreciation went around the room. I was thinking about my dad and wondering how much money it would take to mount a rescue. I'd need to get Sophie's take on that after the conference. If smuggling was as profitable as my trip to *Ocelot* had shown, we might be able to make enough to hire a rescue team.

The captain then went down through the chain of command. "Mark, you're the intelligence officer. What have we got?"

This was a bit more informal than I was used to, but when on Mars, do as the Martians do. "I've downloaded all available navigation updates and loaded them into the computer. We're not in a star system, per se, so there's not much in the way of navigation hazards. The Erethizon have occupied Yale." I did my best to keep my voice even. I noticed Sophie closed her eyes and grimaced. "But they don't have complete control of the system. Reports of armed resistance suggest that their usual plan isn't working." I felt a bit of pride reporting that last bit of information. "The fleet there isn't waiting, though. They've moved most of the assets to a new system, Aspen, and started to engage defenses there. That means they're either fighting or blockading the three remaining independent human systems. There's no news of scouting around the Terran Confederation. No change with the blockades at Freya or Saggita."

The captain smiled. "Good work, Mark. I'll want course plots in four hours."

"Aye, aye, ma'am."

She looked at Aasha. "How are we for arms?"

Aasha looked at her tablet. "We've added a sniper rifle to the small arms locker. We've run into a few engagements where it would have been handy, so with your permission, we've restructured one of the squads. They'll train on the new tactics along the way to Gra'nome. We shouldn't need marine support there, but it doesn't hurt to be prepared. We've restocked the ship's armament of missiles and rounds. It was expensive, but it beats the alternative."

The captain nodded her agreement. "Rowdy?"

Rowdy bounced on the edge of his seat. "We're refueled and we're full on volatiles and reaction mass. We've restocked spares, filters, water, and environmental gases. Repairs to battle damage are complete. There were no software updates needed. I've added raw materials for our onboard replicators."

"Good. Dr. Martin?"

I'd coached Sophie on what to do. She rattled her report off like a pro. "We're restocked on the most important medical supplies and except for a few hangovers and bruises, the crew is in good health. There are a few of the crew that have not made time to come by for their physicals and I've sent a message to your inbox with their names. I'll lay in some of the more hard-to-find vaccines, medi-nano, and anti-virals when we reach a port that stocks them."

"Are the physicals necessary?" asked the captain.

Sophie didn't mince words. "Yes. In tight quarters like these, a bout of reaper fever would infect the whole crew in a week. The vaccine is dirt cheap anywhere, and it would be a shame to lose half the crew to something preventable."

The captain apologized. "Sorry, Doc. We haven't had a real doctor on board for some time. You should be able to stock up on Gra'nome."

She turned to Boldrini. "How are we for stores?"

"We have enough food on hand for ninety days. We weren't able to pick up any fresh fruits or vegetables on *Ocelot*. They're just too expensive here. I was able to add in some of the rarer spices for my spice locker, though. Rafe may have had something to do with that."

There was a round of stifled giggles around the table. It was well known that Rafe was an artist when it came to obtaining the unattainable.

***

I was reviewing a map of the surrounding space. The holo-tank on the bridge provided the best interface. It also gave a perspective that a screen never could.

The captain came up beside me and gazed into the multicolored pinpricks of light. "What are ya thinkin'?"

I pointed to a dull red star. "There is a Terran Confederation mining colony here called Eureka. It's rich in precious metals, radioactives, and even some exotic matter. Something about a stellar event long ago—an exploded pulsar or some such. Whatever the reason, the colony there generates enough profit to justify a warp gate. Most of Muscat space doesn't have them, but their homeworld Gra'nome does. We can shave two weeks off our trip by going to Eureka and using the gate."

I had other reasons for wanting to go through that system. I mentally crossed my fingers as Houston tapped her chin with her finger.

Captain Houston nodded. "Two weeks of operating expenses. That'll save a hen or two. Not a lot of traffic out that way. Could be questions. No one in that parcel makes engine parts. Gate authorities will want to know who, what, where from, and where to."

Inwardly I cheered. Outwardly I shrugged. "Is that a problem?"

She grinned wryly. "Sometimes. We ain't picky on how we make our profit. We may have run afoul of the Confederation a time or two."

"You've been at this awhile. Don't tell me you can't handle that kind of problem."

The captain wagged her head back and forth. "We may or may not have an extra identity tucked away."

"You can't play with transponder settings without visiting a port. The encryption on those things is tough and cracking them open destroys them."

"It does, so us less-than law-abiding citizens don't do it. We register more than once instead."

I gave her a curious look. "What?"

She grinned. "We have more than one transponder on board."

"But how?"

"We have the maintenance code. We use it to shut down the ones we aren't currently using. The trick is to come up with a believable story."

I followed her line of thinking. "We need a plausible story boring enough that no one asks questions."

We stood there staring at the star map. I walked to the other side of the holo-tank to see if it gave me a better perspective. One or the other of us manipulated it periodically to get a closer view of various systems.

Then it came to me. "Here."

The captain shook her head. "New Hawaii? They don't make machine parts. It's a resort world."

I pointed into the star map. "Yes, but it's on the way from Hephaestus, where they *do* make machine parts. If we had a passenger fare from Hephaestus to New Hawaii, we'd take the gate to Cassini. There's no gate in New Hawaii, and we might just leg it over to Eureka rather than go back to Cassini."

She continued where I left off. "And no one needs to know that we aren't set up for passengers, because no one is going to board us for inspection in Eureka. We're just passing through. Not stopping."

"Brilliant."

***

Three days out from *Ocelot*, I entered the mess deck to find Boldrini sitting with my sister. It occurred to me that most times I'd been in the mess I'd found him sitting with her. Which wasn't odd in and of itself, but he usually got up when I arrived. I suppose it made sense, him being the chef and all, but Rafe usually handled the serving duties.

Today was no exception, as Boldrini got up and made it a point to personally serve me his Chicken Cacciatore. I thanked him and returned to sit with Sophie. As usual, he returned with me.

It was only then that I noticed where he sat and it all clicked into place. In fact, I must have been pretty dense not to see it before. He sat next to my sister. She looked him in the eyes and moved a little closer as they picked up the conversation where they'd left off. I chuckled to myself.

Sophie narrowed her eyes at me. "What?"

I eyed the two of them. "How long?"

"How long what?"

"How long have the two of you been seeing each other?"

Boldrini blushed, but Sophie scowled. I laughed.

Boldrini spoke up first. "I, uh, asked Sophie out on a date while we were in *Ocelot*. In port mess is pretty easy, so I begged off one night and let Rafe handle it."

My sister picked up the story there. "We went to a nice restaurant called Vacini's. They serve the best Sagitta food I've ever had. We had a nice dinner and a few drinks."

"And you shared a room on the station?" I suggested.

Boldrini looked abashed. My sister gave me an innocent look. "Not that it's any of your business."

I could have pressed it, but the truth was I was happy for them and told them so.

Sara came into the mess soon after that. She eyed us from the serving line and took a table as far from us as she could get and still be in the mess hall.

We'd left Dan on the station. She must have been feeling especially heartbroken. But then, I also remembered seeing Sara coming out of the Erethizon parts shop. What had she been doing there? My mind shied away from the thought that anyone on the crew might be working with the Erethizon. Shopkeepers aside, the Porcu-bears would kill all of us if they could.

I shook my head. There wasn't anything I could do about it, so there wasn't much use in worrying. I dug into the chicken and enjoyed the company at my table.

CHAPTER 18: EUREKA

Racy continued to help me with the Muscat language in my off hours. I was getting the hang of it, but I still had trouble with tenses.

"No. Roll the 'R' sound. *Rrrin'to gala da miso*," Racy corrected me, stressing the "R." "My father is a good being."

I repeated the words exactly as she'd said. I tried to keep the emotion out of my face and words.

"Much better." She put her hand on my arm. "I'm sorry. Do you miss him?"

I looked away and tried to compose myself. "Yes. I do." We were seated at the small desk in my quarters, no one else around. "Racy, what would you do if something happened to Rowdy?"

Her answer was immediate. "I'd do everything in my power to save him. He's my dad."

"Yeah, me too. Only, I can't even begin to think how to do it." I'd been racking my brains for weeks trying to come up with a plan, but every plan I came up with ended with my capture or death.

"Maybe there isn't an answer?" she suggested.

I looked at her.

Racy shrugged. "You're right. I wouldn't accept that either. Perhaps if you wait and look, an answer will present itself."

I looked down at the lesson plan. It was simple, organized, and would get me to the goal of learning a new language. I needed a rescue plan that would do the same thing. Right now there wasn't a plan to defeat the Porcu-bears, much less save my world. The

Erethizon would continue to gobble up independent systems until they were strong enough to take on the Terran Confederation, the Muscat Empire, and finally the Dru. They had a plan, and the rest of the galaxy did not.

Racy looked at me. "How did the Erethizon Theocracy get to where they are? I mean, I know that they are a religious movement, and that it grew to encompass the whole of Erethizon culture before they became a space-faring race. What I want to know is how it all started. How did it get to be so big?"

I collected my thoughts. "Well, they were originally a race of small fiefdoms. Each small kingdom carved out a living where they could. Their homeworld is mountainous, so a lot of enclaves were defensible by natural barriers. Then along comes the prophet Coachenic. He developed a form of gunpowder on their world and started a crusade to bring all Erethizon under one rule. It took several centuries, but it happened."

She flattened her ears and cocked her head to the side. "Theocracies aren't creative, so how did they ever develop space flight?"

"Dumb luck. A Dru ship on a survey mission crash-landed on their planet. The church said it was a sign from Coachenic and set about to learn everything they could about the ship. It took another hundred years, but they did figure out how much of it worked. The core of their religion is based on expansion, and they hadn't been able to expand for a long time. The church leadership jumped on the possibility of unconquered lands beyond their homeworld."

Her ears popped back up. "Okay, that lines up. The Porcubears colonize five worlds, then expand by conquering, picking on weak independent colonies in Terran space."

I sighed. "There has to be some way to get the three races to work together against them."

Racy shook her head. "It's a question of trust, Mark. Humans stole several Muscat technologies."

"Hey! That's not true."

"Gravity plates, medical nanites, plasticrete." She ticked them off on her fingers. "I could go on."

"We developed gravity plates on our own."

"Phft. And figured out how to direct it one-way and limit field size using a design almost exactly like ours. Not buying it."

"Okay, what about Frederick's Star?"

She narrowed her eyes at me. "That's Gra'norint. The Muscat named that system first, and it was an accident."

"Ten thousand colonists killed by their own farming equipment is not an accident."

Randy opened the door to my cabin, but she ignored him. "We didn't do that and we made reparations for it. We did it even though it was not our fault. Besides, that was a decade ago."

"We have the comm traffic. The Muscat king ordered the maintenance team to reprogram them."

"That was never proven," she snarled. "And the king died shortly after that."

"It was your government," I pointed out.

Her lips curled back. "What about it? Do you trust the Terran Confederation? They've annexed five systems in the past ten years. No one believes the story about it being for their own good."

"I don't belong to the Confed. I'm from Yale."

At the door, Randy cleared his throat.

"What?" we yelled at him.

"Can you guys keep it down? We can hear you on the mess deck."

"Fine." Racy stormed out.

I took a few deep breaths to calm down. After ten minutes I looked at the still open door. Randy moved his nose in a small circle at me, the Muscat equivalent of "you know what to do."

I hung my head. "You're right. I'll go find her and apologize.

Entering the passage, I wondered where Racy might go. I decided to check her quarters first.

In the thirty years since the Erethizon had started expanding, the situation hadn't changed. No one had enough weaponry or ship tonnage to take on an Erethizon battle fleet, but each race had been building up. If we could work together, then with human industrial power, Muscat technology, and Dru intelligence, it just might be enough.

If we could all get along.

The Muscat were protective of their technology. No one trusted the Dru because they could read everyone's minds. And neither of them trusted the Terrans because they might finish the job if the Erethizon were ever stopped.

Racy was in her quarters near engineering. She opened the door when I knocked. A blast of warm air rushed out. She crossed her arms angrily.

"I'm sorry," I said. "You're right. The Terrans haven't played fair. They've pulled more than a few dirty tricks."

She blew out a breath. "And the Muscat haven't always reacted with restraint."

I held out my hand. "Treaty of Gra'feld?" I deliberately referred to the agreement that set the boundary between Muscat and Terran space, hoping it would at least get a smile out of her.

She ignored my hand and hugged my legs. If only all disagreements could be resolved so easily, there might be hope for the galaxy... or at least the Orion arm of the galaxy.

Racy interrupted my reverie. "Okay dork, we're not going to solve the galaxy's problems today. Now tell me 'The *skrit'caresh* is good here.'"

"Dork?"

"Your sister said to call you that."

I laughed. "U*n Nawit skrit'caresh*," I recited.

"Not bad, but the inflection goes up on the end. Not down."

"But didn't you tell me that syllable goes down?"

She gave me a patient smile. "Not at the end of a sentence."

I slapped the table. "Right. What is *skrit'caresh* anyway?"

"It is a delicacy among the Muscat. A small rodent, similar to a Terran mouse, called a skrit. It's basted with spices and eaten live."

"Ew!"

***

I stepped onto the landing and was immediately hit with a wave of ozone from engineering. The scent took me back to my first solo flight: the freedom, the exhilaration, the awe. For a moment, I experienced it all over again.

Rowdy broke the spell. "Oh good! You're here! Come take a look at this."

I descended the ladder to where Rowdy was sitting at his workbench. "What have you got for me?"

He gave me a toothy grin. "The great equalizer."

I raised an eyebrow. "You found something that will make it a fair fight between us and the Erethizon?"

He shook his head. "No, nothing that great. I found a way to make the Dru mind blind."

I couldn't have been more surprised if he'd hit me with a brick. "You did what?"

He gave me a grin—like he was the cat and I the canary. "I, with Dr. Martin's help, have discovered a way to make the Dru mind blind."

"How..."

"The Dru think at a certain frequency, for lack of a better Terran word. Their homeworld is rich in certain types of cesium isotopes. I theorized that their brain chemistry is designed to enhance the Beta decay and electron capture properties..."

I held my hand up. "Rowdy."

"Fine. In short, I can blanket an area with the same frequency in which they think."

I shook my head. "How does that help us?"

"I don't know," he admitted. "It might be like white noise, or it might be like the screeching of the taunda bird. Either way, it should stop them from picking up everyone's thoughts and communicating with each other."

I had no idea what a taunda bird was, but it sounded unpleasant. The idea had merit. "How do you know it works? There aren't any Dru on board."

Rowdy deflated. "Well, I don't. Like you said, there's no real way to test it out here, but the theory is sound. When we get to a place where it can be tested, I know it will work!"

***

A week later we arrived in the Eureka system. We took our places at the navigation stations a half hour before we entered the system. For this trip, the *Leonard Fox* would become the *Lady Emma*, a name registered with the Terran Confederation. You could feel the nervous tension on the bridge. We'd rehearsed the story several times in the last few days.

We popped out of our R-drive bubble universe and I was immediately reminded of a line from my combat tactics class: "No plan survives enemy contact."

"Whoa!" yelled Wally.

We'd come out within spitting distance of an Erethizon battlecruiser.

Jenna never hesitated. "Helm, bring us thirty degrees to port and all ahead full! Tactical, arm everything! Astrogation, plot me a course to the warp gate! Engineering, give us everything you got!"

The ship's AI was a voice of calm in a sea of chaos. "Captain, they're hailing us. A Commander Grova is asking us to heave to for boarding."

CHAPTER 19: COMMANDER GROVA

"Like hell, we will," responded Captain Houston through clenched teeth.

It was the same Porcu-bear CO from above Yale. But how did he get to Eureka ahead of us? My plot updated. "I've got the gate. Wally, bring us to port 23.2 degrees and down 2.7."

"Port 32.2, down 2.7. Aye, sir."

Sara shouted from tactical, "Ma'am, the Porcu-bears are powering up weapons."

Jenna almost stood up in her chair. "Mother fucking farthogs!"

My plot refreshed again. If my heart was in my throat before, it sank and became a puddle in my shoes. "New contact: possible Porcu-bear battleship complete with screening elements on the other side of the warp portal. They're accelerating on an intercept course."

The captain shook her head. "Mark, Sara, do y'all have any ideas, 'cause I'm fresh out."

Sara shook her head. "No, ma'am."

I looked at the plot for a couple of heartbeats. "No. Even if we go vertical to the plane, it will still be three days before we can fire up the R-drive again. We're faster than the cruiser, but they'll take pot shots at us for hours."

She grimaced. "Why haven't they?"

The ship's AI spoke again. "We have a transmission from the battleship."

"Put it through," Houston ordered.

"Attention Erethizon battle cruiser *Granza*," the speakers rang out, "This is Captain Rod McCormick of the Terran Battleship *George Washington*. As you were warned when you arrived in this system, you can look all you want, but you can't touch. You have no authority in this system and will not be allowed to harass industrial activities or merchant shipping."

"Terran battleship *George Washington*, this is Commander Grova of the Divine Battle Cruiser *Granza*," came the response. "The ship we are pursuing matches the description of a ship known to supply aid and arms to the enemies of the Erethizon."

"Cruiser *Granza*, if you are referring to the 'enemies of the Erethizon' on Yale, Grey, Anderson, and Ajax, you aren't going to get any sympathy from the Confederation. If you try to fire on or board any merchant shipping in Terran space, we will consider it an act of aggression against the Terran Confederation. The immediate outcome would be fatal to any Erethizon in the system."

"These systems rejoice at being brought into the fold. They embrace the teachings of the one true way. It is the divine will of the prophet to seek out and convert all beings. That includes those on this freighter. Do not stand in our way."

The voice of Captain McCormick was pleasant. "Battle Cruiser *Granza*, we of the *George Washington* battle group look forward to assisting you in becoming one with the divine. Please feel free to martyr yourselves by attempting to board the *Lady Emma*."

There was a warning tone in the Erethizon captain's voice. "That would be an act of war. Are you so willing to become the next to feel the light of the Righteous Crusade?"

"Your divine prophet Untera is busy converting Aspen and subjugating Yale. I'm sure he doesn't have time to worry about one lowly battleship captain. But when the prophet hears that a captain stupidly got his crew killed in a backwater system, now, that might get his attention."

There were several tense minutes before the AI changed the *Granza*'s image. Sara confirmed, "Ma'am, the cruiser is powering down weapons."

The tension on the bridge went down a few notches. We were still caught between an asteroid and a star kraken, but at least nuclear-fueled death was no longer imminent.

The *Leo* brought us back to reality. "Ma'am, Captain McCormick is requesting a visual conference."

Jenna and Sara shared a grimace. "Okay *Leo*, put him on."

The wide eyes on Captain McCormick's face told me he had a history with Jenna. "Goddamn son of a bitch, Houston! I should'a let that Porcu-bear bastard blow you outta the sky."

Captain Houston gave him a lopsided grin. "It's always nice to see you too, McCormick."

"I should haul you in, impound your ship."

She held her hands up. "There are no active warrants. Have I been accused of something?"

He looked at a screen on his left. "No. You must have done someone a favor. I hope whatever it was hurt like hell."

Houston shook her head. "It's classified, or I'd tell you. If it's any consolation, it did hurt like hell for the other guy."

"Does it have anything to do with why Grova wants you?"

Jenna waited a couple of heartbeats. "No. We were making a delivery on Yale when the planet shield failed. We beat feet. A destroyer might have had a fatal accident in the process."

His face showed he clearly didn't buy it. "No way that tub of yours took out a tin can."

"The evidence is shadowing us a few thousand klicks astern."

He looked more speculative. "All right. Are you carrying anything I don't want to know about?"

Captain Houston shrugged. "Engine parts. Feel free to come over and check if you like."

"Nah. I'll give you a pass this time and a couple of frigates for company. Safe voyage, Houston."

"Safe voyage, Captain McCormick. And thanks for the escort."

I suspected the escort may have been more to keep an eye on us than to protect us from roving Porcu-bears, but I welcomed it all the same.

***

"*Leo*, open a secure comm with Eureka, Songbird Mining and Manufacturing." I was back in my quarters. I had an ulterior motive for choosing this system. I'd neglected to share it with the captain, but Sophie knew.

"Songbird. This is Ellen. How may I direct your call?" A serious-looking brunette appeared on my screen.

"Hi, Ellen. Can you connect me with Ike Fullerton?"

"I'm sorry, sir. Mr. Fullerton is busy. Can I take a message?"

"Just tell him his roommate from University of Aurora wants to speak with him."

Her look said she thought I was a nutjob, but what came out of her mouth was, "Just a moment, sir."

A few seconds later, the image of a large, solid man with a ruddy complexion filled the screen. "Mark! Goddamn son of a bitch. Slugging tell me it's really you!"

I grinned. It was nice that someone was happy to see me. I held up my coin so he could see it. "Coin and all. Hey Ike. How's Yappie?"

"Oh, thank fucking God!" Relief spread across his whole body. "Cordie's fine, the kids too. Where the hell are you?"

"I'm on a freighter in-system. We're not stopping, though. Sophie's with me."

"Your dad?"

"Didn't make it. The Porcu-bears got him." Just saying it still felt like a punch to the gut.

"Damn it. I'm sorry, Mark. At least you two made it out. Is there anything you need? You name it and it's done."

"I'll get to that," I said. "Right now I want to know how life is down at the ass end of nowhere?"

"Not as bad as you might think. Almost everyone has those big screens. You know, the ones that take up a whole damn wall. Fill 'em with scenes from Yale, and you can almost forget you're trapped in a rock dungeon. I have deep scans of the old magnapple orchard. Helps me forget about the damn radiation storms outside." He sighed. "What about you?"

"On a freighter carrying parts to places unknown. Going to keep it that way too, if you know what I mean."

"Yeah, I can't tell what I don't know. Gotcha. What can you tell me?"

"That I'm going to get my dad back. Yale too, if I can swing it."

"No shit? Give me a chance to spit in their eyes. What can I do to help?"

"Thanks. A little short on details at the moment, but there is something you can help me with. Your sales agents go everywhere in Confed space. We need to start building a government in exile. Can you start rounding up Yale's off-world assets? Bank accounts, other mining colonies, shipping, everything. Convince them that you represent what's left of the independent government. Collect the taxes. Build a war chest."

He was quiet for a few moments. "You don't ask for much, do you?"

"Use my name if you need to. It may not count for much, but you never know—son of such and such and so forth..." If I couldn't hire mercenaries, I'd find a different way. We'd find people as dedicated as we were to seeing Yale free. It would require ships, soldiers, supplies, and intelligence. Most of all, it would require money.

"Okay. I can do that," he said soberly.

***

It took us another two and a half days to make it to the gate. The Erethizon cruiser shadowed us the whole way. And while it didn't get close enough to threaten us, it did stay close enough to keep an eye on what we were doing.

Knowing they were out there was intimidating, but they'd never be able to tell where we were going; there was no way for them to know where our wormhole led. Gate traffic control certainly wouldn't tell them. One of the first things Porcu-bears did when they blockaded a system was to take over the gate, which usually meant killing its crew. Gate crews everywhere hated them.

The Erethizon knew how to work the gates, but they didn't understand the technology. So while they could use the gates to transport their fleets, if a gate broke, the Porcu-bears didn't know how to fix it.

They also didn't know how to repair R-drives, even though their fleets were upgrading to incorporate the technology. They'd found someone willing to sell them the drives, but not the know-how to build or maintain them. Somewhere, someone was making a massive profit.

We arrived at the gate with our shadow in tow and our escorts firmly between us and them. Gate control received our request and added us to the queue behind a couple of ore haulers. I'd never been privy to the cost of gate transport before. I was on the bridge when the captain worked out the details. The cost to use the gate was modest. Well, modest compared to the cost to run the ship if we'd completed the journey the long way.

Within a couple of hours, it was our turn at the gate. I'd been through gate transitions before, so I knew what to expect. I understood that the wormhole created a bend in space-time that temporarily made two distant points contiguous. It was like drawing two circles on a piece of paper and then folding it in half so the holes matched up. We just passed through the holes from one side of the paper to the other.

It seemed to me that when traveling a few hundred light years in an instant, you should feel stretched or pulled or something. The reality was that it didn't feel like anything. One instant we were one place, the next instant we were someplace else. The travel took no time at all. The view changed from one star-speckled black panorama to a different star-speckled black panorama with a brighter dot in the middle.

The captain called us to navigation stations a half hour before we transited the wormhole. Like when starting up the R-drive, this meant all the officers and the most senior helm crew were on duty on the bridge. This evolution was different in that Racy was also on the bridge. Going into a non-human system, the captain felt it was important to have a native guide on the bridge. Rowdy and Randy both had duties in Engineering during transitions, but Racy, being the Systems Specialist, was unoccupied. She was sitting at a spare console at the back of the bridge between Sara and the captain.

I was settling into my Astrogation station when a message popped up on my screen. It was Sophie, asking me what it would feel like going through the wormhole and if there was anything she needed to do to prepare. I typed back to her:

Nope. You won't even notice anything has happened.

Sophie had settled in faster than I had expected for a civilian who had never served on a spaceship before. We talked a lot more now, most of our conversations centering around why we did things a certain way on the ship.

The bridge crew settled in and assumed the exact course and speed gate control had provided. When we were a minute out from the wormhole, the captain addressed the AI. "*Leo*, please make the announcement."

"All hands, prepare to transit the wormhole." The announcement would be heard throughout the ship.

I watched the timer on the main display. When it was within ten seconds Wally counted it down. "...Four, three, two, one. Transit complete."

Information flooded the screens, our systems updating data from sensors and the gate beacon. In less than a minute, we knew something was wrong.

Sara and I spoke at the same time. "Ma'am..."

"I see it."

On the edge of the system, far enough away that we weren't in any immediate danger, waited three Erethizon destroyers.

CHAPTER 20: GRA'NOME

The captain addressed the AI. "*Leo*, please contact gate control. Ask about the destroyers."

"Aye, ma'am." After a few minutes the AI said, "Ma'am, gate control says that the destroyers showed up a week ago. They were allowed in-system as long as they did not threaten, proselytize, or enter restricted space. It took them only three days to break all three of those conditions. They were told to leave the system. They then retreated to the edge of the system as defined by interstellar law and have been there ever since."

The captain turned to face me. "Your assessment Mr. Martin? What are the chances of two weasels showing up in neutral hen houses within a week?"

I looked her right in the eye. "Astronomical, ma'am." I glanced at Sara. She was still being cold to me. Could she be tipping off the Erethizon?

She nodded. "My thoughts exactly. Mr. Martin, plot our course to Gra'nome primary orbital. Section heads are to report to the conference room in an hour. Racy, please be there as well."

***

The conference room was full, but not to the point of being crowded. The captain started without preamble. "We've got a problem, people. The Porcu-bears are showing up along our route. They can't be following us, because they're arriving before we are.

So I want options. How are they getting their information? What is their purpose?"

Sara began. "Are they trying to punish us for destroying the frigate?"

I shook my head. "Not likely. It stung them to be sure, but they are not a vengeful people. They'd look at it as a cost of war, tag the vessel, and send reports to all fleets to be on the lookout. They wouldn't spend the resources it takes to send task forces to the far ends of the galaxy. There's something we're not seeing."

Aasha shrugged. "Something we're carrying? Didn't Commander Grova say something in Yale about Hedgehog property of some such? Did we pick up something important?"

The captain looked dubious. "We're carrying engine parts. Hardly precious cargo."

Sara glowered at me. "What if it's not some*thing* but some*one*?"

Sophie looked at me with an unspoken question. I could tell them that it might be us, but the idea that they would spend so many resources to track down the children of a senator seemed ludicrous. I rubbed the coin in my pocket for luck and lied. "Sophie is a doctor and I'm a fighter pilot. Useful, but hardly the kind of people to warrant this much attention."

Sophie gave me a meaningful look. "Mark. Tell them."

I sighed. "It doesn't have anything to do with this."

The captain speared me with her gaze. "Tell us what?"

As we sat there, the silence seemed to gather and press in on me. As much as I didn't want to bring it out in the open, my sister had just forced my hand. "Fine. Sophie and I are the son and daughter of a Yale senator. There are ninety-nine other senators. Also, two generations ago, my grandfather was the king. He isn't the king now. So while the Porcu-bears would like to get their hands on us to force our dad to support them, we're not important enough to warrant this much attention. "

Aasha gave me a curious look.

The captain frowned. "We will discuss what I need to know later, Mr. Martin. That aside, you're right. Racy, Rowdy, what's the political climate like here in Muscat space?"

Racy wore an expression I couldn't quite read. Rowdy answered the question, though. "The Erethizon have been trying to spread their faith throughout the Muscat worlds. Often they are pushy and forceful, so their missionaries are monitored. There have been some scandals: kidnapped kits, re-education camps, intimidation. The Council of Lords has passed laws to curb their activities. They are still seen in Muscat space. Not so much on Gra'nome, but many other places. In a word: shaky."

Rowdy looked over at his daughter to see if there was anything she wanted to add. Racy shook her head.

Rowdy continued. "There have been some legal difficulties between the Muscat and the Terran Confederacy regarding intellectual property rights. There is some evidence to support this. But there are similar problems with the Dru. We've intercepted enough sensitive documents, classified technology, and information on military deployments to be certain. As a result, the Dru are increasingly restricted in Muscat space."

The captain brought the conversation back to the main point. "Anything your family has done to warrant extra attention?"

Rowdy looked at Racy and opened his mouth as if to say something but then closed it. The captain didn't miss it. "Racy, is there something we should know about?"

Racy jumped as if she'd been shocked. "Uh, no ma'am. I had a boyfriend who was high up in the Muscat aristocracy, but that ended a long time ago. He'll be mated to someone else soon."

The captain sighed. "Any other skeletons to drag out? Any more senators and aristocrats I don't know about?"

Everyone looked around the table and shrugged.

"Two unlikely reasons. Let's forget the 'why' for a moment and focus on the 'how.' How do they know where we're going?"

Sara looked thoughtful. "Anubis?"

The captain shook her head. "Unlikely. Anubis set up the arms deal in Aspen, but he didn't know we'd get to Gra'nome by way of Eureka."

Rowdy spoke up. "Locator beacon?"

Sara waved her hand. "They got here before we did, but to be safe can you sweep the ship for beacons and bugs?"

Rowdy looked offended. "There are no pests on my ship."

Aasha laughed. "She means listening devices, not actual insects. Can you scan for them?"

He looked a little less offended. "Oh, yes I can put something together and run a sweep."

The captain nodded. "Good. As much as I hate to say it, let's check message traffic as well. Racy, get with *Leo* and go over the messages to and from the ship. See if you find any suspicious messages or hidden codes. I'd hate to think that any of the crew could be spying on us, but we can't rule it out."

Racy nodded. "Aye, ma'am."

Aasha sat forward. "Can I help, ma'am?"

"No. As my head of security, I want you to go over everyone's file. See if there's anyone sympathetic to the Erethizon for any reason."

Aasha grimaced. "Aye, ma'am."

I didn't envy her the task. Doing background checks on the whole crew was going to be tedious. If word got out, it could affect the marines' trust in her.

The captain slapped her hand on the table. "All right then. Let's get to it. We've got some engine parts to deliver and a few pop-guns to pick up. I don't want to show up on Aspen and find a Porcu-bear reception."

***

The trip to the space station orbiting Gra'nome took five days from the jump gate. Gra'nome was on the opposite side of the sun from the gate when we arrived, so it took a little longer. Docking with the station went off without a hitch. While the stevedores started unloading, I decided to take a walk around the station. It was my first time to Gra'nome and if I couldn't see the planet, I wanted to at least experience the culture.

I'm a tall guy. At 1.93 meters tall, I'm used to being a little taller than the average Terran. The average height for a Muscat is 1.12 meters. As a result, I felt like Gulliver among the Lilliputians when I stepped off the ship. The cinnamon scent I'd come to associate with the Muscat filled the air. And of course, the patented Muscat disregard for personal space meant I was constantly worried I'd step on someone.

I thought it might be hard to tell them apart. It wasn't. I saw fur ranging from white to red to rich browns and blacks. Most of the Muscat had distinct facial markings: different colored ears, muzzles, or fur around their eyes. Telling the sexes was a bit harder. After a time, I figured out that the women were more graceful.

I hadn't seen any dwellings, but the space station was set up for multispecies habitation. The overheads were high enough for me, but a full-grown Erethizon would have to stoop.

I heard someone call my name from behind me and saw Racy and Rowdy approaching from the lock.

Racy gave me a wicked grin. "Hey, Mark. What are you up to?"

"I wanted to step off the ship and see if there was anything a Terran could do on the station. Maybe get some food."

She shrugged. "You'll want to stay away from the dishes that are served live or raw. There is a restaurant on deck four that has some dishes for Terrans."

Rowdy nodded. "We can show you where it is."

I shrugged. "Lead on, Macduff."

Their ears and whiskers twitched in confusion.

"Sorry, a line from an old Terran story. Show me the way."

We took the lift up to deck four and found the restaurant almost across from the lift doors. The sign out front was written in Muscat, but there was a translation in Terran below: Growler's Grill. The smells wafting out the door were wonderful and the host showed us to a booth with enough room under the table for my legs.

The waiter gave us each different menus. I was pleased to see that mine was written in Terran and Muscat. I ordered a fish dish grilled with local spices and spent some time expanding my vocabulary. Racy helped me get the accents right and introduced me to a fermented fruit juice. It tasted like cashews. Rowdy enjoyed it a lot.

The waiter, the manager, and several restaurant patrons stopped by the table to practice their Terran on me. Most were pretty good. A few made me laugh. One timid Muscat girl asked me if I was a potato. Racy and Rowdy burst out laughing. They explained what she said to me, and she looked embarrassed. She shrugged and left.

"What was she trying to ask me?"

His giggles under control, Rowdy explained, "She was trying to ask you if you were a pilot."

"What should we expect while we're in port here?"

Rowdy looked thoughtful. "Well, we'll need a day to unload the engine parts. After that, we find out where to pick up the cargo. They won't deliver something like that on-station. We'll pick it up someplace out of the way, Gra'nome or one of the moons. I'm hoping that we'll have a day or so. I want to find someplace to test out my newest invention."

"Where would we find any Dru?"

Racy pulled out her tablet and soon turned it around so we could see it. It showed a news article in Muscat. The picture displayed a rocky beach and several Dru.

"That's perfect!" Rowdy exclaimed. "There's a Dru science team on-planet studying the biosphere near Tra'zan." He turned to me. "It's a famous island in the northern ocean. It was isolated for millions of years. There are creatures above and below the water there that you won't find anywhere else on Gra'nome."

I played devil's advocate. "Do you think you can get them to agree to be your guinea pigs?"

Rowdy stared at me, confusion causing his ears to tilt in opposite directions. "What's a guinea pig?"

"Small Terran mammal commonly used as a test subject for experiments."

"Oh. Why wouldn't they?"

I ticked the points off on my fingers. "They have a different culture than you do. They may not like the idea of not being able to read thoughts. They're busy doing their own research. There may be local regulations on experiments. They may not speak Muscat or Terran."

Rowdy shrugged. "Why don't we just ask them? They can always say no. Let's ask Lavesh if he'd like to join us. He speaks Dru."

I had a bad feeling about it, but seeing the excitement in Rowdy's eyes I decided to stop uncovering problems.

We settled the tab and walked back to the ship. I told them about other planets I'd been to, such as Aspen and Earth, and they told me more about Muscat culture and the planet below.

We checked in with Wally on watch when we got back aboard. "Is my sister around?"

He looked up from his screen. "No, sir. She went ashore with Mr. Boldrini about an hour ago."

"Thanks." I hoped they were having fun.

I was about to head into the ship when Aasha approached the watch stand. She stopped me by collecting a kiss. "Hey flyboy, take a girl to dinner?"

"I just ate."

She gave me pouty lips. "Well, you're taking me anyway." Her face dared me to contradict her.

I laughed. "And so I am. Wally, log us ashore."

***

We had three days before we picked up our outbound shipment and there was some paperwork to be sorted out before we could pick up the weapons. So we had time for Rowdy's experiment with the Dru.

Lavesh was eager to use his language skills and agreed to be our interpreter. We took a shuttle down to the planet. There were no transports scheduled for Tra'zan, so we chartered one. I winced at the cost, but Rowdy didn't even blink. Two hours later we were on the island. Pretty much anywhere you go on Muscat is either ocean, swamp, or forest. Tra'zan was... different. It was still a forest, but it was more raw, more primal than any forest I'd ever seen before. Rowdy explained that the whole island was a nature preserve. There was a small airstrip and some basic living arrangements, but otherwise, no development of any kind was allowed on the island.

We rented an aircar and sped toward the beach, flying over the science site where the blue faces of Dru looked up as we passed. We landed in a clearing not far from the science camp. When we popped the canopy, I was hit with the smell of saltwater and seaweed. Three tall, willowy Dru in loose white robes came out of the forest.

I realized at that moment that I was the only trained soldier in this group. We weren't expecting trouble, but if something happened, I would be the only one there to protect my friends. One look at the Dru scientists told me that I didn't need to worry: they appeared curious rather than tense or hostile. We'd get our test.

The leader approached us as we stepped out of the car. I noticed he wore some kind of circlet on his head. Putting his hand to his chest, he bowed. "Welcome to our camp, Rowdy, Racy, Mr. Patel, and Mr. Martin. I am Chief Scientist Wanata. These are my colleagues, Burnta and Goona."

I stopped myself just short of asking how they knew who we were. Of course, they knew who we were—they'd picked the information out of our heads before we landed.

Rowdy stepped forward and shook hands with Wanata. "Thank you, Chief Scientist Wanata. You know why we're here, of course."

The Dru scientist inclined his head. "Yes, but to be polite I was going to let you ask."

Rowdy gave him a toothy smile. "I've invented a device that might turn off the Dru telepathic ability within a certain area. I was wondering if some of your scientists would like to help us test it."

Wanata favored us with what I believe was a patient smile. Since Dru don't have many facial muscles, their expressions can be hard to read. "Several scientists and engineers have attempted to curtail our telepathy. None have succeeded in anything more than giving us headaches. Your approach may be a little different, but I believe this will be a waste of time."

Rowdy's ears pointed forward and his face broke out into a feral grin. "If you intended to tell us no, you would have come here by yourself. You know we would have accepted your answer and gone away. But you lost the argument and curiosity won out."

We waited in silence for a few heartbeats. I noticed that all three of the Dru focused their eyes on Rowdy, me, then Rowdy again.

Burnta and Goona smiled at each other and then looked at Wanata. Wanata just looked annoyed. I had the odd feeling we'd just passed a test we hadn't been aware we were even taking.

Wanata spoke again. "Burnta and Goona will go with you two kilometers up the beach. I don't want this foolishness interrupting any more of our work here than it already has. They don't speak Terran or Muscat, so you will need Mr. Patel to translate that you are wasting your time."

With that, Wanata strode back the way he'd come. Burnta and Goona started talking at once to Lavesh. From the gestures and sounds he was making, I can only guess he was asking them to slow down, stop talking at the same time, and repeat that again.

I tried not to laugh as we walked up the beach. Burnta and Goona made up for Wanata's lack of excitement. It also became clear that while Lavesh had a pretty good Dru vocabulary, it broke down when the discussion got too technical. Goona was a woman, but don't ask me how I figured that out. I could tell Goona was able to work out what she wanted to say quickly and was able to keep Burnta calm when he got frustrated about speaking aloud. I guess when you live in a telepathic society where everyone around you is instantly aware of your every thought, having to wait a couple of minutes to get your point across could be taxing.

Lavesh was getting a mental workout, but his face was plastered with a grin. There were some concepts of language or engineering they couldn't get around, but all in all, it was fun. It was a little like watching a couple of hyperactive kids pester their parents at an amusement park—Can it do this? Does it do this? Can we get cotton candy after the roller coaster, Dad?

We reached a stretch of the beach far enough away from Wanata's research site. Racy and I sat at the edge of the jungle to watch.

When test after test ended with Burnta and Goona stating there was no difference, Rowdy made adjustments. The box itself was about a half-meter by a half-meter in size and Rowdy completely took it apart and put it back together again at least four times. I was beginning to believe Wanata was right—we were wasting our time. An hour and a half later, I could see our Dru friends' excitement was waning. But Rowdy kept going at it. I knew I'd have to step in soon.

Rowdy had just started the machine up again and was adjusting something when Burnta gave him a signal that clearly meant stop. I thought he was about to signal that he was done, but he made a backwards rolling motion with one of his webbed hands. He spoke in rapid-fire Dru and Lavesh had to ask him to repeat himself twice.

Lavesh turned to Rowdy. "He says, whatever adjustment you're making, back it off a bit."

Rowdy glanced at them curiously but started twisting a tool that looked like a screwdriver.

Burnta held up his hand in a clear signal to stop. He looked at Goona, who gave him a gesture that looked something like a shrug before she spoke.

Lavesh had no trouble this time. "She says she has a ringing in her head."

Rowdy looked puzzled. "But they can still hear each other's thoughts?"

There was a little back and forth before Lavesh replied, "Yes."

Rowdy made another adjustment, after which both of them held their heads with one hand and waved at Rowdy in a sign that clearly meant "turn it down." Rowdy turned the machine off.

I cocked my head toward Racy. "That must be the headache they were talking about." She nodded in agreement.

Rowdy sat on the beach in deep concentration. Lavesh, Burnta, and Goona all attempted to talk to him. He waved them off.

After about fifteen minutes of this Rowdy approached me. "Mark, can I borrow your communicator?"

The comm I'd brought along would work fine as long as long as the *Leo* was above us and not over the horizon. I did a quick calculation in my head and figured that the *Leo* and the main space station should still be in range for another couple of hours. I handed him the communicator.

He was routed through *Leo*'s comms to the medical bay. I realized he was talking to Sophie. About twenty minutes later he ended the conversation and threw the communicator back to me as he headed back to the box on the beach. "Your sister says hi!"

Fifteen minutes later Rowdy signaled that he was ready to try it again. I expected the Dru to quit, or at least hold their heads again. But he turned the machine on and Burnta looked at Goona before speaking to Lavesh.

"He says, 'Goona's thinking is fuzzy.' Also, thank you for not giving them another headache," Lavesh translated

Rowdy let out a small yip of triumph. It took them another hour to work out the exact frequencies. After that, they played around with how much power was required to jam how much area.

The next thing I knew, Wanata was pounding up the beach. The body language screamed, "I'm not happy, and I'm going to make sure you're not happy either."

I thought he might try to take the machine. Instead, he was just there to collect his research assistants. Burnta and Goona thanked Rowdy for allowing them to be a part of his experiment. I remembered then that the Dru believed information should be free to all. Wanata, while unhappy that Rowdy had been successful, wouldn't believe it was right to keep that information to himself.

Rowdy, Racy, and Lavesh congratulated each other all the way back to the aircar. If they noticed me being a little less enthusiastic, no one mentioned it. I was excited for my friend and I told him so over and over again. What bothered me, though, was the realization that the genie was out of its lamp. The reality, the enormity, of what had just happened hadn't hit me until that very moment. The nuclear bomb and warp gate technology had profoundly shaken Terran civilization. I couldn't help thinking that the same kind of thing was about to happen to the Dru because of Rowdy's device. This tiny stretch of beach was about to become their Hiroshima. And I had been there when it happened. I had seen it with my own eyes.

I wondered what it would do to them. Did they even realize the potential impact? How would their culture evolve after this?

I didn't think Burnta and Goona understood. Could anyone predict the implications? I saw the look in Wanata's eyes as he escorted his assistants down the beach. He might.

CHAPTER 21: THE DELIVERY

Back aboard the ship, I asked Rafe if he minded me eating in the conference room just off the bridge. He gave me a strange look, but told me it was okay. "Leave the plates on the side table. I'll grab them when dinner mess is over.

I took my tray up to the conference room and sat there in my normal chair just to the left of where the captain would sit. I wanted to be alone. I took the coin out of my pocket and studied it a moment before putting it back. I didn't so much eat my food, as stir the beef stroganoff about a bit. I'm sure it tasted good—Boldrini was an excellent chef—but I was too distracted. I was flicking a noodle back and forth when I heard a throat clearing.

Captain Houston was leaning against the doorframe, a coffee cup in one hand.

"I'm sorry, Jenna. Do you need the conference room? I didn't see anything scheduled." I started to get up, but she waved me back down.

She crossed to the chair across from me but didn't sit. "Want to tell me about it?"

I was silent a long time before responding. "Do you know what Rowdy and all of us were doing on the planet this afternoon?"

The captain shrugged. "Yeah. Lavesh asked to trade watches so he could go. Something about testing a device that Rowdy came up with." She gave me a questioning look. "Everyone make it back okay? No one got hurt, did they?"

I shook my head.

"Then what's got you so spooked?"

"It worked."

Her face split into a grin from ear to ear. "That's great!"

"Is it? What will it do to the Dru?"

It took a moment before she dropped her coffee cup. It shattered against the edge of the conference table. Coffee splashed onto two chairs and all over the floor. She pulled out a chair and sat down heavily.

I'm not sure how much later it was before she said, "I can order him not to tell anyone. Keep it a secret."

I could tell by her voice that she didn't think that was a good idea either. "No, word will get out. People will know it's possible. It will only delay the inevitable."

She waggled her head back and forth. "If it's going to get out anyway, we owe it to Rowdy to help him get the manufacturing contracts so he can at least get credit for it."

I nodded.

Jenna continued, "The Dru are going to feel threatened. They may target us. Getting the information out there may help with that, but they will retreat to their sector of space. The Terrans and the Muscat will lose their source of intelligence on the Erethizon. The Terrans and the Muscat will be even more distrustful of each other. It will divide the three races even further. It will be easier for the Porcu-bears to pick us off."

I nodded again.

Her voice was almost a whisper. "Oh fuck."

My eyes closed. "Now you know why I've been in here. We need another option."

Captain Houston gave me a wicked grin. "When you come up with that idea, make sure we can make a profit on it!"

That broke my somber mood and I snorted.

***

I had recovered by the mission briefing the next day. The captain called the meeting to order. "Before we talk about the pickup tomorrow, I want to show you something. Sara?"

She glared at me and tapped her tablet. A tactical plot image came up on the conference room screen. "The Erethizon have not been idle."

My eyes nearly bulged out of their sockets. "Is that what I think it is?"

The accusing glare did not abate. "If you think it's an Erethizon battle group consisting of three battlecruisers and five destroyers, then yes. They've been showing up in ones and twos."

Jenna gave Sara a look and she backed down. "The Muscat response has been to move an equal weight of their own warships to a position just inside the border. There have been several encrypted transmissions back and forth between the Porcu-bear ships. There hasn't been any official word from the government of either side, but I suspect a lot of posturing."

Rowdy shook his head. "The Muscat will not back down. If the Erethizon threaten our home system, expect a swift and final response from the queen. Our ships have more reach and a better capacity for electronic warfare."

The captain nodded in agreement. "That's true. I don't see the Erethizon pushing it. For all its small size, the Muscat navy could take on three times an equal weight in Porcu-bear ships. Even with all their religious dogma, they aren't stupid. They have to know coming in here is a bad idea. That brings us back to the issue at hand: what are they doing here and why are they doing it? Anyone have any bright ideas on that subject? I think we can all agree that the Martins' father isn't enough of a reason."

Sara fumed. Aasha gave me an encouraging smile, to let me know she at least would back me up.

The captain continued, "That brings us to the pick up tomorrow. Aasha, will you be leading the security detail?"

She shook her head. "Ma'am, may I suggest you ask Jay to run the ground ops? Those ships have me spooked. I'd like to continue background checks and run tactical from inside the ship on site."

I liked Jay. Moreover, I trusted Aasha, and not just because we were sleeping together. If she thought Jay was a good substitute, I wasn't going to argue. No one else objected either. But I did wonder about her reasons.

Aasha continued, "The plan is to come from the south. We're landing the ship for this one, so we'll come in on full stealth, avoiding the major population centers. We'll play it cool. An advanced team of three marines will scout the location out an hour before we arrive and let us know if there are any surprises. We'll take both Galvins to provide our own air support. Our contact stated that they would provide two fighters of their own as well, so we should be well covered."

I interrupted her. "Do you want me in one of the Galvins?"

She shook her head. "No Mark. I want two officers on the ground in case one of you gets hurt, and the captain is going to be in the ship supervising the loading. If things go woolly I want one of you organizing and rallying the troops on the ground."

Aasha pulled up a map of the site on the screen and went over the troop placements and cargo loaders. It all seemed pretty straightforward to me.

Sara studied the map. "We only have five for loading security. Isn't that a bit light for this op?"

"Rowdy hit the nail on the head. The Erethizon would be foolish to try anything. This should be more than enough for what we're doing. Also, our contacts are high in the Muscat government. They were able to get some Gra'nome military hardware for their own security. I think we have things pretty well covered."

While Aasha addressed everyone's concerns and answered questions, it still struck me as odd was that she wasn't leading the ground forces herself. The captain being on the ship I could understand, but my experience with small unit leaders like Aasha was that they liked to lead from the ground. Maybe Aasha was trying to act more like an officer and less like a foot soldier, delegating leadership of the ground forces to Jay. More power to her if she was. It would be a difficult transition to make.

***

I walked into the squad bay. "Jay? You in here?"

His voice came from the door to the armory. "In here, Mark."

In the couple of months I'd been aboard, I'd gotten somewhat used to the pseudomilitary formality of the crew. I knew I was just as likely to hear my name as I was to get a "sir" or "Mr. Martin." I walked into the armory to find Jay reassembling a gauss carbine. I waited while he finished the process and hit the stopwatch.

"Damn." He showed me the time. "Five minutes, nineteen seconds."

"It looked impressive to me."

"Yeah, but Aasha can do it four minutes and thirty seconds."

I grinned at him. "She's also got a few artificial parts. I'm sure that speeds up her reflexes a bit."

He shrugged. "What can I do for you, sir?"

"I'm sure you've heard by now that I'm going to be on the ground for this one."

Jay took the carbine over to the arms locker. "Yeah. Not sure I agree with that, but I understand the logic. Did you want to look over the duty assignments?"

Leaning against the door jam, I shook my head. "No. Aasha knows her people and the assignments look good to me. I'm just feeling a bit exposed being out in the open like that."

He grinned at me, sizing me up. "You want something between you and any unfortunate circumstances. You do realize, though, that we're deep in friendly territory and doing business with people we trust?"

"Fine. Call me paranoid."

Jay closed the small arms locker and set the security. "All right, sir. Well, you're here talking to me, and you don't want to change the duty roster. That must mean you want arms or armor."

I felt the smile creep across my face. "How about both?"

He walked to the back of the armory where the combat armor was kept and I followed. "I have one extra suit and enough parts to make two more. The problem is size."

"Size?"

"Yes, sir. You're too tall. Let's see if we can squeeze you into it anyway."

I'd worn combat armor a couple of times, so I knew the drill. For weaponry, I had the choice of a pistol, the gauss carbine, or a grenade launcher. All of them could integrate with the armor. I thought about going with the pistol, and almost did, as it was my preferred small arm. In the end I decided I didn't want to stand out as an officer. I opted for the gauss carbine, a TR32. The grenade launcher seemed a bit like overkill.

***

Wally was following the glide plane I'd set perfectly. I should have been concentrating on the ground mission, but I had my wrist AI set to show the navigation display. We'd made our descent to Gra'nome and there hadn't been a peep out of traffic control. Our contacts must have been well connected.

I watched as Wally maneuvered the *Leo* right above a group of warehouses and hangars in the middle of nowhere. The landing pad was big enough to hold two freighters of the *Leo*'s size, so I switched off the feed and got ready to disembark. Wally didn't need me looking over his shoulder while he landed the ship.

Sara was shaking her head at me.

"What?"

"Combat armor, Martin? Are you expecting trouble?" Her tone was more playful jibe than an admonishment from the senior officer.

I had to admit. It did seem rather silly. As Jay had pointed out, we were in friendly territory working with contacts we had a good reason to trust. "You can't be too careful."

There was a jarring lurch that almost threw me off my feet. We hadn't been hit or anything. Apparently, Wally *did* need me looking over his shoulder during landing.

The cargo bay doors opened up and the marines and cargo handlers spilled out ahead of us. In our case, the cargo handlers were marines pulling double duty.

Sara and I walked out onto the landing field. A group of five Muscat were there to greet us. Four of them were in Muscat combat armor. There were two in the middle and three playing bodyguard. The one without the armor came forward and shook hands with Sara. He introduced himself as Graff. I couldn't tell for sure, but it seemed to me that the one without the armor deferred to the one behind him, whose armor looked newer and had a full helmet that kept his features obscured.

Sara and Graff spoke in Terran and both of them nodded as they confirmed the details of the cargo and payment. Without another word, they moved apart and signaled their crews to begin loading.

It took them only an hour to load everything. Racy, who had the greatest fluency in both Terran and Muscat, stood by at our cargo lock and checked everything aboard. Our small fighters, the Galvins, whizzed overhead, keeping constant watch over us. The shipment included two shield generators, monstrous things heavy enough we had to use one of the Galvins as a sky crane to help us get them aboard.

I had to admit, watching that last generator being eased into place, that I was glad all the extra preparation and paranoia had been for nothing.

That's when it happened. An explosion bloomed on one side of the Galvin loading the last generator. The loading cables treated the fighter like a yo-yo. It flew sideways, snapping two of the cables before crashing into the landing pad. One of the two snapped cables sliced clean through a Muscat loader who had been standing too close. The generator crashed to the deck, crushing one of the marines beneath its massive weight.

CHAPTER 22: BATTLE ON THE GROUND

My first thought was that there had been some sort of malfunction aboard the Galvin. But then I jumped at another explosion behind me and realized we were under attack. Sara and I sped into motion. I took charge of the cargo bay while she commanded the marines. In hindsight, we should have done it the other way around, but in the confusion of the moment, my concern was for my crew.

"Medical to Cargo Pod Four! Smith, Anderson, do what you can for the injured. War, Pace, cut those two remaining cables. We can't button up *Leo* while they're still attached. Daniels, Weber, get Cox out from under that thing and get it strapped down to the deck. When we bug out, we can't have it loose."

Orders issued, I turned around to bedlam. Thirty Porcu-bears in stealth armor were advancing two by two across the landing pad using buildings and vehicles for cover. Fortunately for us, the stealth armor wasn't working anymore—someone on our side had the bright idea to use paint grenades. I'd give them a hearty thank you and a bonus if we survived this. In the air were our last Galvin and three ESF28s, the Erethizon stealth model starfighter. I'd seen enough of their tactics to immediately grasp the situation. On Yale, a Porcu-bear strike force using these stealth fighters would sometimes get through the planet shield in a coordinated attack on a soft target. But these 28s were visible, which meant they'd already been damaged.

I used my suit's greater strength to flip a grav pallet to use as a shield. Sara and one of the marines joined me behind it as we picked our targets.

I shot a Porcu-bear trooper as he came out into the open. Our people were doing it by the numbers, making an organized retreat back to the ship using whatever cover they could find. Meanwhile, the Muscat were trying to make it back to the shelter of a hangar. It was the nearest structure, but there wasn't a lot of cover between here and there. The Erethizon strike force was picking them off one by one.

On the ground, only one of our ship-mounted gauss cannons was usable. It was firing almost nonstop, but the ESF28s were hard targets.

I ducked behind the pallet as I heard three thuds and a zing. The zing surprised me. The strike force was using a combination of gauss rifles, plasma rifles, and grenades. The zing was a plasma rifle—an odd choice of weaponry. They were used to take out equipment without destroying it. It would shut down combat armor, but the explosive rounds they used would do a better job. Plasma rounds were slow: at the range they were using them, the marines and Muscat troops would have half a second to dodge. I grimaced as I saw a Muscat soldier hit by a plasma round. He'd be unconscious for a half a day or more, and when he woke up it would hurt like hell, like an all-over sunburn.

One of the ESF28s fired a pair of missiles at the hangar. It exploded in a huge fireball. The one Muscat soldier that had almost made it inside was incinerated.

The remaining Muscat switched directions. They ran for us. Our contacts were down to three.

From behind me, I heard Reeves. "Sir, we're ready to button up."

I yelled over my shoulder, "Close the overhead, but leave this hatch open! Let's save as many of these people as we can!"

"But sir!"

I growled at him and put my finger in his face.

He held his hands up "Whatever you say, sir."

Across the pad, I saw the Muscat in the fancy armor go down. He'd taken a direct hit from a plasma rifle. Graff and the last bodyguard managed to get him behind a tractor before the bodyguard caught an explosive round in the back.

I swore and yelled behind me, "Cover me!"

I didn't stop to see if they heard me. I ran toward the tractor, my combat armor enhancing my speed. From behind me, I heard a surprised "What?" from Sara, and an "Aye, aye, sir!" from Reeves.

It seemed to take forever to reach the tractor. In reality, it was only ten seconds, but when you're sprinting in the open through enemy fire, that feels like an eternity.

I reached the tractor. Graff was wide-eyed with panic. I remembered to speak in Muscat. "Climb on!" I indicated my back as I scooped up the guy in the fancy armor.

Graff stared at me for half a second as I grabbed his boss. That seemed to snap him out of it and he climbed onto my back.

I got to the edge of the tractor and took in the battlefield. The ESF28s were nowhere to be seen. The last Galvin was back aboard the *Leo*. I took three quick breaths and decided to go for a fake. I stepped out of cover and then back. I was rewarded with three thuds and two zings. Before I could think about how suicidal of an idea it was, I sprinted the space between the tractor and the *Leo*. This time I remembered to vary my speed.

I didn't stop at the overturned pallet but ran straight into the open hatch. Sophie and Racy were there and helped me lay the armored Muscat on the deck. Graff helped get his helmet off.

Racy gasped when his face was revealed. It looked to me like the armor had taken the worst of it. He'd be okay.

I turned back to the door and saw Sara and two marines returning fire. I went to the edge of the door and gave a quick peek around. That was it. Everyone who was going to make it was on board.

I pulled out my carbine and fired a long burst at the closest enemy positions. "Time to go, Sara!"

I shot another long burst as Sara and the two marines ran for the hatch. The indicator on my heads-up display was telling me I was almost out of ammo, but I didn't let up. After the door was closed I wouldn't need it.

It only takes the cargo bay door five seconds to close, but I ran out of ammo after two. I saw two Porcu-bears jump up and start firing at the closing door. Sara wasn't clear yet. Time slowed to a crawl. A plasma bolt. "Sara, get down!" I yanked her clear.

I didn't feel it, but I heard it.

Thud! My left shoulder swung around.

Thud! My left spin stopped. I fell straight back.

Then there was a zing. An ocean wave crashed over me, setting every nerve on fire. Then, nothing.

CHAPTER 23: BACK TO SPACE

Pain. Not the kind of pain you get from a sprained ankle or a stomachache, but real, overwhelming, everywhere pain: the kind of pain you want to douse with buckets of ice-cold water or cut away completely. "Ugh! Turn down the heat."

"Lie still. I'll give you something for the pain."

That voice. I knew that voice. Who was it? I couldn't focus my eyes; they hurt as much as the rest of me. Who was I hearing? A voice I hadn't heard since I was a kid. "Mom?"

My arm. A sharpness mixed with the burning. The pain didn't go away, but it changed. I was no longer standing-on-the-sun hot. I was just sitting-too-close-to-the-campfire hot. A massive improvement

My eyes focused on my savior. A whimper escaped my lips. My voice sounded like I was trying to talk underwater. I slurred, "Hey, sis. I promise I didn't cut the hair off your dolls. Make it stop, please."

My mom—sister?—sounded far away. "That's the best I can give him at the moment. I need Mark awake so he can tell me what he feels. Any more and I'll send him back off to sleep. You can talk to him, but don't expect coherent answers."

There was a taste like metal in my mouth. What kind of metal? Was the metal important? A face with a smile hovered into view. "Mark, do you know who I am?"

Her face looked stretchy. "Jenny! Let's take the gang someplace fun. Is there a carnival near here? I'm on a Ferris wheel."

"What's the last thing you remember?"

The memories were there, but I couldn't reach them. Something had happened. Someone had been fighting. "Fight! There was a fight on the playground! I saved a kid and some girl named Cindy... Samantha? See something." I shook my head in confusion. Something wasn't right, but I couldn't put my finger on it. "That big bully Eric was trying to hurt them. It was all weird. He had spikes and stuff in his skin. I made him go away."

That girl I was trying to think of stood next to Jenny. Cindy? No, that wasn't right. It was definitely a C-name. "Oh. There you are, pretty girl. Are you okay? I tried to stop the bully from hurting you." I felt a big rubbery grin take over my face.

Mom/Sophie put her hand on my cheek and I felt my face moving toward her and away from Cindy and Jenny. "Mark. Pay attention."

I nodded, but it felt like a combination of a shake and a nod.

"I know you hurt all over, but does anything hurt other than the burning feeling?"

Burning feeling? Oh yeah. My body was on fire. "Ow."

"Yes, does anything else hurt?"

Mom/Sophie looked so serious, but I did my best to answer her. "Chest hurts. Eric hit me in the chest."

Mom/Sophie smiled. "Yes, I bet it does. Is it an achy chest pain or a stabbing chest pain?"

I tried to concentrate on the pain in my chest. What did it feel like? Burning. It felt like burning. No, she knew about the fire feeling. She wanted to know about the other pain. What did that feel like? It felt heavy, like someone sitting on my chest.

Mom/Sophie said something. "Thanks, Mark. I'm going to give you something to help you sleep."

Had I said something? I didn't remember saying anything. Sleep. Did I want to sleep? Help. I needed to help someone. Cindy! That's who I needed to help. I groped for Cindy's hand and my vision swam until I could focus on her. "Cindy!"

She gave me a patient smile. "It's Sara."

Her name was Sara. Was that important? I didn't think so. "Sara, I have to tell you something. You're such a pretty girl. I know something hurt you and that's why you cry and get angry so much, but there are still so many wonderful things. Great things like flowers, and puppies, and angels, and... and..." I couldn't think of anything else. I refocused on her face, which was getting blurrier by the second. "And you have such a great smile. Try and spend some time thinking about the good things... too..."

Sara's eyes went wide and she put her hand to her mouth. Water was in her eyes. How did the water get in her eyes?

A warm, soft blanket covered my mind and the pain went away. The room went away too and in its place was a field of flowers filled with angels playing with puppies.

***

Pain. Again. An all-over sunburn. Someone was sitting on my chest. I opened my eyes. No one was sitting on my chest, even though it felt that way. Sickbay. Antiseptic smells. Sophie always had that smell when I saw her after work.

What happened? Sunburn feeling. Then it all came back to me: I got hit with a plasma bolt. And a gauss round. Crap.

I looked around. Sickbay was as full as I had ever seen it. Sophie was crashed out on her desk. I'd found her like that a few times when she was in medical school. I smiled a bit at the memory.

Racy and Graff were sitting next to a bed not far away. Racy was holding the hand of the Muscat who had been wearing that fancy armor. The left half of his face was all black fur even though most of the rest of his fur was a soft brown. He had a white spot around his right eye.

I sat up and rolled my neck. "Anyone get the registration number of the space tug that hit me?"

Racy laughed softly and set the guy's hand down gently. Coming over to me, she wrapped her arms around my neck. "Thank you, Mark." Her eyes sought out mine. "How do you feel?"

I gave her a weak nod. "Everything hurts, but I'll be fine in a couple of days." I jerked my head in the direction of the Muscat in the other bed. "Friend of yours?"

"Yes. You remember that one of the reasons I came out here was to put some distance between me and my ex-boyfriend?"

It came back to me then. "Yeah. You told me he was some important guy back on Gra'nome. That's him?"

She nodded. "I had to leave because he was engaged to

someone else. An arranged marriage. I believe some Terran cultures still practice that too, don't they?"

"Yes. Kinda outdated, but it still happens in some places."

"He wanted me to stay and be his mistress. I loved him, but I'm not going to be anyone's mistress. That's just not me. He couldn't get out of the arrangement, and I wouldn't stay and be a part of it, so my dad hired on with Captain Houston and we all came to live on the *Leo*."

I smiled. "Tough choice. I don't envy you."

I stared at the Muscat in the bed for a few heartbeats. "What's his name?"

"Granta Gra'tau'ganteedi."

Something about that name bothered me, but I couldn't place it. "He must be pretty important to be out and about with three bodyguards and a retainer."

"He is."

The Muscat in question started to stir. Racy went to his side and held his hand again.

I tried to reason it out while I grabbed my tablet from the table beside my bed. That name should mean something to me. A quick check of the ship's status had us on final approach to the space station. It also told me I'd been out cold for seven hours.

The Muscat with the half black face shifted under the sheets. Graff said something to him and as my mind translated it into Terran everything slipped into place.

"Your Highness, please try not to move. You're safe."

The words echoed in my mind. "Your Highness." I thought back to Racy's language lessons. Granta was the honorific for Muscat royalty. I was sharing a room with a prince.

CHAPTER 24: THE INVITATION

There were a dozen Muscat in powered armor waiting for us when we docked at a completely different station, this one less crowded and more lavishly furnished than the first space station we'd visited over Gra'nome. Even the main promenade was carpeted.

Sophie cleared me for light duty and slapped the back of my head. "Ow! What was that for?"

"For cutting all the hair off of my dolls, you jerk!"

I rubbed the back of my head. "I did that when you were eight, and I was like, six. You're beating me up for it now?"

Her look said she was equal parts concerned and pissed off. "I didn't find out it was you until today!"

That confused the hell out of me. How'd she found that out way the scrut out here?

Weirder still was how Sara had changed toward me. I was used to the open hostility and glaring. Now she avoided me completely. An improvement, I guess. Whenever we had to interact with each other, she wouldn't look me in the eye. It made changing watches a little odd.

Aasha, however, was as I expected Aasha would be after her op went south and several marines under her command were killed. She was moody and withdrawn.

We'd slept together a few times since that drunken night on *Ocelot*. I tried not to read anything into it. She still kept her distance in public, but the rumor mill had the right of it. I wanted to go to her to offer some comfort, but she didn't want me around just then. I knew enough to give her space. Maybe she would pick a fight at the next port, blow off some steam, get her head on straight.

All of that I could understand. I mentally replayed everything that had happened down on the planet. It got unpleasant when I remembered the Erethizon I'd had to kill. The intellectual side of me could reason that I was protecting my friends and I didn't have a choice. The emotional side of me was a little less understanding.

Everything got fuzzy after I picked up Graff and Gratsi from behind the tractor. I know I made it back to the ship after that. There was evidence to prove the point, but the plasma bolt had scrambled my short-term memory. Everything, after I grabbed them, was a blur.

The captain called a briefing a couple of hours after we got to the station. She called the meeting to order as soon as Aasha stepped through the door, the last one to arrive. "Sorry, I'm late."

The captain gave her a friendly smile. "It's okay, Aasha." As everyone took a seat she continued, "Ladies and gentlemen, we'll put aside the fact that we were sold out again. Let's concentrate on the opportunity before us. The queen has invited us to the palace for a formal reception tomorrow. Sara, Mark, and myself are required to be there. I'll make it optional for any of the other section heads who want to attend. Rowdy, I'd really appreciate it if your family would attend."

He gave a toothy grin. "We wouldn't miss it, ma'am."

Sophie still had patients in the infirmary, so she begged off the queen's reception. Unsurprisingly, Boldrini said he'd stay aboard with Sophie.

Captain Houston turned to Aasha. "You up for it, sergeant?"

Aasha's eyes never came up from the table in front of her. "No, ma'am."

"We need to replace the men we lost before we leave. Do you have a problem with hiring Muscat to fill those roles? We aren't likely to find many Terrans to fill those posts here."

She did look up then, but it was several moments before she spoke. "No, ma'am. I don't have a problem with it." It looked like she wanted to say more, but it took a few minutes before she could continue. The captain waited her out and seemed inclined to give her all the time she needed. "Ma'am, I'd like to ask Mr. Martin and

Rowdy to handle the interviews. I... I don't think I can do it right now."

"How about it? Mark, Rowdy, you two up for a couple days of extra duty?"

Rowdy and I shared a look. We answered in unison, "No problem, ma'am."

***

The captain had a set of dress blues from when she was a Confederation captain. Neither Sara nor I had anything appropriate for the queen's reception. Rowdy and Racy offered to take us shopping for formalwear on the station. It was a bit awkward since Sara wouldn't speak to me, but we got by. She wasn't hostile, but she'd get quiet and awkward if I asked her anything. I gave up after a few tries.

Racy and Rowdy took us to a tailor that catered to all races. The lobby was filled with comfortable chairs of various sizes but didn't contain any actual racks of clothes. Instead, there was a measuring booth and a full-length wall screen that showed how we would look once the clothes were fitted to us. The two Muscat tailors bantered back and forth, throwing ideas around about how to dress us. The clothes would be tailored to fit once we made our selections.

I chose a suit in deep blacks and blues. Rowdy kept trying to steer me toward the more revealing suits that were currently the fashion, but I couldn't see myself wearing something like that. I only relented and compromised after he pointed out to me that Muscat didn't wear much in the way of clothes and I'd make my hosts more comfortable if I wore something that "showed more fur."

I decided not to comment on his turn of phrase. My compromise outfit was a nearly skintight pair of midnight blue slacks and a black, tailored shirt made out of a shimmery material. I also got a half jacket with long sleeves of the same midnight blue fabric. A pair of black leather boots completed the ensemble. I thought I looked more like I was going out to a nightclub, but Rowdy assured me it was appropriate for the occasion.

I came out first and posed dramatically with one hand on my hip and the other at my side. Racy yipped and clapped appreciatively.

Then Sara came out of her dressing room.

She had chosen a burgundy evening gown. It plunged and flowed in a variety of distracting ways and I had to look away to keep from staring. Though it was floor length, it showed way more skin than I was comfortable with. Black heels and ruby jewelry completed her look.

Racy looked pleased with the selection and gave me a wink behind her back. Sara was standing tall, with an air of confidence. The dress left little to the imagination. In short, it took my breath away.

"Wow," was all I could get out.

She gave me a sidelong look and the edges of her mouth turned up ever so slightly. It was the first time I could ever remember her smiling at me. The smile suited her even more than the dress.

We changed back into our normal attire and grabbed our purchases. I winced a little at the cost, but it couldn't be helped. I needed a nice suit to meet the queen, and I would have to replace a lot more of what I lost on Yale.

***

A Muscat in royal livery showed up later that evening to brief us on royal etiquette. Racy had it all down and even provided some details the courtier missed. The next afternoon, we set off for the private shuttle bay reserved for the occasion. There were a few other races mixed in with the Muscat nobles. I counted five other humans and two Erethizon. I asked a small Muscat consulting a guest list if any Dru were attending the event. He gave a short laugh and informed me that Dru were not allowed near the palace.

We were scanned before boarding the shuttle. We were scanned when we got off the shuttle. And as if that wasn't enough, we were scanned before the herald announced us at the palace.

The banquet hall was huge: three stories tall and a hundred meters long. Dinner was a social affair. The guests ate and switched places and ate some more. Our hosts were considerate and made sure there was food appropriate for the non-Muscats available. The smells and appearance of the Muscat food ranged from tantalizing to bizarre. There was a buffet around the raised royal table at the end of the hall where the Queen and her family dined. No one approached them unless invited.

When everyone had finished eating and the remnants of dinner had been cleared away, large doors opened along one side of the hall. We adjourned to a hall twice as large as the banquet hall. The royal family was again seated on a raised dais at the far end of the room. Plush carpet and comfortable, Muscat-sized seats near small tables lined the outside of a considerable dance floor. "Ballroom" would have been a more appropriate name for the space, but nothing about the Muscats' gyrations even remotely resembled the Terran concept of formal dance.

Other than the royal family, the humans seemed to be the star attraction. A man who turned out to be the Terran ambassador looked like he was holding court on one side of the room. He was telling stories about what life was like in the Terran Core Worlds. I followed his lead by sitting on a sturdy table; none of the chairs were big enough for a human.

Sara and Jenna didn't speak the language, so the small crowd of Muscat gathered around them were practicing their Terran phrases. It wasn't the most engaging conversation, but it kept them all entertained. My limited understanding of the dialect attracted my own herd of followers. I kept them entertained with stories about Yale before the war. They loved hearing about the songs, writers, and playwrights for which my world had been famous. In turn, I asked them about their history, art, and literature.

By contrast, the Erethizon were the pariahs of the evening. No one went near them. That didn't keep them from trying to extoll the wonders of their religion to whoever let them get close enough. They glanced several times in our direction but never approached us.

I knew my grammar was a bit rough, but the locals were coaching me in good humor. I was in the middle of describing a magnapple tree when the Muscat around me got quiet and bowed their heads. Looking around, I found my neighbor from the medical bay.

I bowed low. "Your Highness."

He inclined his head toward me but addressed the gathered throng. "I wonder if I might have a moment of Lieutenant Martin's time."

I didn't know Muscat could scatter like frightened mice, but scatter they did.

The Prince, Gratsi, gave me a small smile and spoke to me in Terran. "Would you walk with me?" He said it as if I could have said no. I recognized a royal command when I heard it, and followed him.

CHAPTER 25: THE QUEEN

We walked along the right wall of the ballroom in a bubble of space created by Muscat bowing and moving out of our way.

He didn't look at me when he spoke. "Did you know who I was when you ran out to get me?"

"No, sire. I knew you were someone important, but I didn't know who you were."

He looked at me intently then, focusing on my eyes. "Would it have mattered if you did?"

I thought about that for a moment before responding. I shook my head. "No. You were in trouble and pinned down. I would have done it even if it had been one of the cargo handlers."

He stopped and searched my face closely as if he were looking for freckles. "Raw'scadi tells me that you were in the Yale military prior to joining the *Leonard Fox*." Call me slow, but it took me a second to remember that was Racy's real name.

"Yes, sire. I was a navigator and fighter pilot. Captain Houston needed my skills and we needed to get off the planet to stay safe."

The prince gave me a questioning look. "We?"

"My sister was with me."

I'd gotten pretty good at reading Muscat emotions through their facial expressions. Something about what I'd said had struck him as both curious and deserving of his respect. I expected him to press me on what he was curious about, but he didn't. We'd reached the other end of the hall and he motioned for me to join him on the dais with his family. "The queen would like a word with you."

He bowed low before his mother and I did the same. He said some words of formal introduction in Muscat. I confess I didn't catch all of it.

"Arise and sit with me, Lieutenant Martin." She indicated a settee just to her left. Gratsi sat on her right.

Her eyes were dark, intelligent, and mysterious. Her face was all black except for her ears, which were a soft brown. Unlike most Muscat, who I'd found radiated a constant state of nervous energy, her movements were relaxed yet precise. She had a Zen-like quality about her.

She also spoke to me in flawless Terran. "I'd like to formally thank you for saving my son."

I bowed my head. "It was my pleasure, Your Majesty."

"Do you know why the Erethizon were there?"

"No, Your Majesty. The idea that they would be there to intercept the cargo we were picking up doesn't make sense."

She smiled slightly. "No?"

"The Erethizon I've met are brash and fanatical, but they're also smart. It's an odd misstep for them to violate your sovereignty in this manner."

Her eyes darted to the other end of the room where the two Erethizon present were speaking with a trio of Muscat who looked rather annoyed. "It does seem a bit out of character for them. The fleet commander at the edge of our system, a Commander Grova, says that all of his people and equipment are accounted for. He suggested the attack was made by rogue elements."

I grimaced. "Unlikely."

She favored me with an enigmatic smile. "I'd like to thank you properly, but..."

She left the statement hanging there, waiting for me to pick it up. "But we can't admit to anyone what we were doing out there in the first place. I understand your delicate position. Your gratitude is enough."

The queen gave a slight nod. "Still, you will receive the title of Gran'osida. The credentials will arrive by encrypted message tomorrow. The password will be the name of my son's love interest aboard your vessel."

I was a bit taken aback that she knew about Racy and Gratsi's relationship, but I guess I shouldn't have been. "I'm not familiar with the term 'Gran'osida,' Your Majesty."

"It means 'Friend of the Empire.' It is the highest honor we can give to a non-Muscat."

I was shocked into silence. An objection on the tip of my tongue, something occurred to me just then. Pythia's prophecy. This was the wolf mother and she was offering me a gift. Pythia had been right on the credits. It was several heartbeats later before I could respond. She waited me out. "I am humbled, Your Majesty."

"Well, perhaps you can do me a couple of favors in return?"

"Your Grace need only name it. It would be my pleasure to serve the Muscat Empire."

She gave me that same enigmatic smile. "You are aware of Raw'noriede's recent breakthrough?"

It took me only a moment to recognize Rowdy's proper name. How this monarch had already come to know what he'd accomplished I'd never guess. I could imagine quite well what she might want. I just wasn't sure I'd be able to do it for her.

"Yes, Your Majesty. You should know that I have very grave concerns about the invention."

Her smile disappeared and she looked me straight in the eye. Her voice was still soft, but there was an edge of steel just under the surface. "Pray, enlighten me, Lieutenant Martin."

I chose my words carefully. This was a powerful woman who could have me killed before I left the room. Every Muscat in the hall would swear it was an accident.

***

"The device blankets an area with white noise at the same frequency that the Dru use to communicate." I took a deep breath. "As a race, they believe everyone should have the same information."

She made a stuttering sound I had learned to interpret as a Muscat being thoughtful. "How will the Terran react?"

"Much the same as your own people, I would expect. Every government everywhere is going to want one for all government buildings. Every corporation is going to want one for every one of their boardrooms and labs."

"Yes," she acknowledged, "and the Dru?"

"They're going to have tadpoles or whatever the equivalent of kittens is. Their intelligence network will be in shambles. While individual Dru might not think much of the invention, the government is going to view it as an attack on their way of life." I shrugged, "The Dru will withdraw to their own area of space. The Terran and Muscat governments will become more cautious, less trusting than normal. Both governments rely too much on the Dru for information gathering."

She nodded, "How would you deal with the situation? If you had the kind of influence to make a difference?"

"I'd license the technology to the Terrans, Muscat, and Dru civilizations and exclude only the Erethizon. They'd get it eventually anyway, but this would slow them down."

As I ran down she looked at me speculatively. "Your insights are remarkably mature and carefully considered for a mere lieutenant."

"My father was a senator on Yale."

She nodded in understanding. "That must be it. As it stands, you are correct. My proxies will be providing Raw'noriede with recommendations—companies he should contact regarding distribution, known entities to the crown who can be trusted to deal fairly with him. Can you find trustworthy Terran and Dru manufactories? I have it on good authority that you have his trust and he could use your insight on this."

I was a bit shocked. She knew about the device that could nullify the Dru psychic ability. A more cautious monarch would convince me to keep the device a secret. Keep it as a Muscat only technology where she could keep an eye on it and keep it from being misused. That would drive a wedge in everyone's relations. Instead, she had the long game in mind. The effect couldn't be avoided, but it could be decreased. Minimize the impact by giving everyone the technology. This was a monarch I could get behind. I could see why she instilled such loyalty in her subjects.

"What was the other thing you wanted?"

The crafty woman gave me that enigmatic smile again. "I'd like you to look after Raw'scadi for me."

Muscat don't blush. I suppose if their skin was visible it might, but that was a question best left to my sister. What I did observe was on the other side of the Queen, Gratsi's pupils dilated and his head bowed in embarrassment.

She continued, "I'm quite fond of the girl. A shame about her birth. Were she from a family of better breeding, she'd be a good match for my son."

The Prince closed his eyes but otherwise kept his emotions under control.

The queen pretended not to notice. "Political realities, unfortunately, take precedence. His fiancé is a good girl as well. I know they'll make a fine couple."

She dismissed me with a wave of her hand and I stood to leave. The queen and her son spoke briefly. I was almost off the dais when the regent called me back again.

"Lieutenant Martin. My son tells me that you saved your sister when you left Yale."

I knew family was a cornerstone of Muscat culture. The observation didn't catch me off guard. "Yes, Your Majesty."

"What is her name?" She was trying to be casual—or at least as casual as a queen can get in public. There was an intensity in her eyes that was more than simple curiosity. It told me the answer was important to her.

Maybe that was why I hesitated a moment before replying. "Sophia, Your Majesty."

The look on her face hardened into an impenetrable mask. It was clear that something had spooked her and she was working hard to keep her expression neutral. She beckoned me closer, so close she spoke right into my ear.

"Your father is George Martin?"

I pulled back in astonishment so I could look into her eyes. "Yes. How..."

Her look stopped me cold. After a long, uncomfortable pause she said, "My Gods. You don't know."

I was dumbfounded. I wanted to ask what I didn't know, but I never got the chance. Quickly and quietly, with an efficiency that surprised me, she issued orders to the guards behind her. They approached and took my arms gently but firmly.

She whispered in my ear, "You can't stay here. You and your sister must leave Muscat space. All will be explained."

CHAPTER 26: HASTY EXIT

The guards led me back to the palace shuttle bay through back hallways. It was the royal treatment: two of the Muscat escorting me to the private shuttle joined me for the trip up and walked with me through the space station to the *Leo*. I got the impression they were trying to keep me safe, but from what? The situation felt so odd I checked my messages every half hour to see if the queen's promised dispatch had arrived.

Once aboard, I went down to medical to check on my sister. I found her in the small office just off Sickbay. She was keeping one eye on the view screen displaying patient data and the other on Boldrini sitting across from her.

"Hey, guys."

Boldrini smiled, but Sophie knitted her brows at me. "Don't state functions usually last couple hours longer? I'm not sure you were tortured enough."

Boldrini laughed. "Have you been to many?"

We smiled weakly at each other before answering in unison, "Yes."

He snapped his fingers. "That's right, your father is a senator."

Sophie grimaced. "Worse. He's *the* senator. The Senate majority leader. Still, it could have been worse."

I nodded. Boldrini looked confused. "Worse how?"

Sophie and I considered each other a moment, in the way siblings have of communicating without words. How much should we tell Boldrini? Did it really matter at this point? Finally, we came to an unspoken decision. I shrugged and explained, "About sixty years ago our government transitioned from a constitutional monarchy to a democratic republic. If it hadn't, we'd be the Prince and Princess of Yale."

He looked stunned. "You're joking."

We watched him and waited for his brain to catch up.

"Soph, you're a princess?"

She shook her head. "No, didn't you hear him? The monarchy was dissolved sixty years ago. Thanks to that, I'm just plain Dr. Martin."

His mouth was moving but no words came out. Finally, something clicked and he found his words again. "How come you never told me?"

She gave him a wicked grin. "Would you have asked me out if you'd known?"

"No!"

She shrugged as if that was all the answer he should need. Which I guess it was.

Boldrini stood up. "I've got to get dinner mess going. You and I are going to have a serious talk after cleanup."

He wandered out of Sickbay in a daze, muttering, "I've been dating a princess."

Mirth bubbled up out of me. "That was mean, Sophie."

"I suppose, but it was fun. Change of subject: why *are* you back so early?"

I held up my hands in confusion. "I don't know." I related the events of the reception leading up to my being asked to leave.

She listened intently and assumed a studied pose of concentration. "It was only after she found out I was your sister, and that Dad was..." she shrugged, "well, *Dad*, that she asked you to leave."

"Yeah. Mean anything to you?"

Sophie frowned in concentration. "No, but it certainly meant something to her. You'll let me see the message when you get it?"

"Of course."

I left Sophie to her patients and went to the ship's office. I wasn't tired yet and thought I'd get a jump on tomorrow's work by putting together the posting for the marine job.

***

The captain and Sara came back aboard a couple hours later. They cornered me in the ship's office.

The captain looked irritated and concerned at the same time. "What happened to you? One minute you're entertaining a bunch of groupies, the next you're gone. I felt a little better when one of the guards told us you left early. They said you felt ill. I didn't know whether I could believe him."

Sara looked concerned too. It wasn't an expression I was used to seeing on her.

"I'm fine, guys. It was a weird evening." I told them about what happened during my audience with the queen. "And then they escorted me back to the ship."

I expected Sara to accuse me of some sort of conspiracy. Instead, she asked, "You have no idea why they asked you to leave?"

"No." By some minor miracle, she looked like she believed me.

The captain looked deep in thought. "You'll tell me right away when that message comes in, right?"

I recognized the order. "Yes, ma'am. I'll come to see you right after I read it."

She nodded absently. I could see her mind working overtime.

A funny thought struck me. "You're not going to have *Leo* read my mail, are you?" I asked with a grin.

That snapped her out of it and she chuckled. "Not just yet, but I might get Rafe to fill me in on the rumors."

***

The encrypted message from the queen arrived midmorning the following day. I had just sent the job posting to the local union hall when it arrived in my inbox. I opened it and was immediately prompted for an encryption key. I typed in Racy's proper name and the message started to decode itself. It took longer than I thought it should. Must have been heavy encryption.

Once it resolved itself I realized the other reason it had taken so long to decode. There was a video file attached to the message.

I read through the content. Most of it was the business information she'd promised to send me for Rowdy. I was thankful since it would give me a great starting point for advising Rowdy on how to proceed.

The credentials for the honor of Gran'osida she bestowed on me were also there and a notice that a medal would be arriving by courier later that day. It was a small pin I was allowed to wear with dress attire and any military uniform, a curious upside down triangle topped by a crown.

I looked up and saw Gina and Rafe standing in the door to the ship's office. "Can I help you?"

They answered much too quickly and almost in unison. "No, sir!"

Great. The rumor mill had already let them know something was up. "Then would you mind clearing the passage? I wouldn't want anyone to trip over you by accident."

They took the hint and left. I had the feeling they were just out of sight of the hatch.

I opened the video file and played it. I recognized the scene immediately. The polished magnapple wood paneling. The microphones. The consoles. I was looking at the Senate chamber back on Yale. If the timestamp could be believed, it was the night we left Yale, but hours before the attack had begun.

They were all there: Mr. Wayne, Mrs. Danby, Mr. Barry, Mr. Spangle, Mrs. Byrne, and of course, my dad. I'd met them all, of course. I knew all the senators from the Conservative Party since we'd been at several family and political functions together over the years. I knew the senators from the Liberal, Royalist, Agriculture, and Fine Arts and Education Parties as well.

The Senate was in session. I watched as Mr. Spangle from the Royalist Party stood up and made a motion for a constitutional amendment. An amendment? That seemed a bit extreme. The constitution was a painstakingly crafted document that had governed Yale for the last sixty years.

To my surprise, I saw Mr. Wayne from the Conservative Party stand up and second the motion. This was unusual since Mr. Wayne and Mr. Spangle rarely agreed on anything. This sent the motion to the floor for a vote to open the discussion. To my shock, everyone in the chamber almost unanimously voted to open discussion on the proposed amendment. My dad abstained.

Mr. Spangle looked exactly like he'd looked in the news report photo—same rhinestone-covered suit with a purple tie. The tie had the house of Martin crest on it. I remembered vaguely that he had been a distant cousin. My grandmother's sister's eldest grandson or something like that. Tenuous claim to the crown, but I'm sure it was close enough for the Porcu-bears.

"My fellow senators," he began, "we have gathered here today to discuss only one topic. You'll find it on the briefing you received as you entered the room. Has everyone had the opportunity to review the proposed amendment?"

There was a murmur of assent.

"Excellent. We have reached a crossroads, ladies and gentlemen. Sixty years ago, the people of this chamber historically voted to abolish the Monarchy in favor of a republic. This was done with much forethought and at the urging of the Terran Confederation ambassador. The ambassador had indicated that an alliance with the Confederation would be forthcoming if changes were made. What followed were years of negotiations. The Terrans repeatedly insisted on language that would strip our proud people of their independence. This we would not abide."

It was a history lesson no one in the room needed, but Spangle was a showman at heart. He'd set the stage before he started the first act.

He continued, "Talks broke down. We came to enjoy other benefits of being a republic. No move was made to reinstate the Monarchy.

"Three years ago, the Erethizon sent missionaries to us. The people of Yale had seen the subjugation of Grey, Anderson, and Ajax. The priests were asked to leave." Mr. Spangle set his jaw. "We saw the writing on the wall. They were coming for us next. We made one last attempt to form an alliance with the Terrans. The cowards on Earth refused to see our representative."

He slowly scanned the room. I rolled my eyes. He was grandstanding, feeding his ego. He leaned over the podium. "My friends, repeatedly in this conflict, this chamber has lacked the two-thirds majority needed to make law. It has become painfully clear that central leadership is required."

That was a twist. Okay, so maybe they'd elected the little snot before the Porcu-bears busted the shield.

Mr. Spangle shook his fist in the air. "Now, more than ever, we need to reinstate the Monarchy. I urge each and every one of you to vote for what the people need. Amendment M must pass. Our way of life hangs in the balance."

The discussion was brief and centered on what proposed powers "the regent" would have. Mr. Spangle got everything he wanted. It took seven minutes—a record as far as I knew. From the discussion, it seemed that they were in the last stages of the process. Everything had already been worked out ahead of time behind closed doors.

A motion was made to bring the discussion to a close and vote on the amendment. It carried. The view switched to the big screen at the front of the Senate chamber. The votes came in. Again, unanimous with only one abstention.

I shook my head in disgust. It was easy to figure out who had abstained, even though the votes were tallied anonymously. Why was my dad not voting on an amendment that would fundamentally change the way the government of Yale worked? He was a powerhouse. I couldn't imagine him not taking a position on this. Granted, he liked Spangle. I knew he admired his dedication, but he had to know the Royalist wasn't monarch material.

The leaders of all five political parties, plus Mr. Wayne, came forward. Mr. Wayne, who was second only to my father in the conservative party leadership, was carrying what I recognized as the crown and scepter from the Royal History Museum. Mr. Spangle carried the royal cape. His grin was so wide I thought his face would split in two. This should be a solemn event. Couldn't the little nut lick at least pretend to gracious about it? I mean, I could imagine why. He'd been working to restore the monarchy for his entire political career. But was he going to be the new monarch? That didn't make much sense. If that were the case, he wouldn't be carrying the cape.

Then it happened. It would have been surreal if it hadn't been so horrifying to me. The three other party leaders knelt while Mr. Spangle draped the cape around Dad's shoulders and Mr. Wayne handed him the scepter and placed the crown on his head. I could hear his voice clearly as he said, "Congratulations, Your Majesty." He and Mr. Spangle knelt before my father, and the entire chamber followed suit.

CHAPTER 27: THE CAT OUT OF THE BAG

"WHAT THE FUCK!!!"

I realized I'd just yelled at the top of my lungs when Rafe and Gina appeared in the doorway, their eyes as big as saucers.

Rafe spoke first, a tentative, "Are you okay, sir?"

An uncomfortably long moment stretched out before I responded. I spoke in what I hoped was a level and calm voice. "I'm not entirely sure, Mr. Sanzio. Do you mind if I get back to you on that?"

"Of course, sir."

I sent a message to Sophia, Sara, and the captain. The content: "If it isn't inconvenient, please meet me in the conference room right away."

I signed out of the workstation and headed for the bridge. Sophie met me in the passageway.

"Mark?"

I didn't stop or respond, just sighed and jerked my head toward the bridge.

She caught up with me. Her look of concern had become one of alarm. "Marky? What's wrong?"

I felt rather than heard Gina following us. I imagine the only reason Rafe wasn't tagging along too was that he couldn't think of an excuse to be on the bridge.

We arrived on the bridge to find the captain, Sara, and Wally staring at the door when it opened. Wally was running an update.

I paused for a second to collect my thoughts. "Captain, Ms.

Chew, if it's not too much trouble, can we speak for a moment in private?"

She returned my careful formality. "Of course, Mr. Martin. I just received your message." She motioned toward the conference room.

We all walked in and I shut the door behind us. I went to the console and fired it up while everyone sat at the table behind me. The small console screen was duplicated on the big screen in the room. I ran a systems query and found that Gina had activated the intercom in the conference room. With a smile, I used my access to lock her out of the ship's communication system and shut off all the intercoms across the ship.

I turned around to find everyone staring at me. "That should keep the ship's rumor mill at bay for a little while longer." I took a deep breath and began, "I know why we've been getting so much attention from the Erethizon."

The captain looked relieved. "You know the identity of the snitch?"

I shook my head. "No. I just know why they're following us. I'm not sure how much you know about the politics of Yale, but we were a constitutional monarchy before we were a democratic republic. Our great-grandfather was the last king, the one who stepped down."

Houston nodded. "Coverin' old ground there, son. I was a might peeved that last time you told us."

"I'm sorry, ma'am." I acknowledged, "I should have told you from the start. Here's a little more. Our father is his firstborn son's son, and a senior senator by the name of George Martin. With that in mind, I'll ask you to watch this clip that was recorded a few hours before you landed on Yale. Sophie and I were not aware that this was taking place."

With that, I played the video.

When it was done, there was a look of surprised shock on everyone's faces. I continued. "I'll find a sparsely inhabited system nearby where you can drop us off. We can't continue to put your ship and your crew at risk."

I looked at my sister and saw her nodding in my direction. I had no doubts that she would agree with me.

"No."

It took me a moment to register that it was Sara who had

objected. "Excuse me?"

"I said, no. I get that you want to protect us, but this is about more than just you. You don't get to be the judge of what trouble we get ourselves into."

Jenna looked me straight in the eyes. "Sara's right. If we drop you off on some random parcel, the spy on board tells them where to pick you up and the resistance on your planet fails. Seems pretty straightforward to me. We're a blockade runner. We're already in trouble with a good many lawmen out here. The *Leo* can deal with the extra risk. Besides," she shrugged, "I just got a first-class navigator and doctor. No way I'm letting them go without a fight."

I rounded on Sara. "I don't get it. You've been trying to get me off this ship since I got here. I find out you're right, that I am a threat, and now you want me to stay?"

She set her jaw. "The captain's correct. You are a good navigator. A lot of the crew like you, so I'm willing to give you a chance. You'll still have plenty of opportunities to prove me right."

My sister chimed in. "Jenna? There's a big difference between weathering a storm and sailing into it."

The captain smiled wolfishly. "I'm thinking that having royalty on board will improve our bottom line. Just having you here will open up markets and jobs I'd never dreamed of getting before."

They were making excuses to keep us aboard. We knew it. They knew it. I looked into Sophie's eyes and could see she was as touched by the gesture as I was.

"In that case, I have a dozen reports to write and marines to hire."

***

The ship rented an office on the station to conduct interviews. I was expecting to have to cobble together a new squad of marines from the rabble who responded to the job listing. In hindsight, that was stupid. The most common response to the job posting was, "How many are you looking to hire?" After the third inquiry, I updated the job posting with the required number of marines.

On the way to the lift, I asked Rowdy, "How many interviews do we have today?"

He checked his tablet. "Three."

My eyebrows bounced off the overhead. "Only three? We need

five."

Rowdy looked confused. "They're all five."

"Huh?"

"Each family is five people. That is what we need, right?"

Understanding dawned on me. "Yes, of course."

Rowdy grinned at me. "You forgot that we travel as families, didn't you?"

I felt my cheeks flush and I laughed. "Yeah, you got me. It completely slipped my mind." I turned the conversation to interview strategy. "I'm going to be looking for someone with a military background. I'd prefer search and rescue, but having someone with shipboard weaponry or special weapons and tactics would be good. We have those skills in our current marines, but a certain amount of doubling up will help."

Rowdy nodded. "That makes sense. I haven't done anything like this before. Can I use my tablet to message you if I have a question? I don't want to say something wrong in front of the candidates."

I gave him a lopsided smile. "Of course. I'll ask the majority of the questions, but if you have something you want to ask, just jump in. I'm more interested in fit than skills."

We arrived in front of the lift. Rowdy hit the call button. I was amused to notice it was at his eye level.

We went up to level five and four doors spinward. The office we had rented came complete with waiting room, office, and conference room. At first, I was surprised that everything looked so nice, then I remembered we were still parked on the most upscale orbital above the planet. Everything would be posh and exclusive. The docking fees must've been outrageous.

Rowdy and I set up our tablets on one side of the conference table, which would allow us to pull up the local net and send messages privately.

The first matriarch came in and settled into the seat across from us. Pur'nika's combat gear was a little worn around the edges but serviceable. We learned that her colony had suffered a natural disaster three standard years ago and her family had turned mercenary. From the skills inventory, her pack must have had training somewhere along the way. She answered our questions well until I started digging into her motivations. Her answers gave me the impression that she was primarily interested in how the job would directly benefit her family—a sort of "What's in it for me?" mentality. Not a bad thing, but I was looking for a family who could truly integrate with the crew. I worried her pack would do their jobs but keep to themselves.

The patriarch that came in next was a bit more professional. Han'torith's combat gear was in excellent condition. His family has been in military service of one kind or another for generations. They were experienced and well trained. Unfortunately, the problem came down to personal motivation again. While he wouldn't go into detail, it quickly became clear that he needed to get out of the system and soon. We had enough wanted fugitives on the crew; I was wary about adding any more.

The last interview was something of a surprise. Tren'groat had a quiet, deadly grace and eyes that spoke volumes about his experiences.

I typed a note to Rowdy.

What does gravinde *mean?*

It took a moment to register, and I saw him scroll through the resume until he found it. His eyes widened before he typed back a response.

It means royal marine. His family served in the palace guard until recently.

His family unit consisted of a sniper, a field medic, a demolitions expert, and a heavy weapons specialist. Tren'groat himself was trained as a forward observer, a scout. His answers were right on the money. He was well versed in what it took to be a cohesive team and was motivated by the success of the whole crew. He was exactly what I was looking for. I could sense the not-so-subtle hand of the queen at work.

I looked him in the eyes, trying to see if his answers were genuine or just rehearsed. "Tren'groat..."

He interrupted me with a small smile. "You can call me Trent, sir."

"Trent, you do know that you're signing on to provide security on a freighter, right?"

"Sir, my family would consider it the highest honor to accompany the Gran'osida on whatever mission he has seen fit to pursue."

If I suspected the queen before, that just removed all doubt. I hadn't told anyone about the honor bestowed on me.

Rowdy looked at Trent in confusion. Then his eyes bugged out and he looked at me, surprised and awed. "Mark?"

I addressed Trent. "In that case, nothing would please me more than to welcome you to our family. When can you report aboard?"

"Two hours, sir. My pack is already on-station and we just need to collect our gear before reporting aboard. Our gear masses two metric tons. Will there be enough room for it in the ship's armory?"

The mass caught me off guard for a moment until it hit me: his family were reporting with their own combat armor and maintenance equipment, an added plus. "Yes. That will be fine."

***

Walking back to the ship, Rowdy kept looking up at me with his ears twitching. I'd come to recognize this as shock. We waited at the lift for the next car to come. "Mark..."

"I know. I should have told you."

The lift doors opened and we rode down to the docks. "But... Mark... no ceremony? There's always a... well, I guess the Terran term would be a 'knighting.'"

"She gave me the honor for saving her son. She can't have a ceremony without admitting what we were doing when it happened."

"But Mark... you outrank every Muscat in the system except for the royal family and the nobility. Generals and admirals have to listen to you. In effect, you've been adopted by the queen."

The lift doors opened and we turned toward the ship. I gave Rowdy a sideways smile. "Does that mean we can't be friends anymore?"

"No, but this is a big deal."

"Then do me a favor and don't tell anyone. I don't want people to know that I'm royalty in two empires. They'd treat me differently."

"Two?"

Oh, right. I winced and let out a long breath. "I just found out that before everything fell apart in Yale, the Senate reinstated the monarchy. They elevated my father to the Regency."

Rowdy took my hand and swung me around. He looked into my eyes. "You're not joking, are you?"

I shook my head. "No. I'm not. My great-grandfather stepped

down when the people asked him to. People thought that if we made nice with the Confederation we would get a treaty. It didn't work. The Terran Confederation was more interested in subverting independent governments than working with them. It made us easier targets." I shrugged.

I started walking down the docks again and Rowdy followed. "Hey," I said, "if Gratzi and Racy could ever get married, I'd be bowing to you, Your Grace." I gave him a haughty look.

Rowdy swished his tail pompously, raised his hand, and strutted with his nose in the air. "Then you'll kiss my paw when I tell you to, lesser being."

I made an exaggerated bow. "Oh, Your Grace is so generous."

We didn't stop laughing until we made it to the lock.

***

"Mark, where did you find these guys?"

We were starting the departure briefing, Rowdy, Boldrini, Sophie, Sara, the captain, and I all stuffed into the conference room behind the bridge. I regarded Jenna with a questioning look. "I'm sorry, Captain?"

She turned her tablet so I could see the screen. "These new marines you've hired. Where did you find them?"

I shrugged my shoulders. "They applied. I hired them."

"Don't get me wrong, I like them, but they could ask for a lot more than we're paying them. I also see that they just recently went on furlough. Their training is current."

I nodded, "And they came with their own gear. I suspect that someone high up suggested they fly with us."

To the right of the captain, Sara frowned with concern. "Spies?"

I shook my head. "More likely they approve of what we're doing, but can't show it for political reasons."

Jenna slapped her hand on the table. "Whatever the reason, I'm happy to have them aboard."

She addressed the table at large. "Okay, let's get the ship moving. Engineering?"

Rowdy piped up. "Tanks are full. Volatiles are topped off. Air, water, and gases are at optimal levels given the current ship's complement. The gravity and heat in one of the two marine berthing areas has been increased consistent with Muscat preferences."

"Good. Boldrini, how are we for stores?"

"The larder's full and we've taken on a load of fresh, local fruits and vegetables. Given the current crew, I don't think anyone would mind if we throw a few Muscat dishes into the menu. Rafe—ahem—acquired some Terran meats and cheeses from somewhere. We'll have bacon with breakfast for the next couple of weeks."

Jenna's eyebrows shot up. "I'd ask where the scrut he got bacon way the scrut out here, but I'm certain I don't want to know the details. Medical?"

Sophie checked her tablet. "I was able to replace most of what we used in the recent battle. We've stocked up on medical supplies and picked up the most recent medical texts on Muscat physiology. I'll be studying them for the next couple of months to make sure I can properly take care of the crew. We're running a bit lower than I'd like on antibiotics, but we should be okay until we reach the next port. Our marine commander is still on no duty rest. She's taking the loss of her men hard. I suggest another two weeks before we put her back on the duty roster."

The captain nodded solemnly. "I can imagine how she feels. Please provide me with daily progress reports, Doc. Astrogation?"

I looked at my calculations. "I've plotted us a course to the gate. We will jump to Sagitta and then hop over to Aspen. I have us dropping out of R-drive a light hour outside the system and well below the plane of the ecliptic. If we come in slowly on full stealth, we should be just another sector of empty space to anyone looking in our direction."

Jenna turned to Sara. "Excellent. First?"

"All crew present or accounted for. Cargo is loaded and secure. The ship is ready for space."

Jenna slapped the table. "Good. Let's be about it, people. 1400 pull out. I'll call navigation stations at 1300. That's a lot to do and little time to do it."

Pull out went off without a hitch. It seemed to me that Gra'nome let out a collective sigh of relief when the *Leo* cleared local space.

I kept an eye on the Erethizon frigates at the edge of the system. They hadn't so much as batted an eyelid with the Muscat battle cruisers sitting in front of them.

Even more unnerving was the message we received from

Commander Grova. He wished us a safe voyage.

We were three days out when out of the corner of my eye I saw Sara frown. She had been pulling double shifts on the bridge to keep an eye on the Porcu-bear ships. I couldn't imagine that they'd try anything with the cruisers right in front of them, but they'd attacked us on the planet. I admired her dedication while I worried about her getting enough rest.

I typed a message to her tablet.

What's wrong?

She glanced up at me with an expression I couldn't read but typed back.

There is some unusual radiation coming from engineering.

Unusual? How?

It was a few moments before I got a response.

It's electromagnetic. The pattern is odd. It could be nothing. One of Rowdy's experiments maybe.

Or it could be our onboard spy trying to communicate with the frigates.

She looked me in the eye.

Yes.

CHAPTER 28: LEAVING GRA'NOME

I sighed.

I don't want to go around accusing shipmates of conspiracy, but one of us needs to look into this. Would you cover the bridge watch while I check it out?

Sara shrugged and nodded.

It amazed me how much our relationship had improved in the past few days. I still hadn't figured out why, but I wasn't going to question it. I stood up. "Ms. Chew. I'd like to check on Ms. Gudka. Would you mind taking over the watch for me? It shouldn't be more than ten minutes."

She gave me a look of bland politeness. "Of course, sir"

I decided to play it formally. "Ms. Chew, no incidents are actions. Standing orders are unchanged. You have the watch."

"Thank you, Mr. Martin. I have the watch."

I left the bridge and wandered down to Aasha's quarters. Checking on her was of course just my excuse for leaving the bridge, but I was still a little concerned for her. When I got to her door, I heard low talking from within. I didn't recognize anyone else's voice, so she was probably composing a message. Aasha sent frequent letters to her sister, so it didn't surprise me. I waited for her to finish. I tried not to listen in, but I caught brief snippets about what sounded like ship gossip anyway.

When she stopped talking, I knocked on the door.

After a couple of long minutes, she opened the door and gave a small start when she realized it was me. "Mark!"

I laughed and let a grin spread across my face. "At ease, soldier.

I just stopped by to make sure you're doing okay."

She smiled in response. A look that said she was still healing. "I'm fine. I mean... I'm feeling better."

I gave her a lopsided grin and tried to calm her down. "Okay. I'm heading down to engineering. See you at lunch?"

She nodded as if she didn't trust herself to speak, then gave me a peck on the cheek and closed the door.

I shrugged and headed down the corridor.

***

In Engineering I found Rowdy working on a project on his workbench while Randy kept an eye on things. I walked up beside him and looked over his shoulder. He was so engrossed in whatever he was working on that he didn't even notice I was there. Randy saw me though and gave me a very human wink.

"Rowdy?"

Poor Rowdy nearly jumped out of his skin. "Mark! You almost gave me feathle shock!" I believed that was the Muscat equivalent of a heart attack. "I'm sorry, my friend. Did I catch you at a bad time?"

Muscats are normally high-strung, but Rowdy practically vibrated. It made me wonder what he had been doing.

He visibly tried to calm himself and took a few deep breaths. "No, not a bad time, but this experiment is fascinating and I just got sucked in."

I looked him in the eyes. "Would this experiment happen to be why we're detecting unusual radiation readings on the bridge?"

"Really?" He turned to a computer and typed a few keys. "Of course! Non-particle, electromagnetic radiation! That's why." He immediately became engrossed in studying the readings.

I waited a handful of heartbeats while Rowdy studied the data on the screen. "Rowdy?"

He turned back to me. "Yes?"

"Well?"

"Well, what?"

"The magnetic radiation, are you responsible?"

He showed lots of teeth. His eyes were wide with excitement. "Oh. Yes, I am."

"And is it a danger to the crew or a method of

communication?"

He thought about it a few minutes. "No. At these levels, it won't pose any risk to the crew. I suppose I could find a way to modulate it if you wanted to make a communication device out of it, but there are much easier ways to do that. An exotic matter lens is hard to come by."

I tilted my head to the side. "Exotic matter lens? Rowdy, what the hell are you working on?"

He jumped up and down in excitement. "A new weapon system! The electromagnetic field is perfect! I didn't have a way to focus the particles. If the field is a byproduct of the reaction, I could harness it to organize the waves!"

I pinched the bridge of my nose. The ship was not in danger... yet. No one was using the radiation to communicate. Rowdy had just been experimenting again. "Rowdy, why do we need another weapon? What makes this one so special?"

"Oh! It ignores conventional armor and shields and increases mass. The effect would be to create a miniature singularity at the point of impact."

"Rowdy, doesn't our R-drive work on the same principle? I thought there wasn't a way to project a singularity more than a few kilometers. Ship-to-ship combat takes place in ranges of several tens of thousands of kilometers. How is this useful?"

He jumped up on his workbench and stuck his face uncomfortably close to mine before I knew it. I needed to have a talk with him about personal space. "This is a different way of doing the same thing. We're not projecting negatively energized particles to stress space. I'm exciting the particles already there. Increasing their gravitational attraction."

I'm not a physicist and I wasn't going to try to pretend I was. "Okay, assuming you can project these particles, the shield technology everyone uses protects from lasers, particle radiation, energy radiation, projectiles, micrometeorites, and dust. So won't it stop this too?"

Rowdy gave me a huge, vulpine grin. "You're not just another ugly face. Shields block only what they are designed to block. They don't block everything, or our sensors and visual pickups wouldn't work either. This particle radiation vibrates at a frequency no one uses. Until they figure it out and design something to stop it, we'll have the advantage."

That thought gave me pause. "You keep the plans on your engineering mainframe computer, right?"

"Of course. It and the navigation computer are the only computers on the whole ship with the processing power to run the simulations."

I looked him in the eyes... which wasn't hard since he was still in my face. "Please have Racy improve the security on your computers at the first opportunity. We don't want this information falling into the wrong hands."

***

I returned to the bridge and Sara and I exchanged the watch again. For the benefit of the listening ears on the bridge, I added, "Ms. Gudka is okay. She was composing a message to her sister."

I pulled Sara to the bridge wing and spoke in low tones. "Rowdy is building a new weapon. The radiation was part of it. He promised to keep it down so as not to wake the neighbors."

She grinned a little at my joke. Bit by bit, I was wearing that girl down. "Well, I'll ask *Leo* to keep an eye on the chatter."

***

Aasha arranged a poker game for a few of the officers and department heads. I took it as a sign that she was feeling better. Sophie, Sara, Boldrini, and I accepted the invitation. We met in the conference room behind the bridge while the captain had the watch. I thought we did a pretty good job of pretending it was all business, but some of the bridge crew gave us knowing looks.

Sophie had just thrown a hand to Boldrini. I'd played with her enough times to know what was going on in her head. I still couldn't read Sara, but was getting better with the chef. His lips twitched.

The real surprise was Aasha. You'd think a woman with cybernetic implants and an AI running half of her body would be harder to read. Not so. Aasha got more still and less natural when she had a good hand. She might as well have lit up a neon sign.

That didn't keep her from trying to distract me, though. She'd been playing footsie with me under the table for the entire game.

At the moment, she was being very still. "One for me, thanks."

The action passed to Sara. "I'll take three. Any headway on the mole investigation?"

Aasha shook her head. "No. I've interviewed half the crew and I'm no closer to finding out who it is. Everything matches up and everyone has alibis. Your play, Mark."

I had a pair of queens, but our head of security wasn't going to sucker me in. "Fold. Do we know how they're communicating with the Porcu-bears?"

"No. Nothing looks odd in the messages going to and from the *Leo*, and we haven't found any other communication devices."

Sophie looked me in the eyes. I tried not to let my body language betray my thoughts. "I'm out, too. Rob?"

Scrut. Sophie had followed me out. She was using me to read the table. Clever.

Boldrini looked at his cards. "I'll take two. What do you think motivates someone to betray their race?"

I shrugged. "Money, blackmail, family, power, revenge? There are lots of reasons."

Aasha looked around the table as if she were considering whether to stay in or not. It didn't fool me. I knew she'd raise any bet. She was going to try to take the table for as much as she thought she could get away with. "Fifteen. I think we're forgetting something important. The Erethizon have some sort of coercive strategy. It may be the whole friends and family thing. It may be more. They seem to be able to control the leaders they reeducate."

Sara didn't betray anything. "Call. But they don't do that with the leaders. Why?"

Aasha grimaced. "I think something about the process makes them dumber. They can't think straight anymore, so they don't make good leaders. You in this, Boldrini?"

He nodded. "I'll see your fifteen and raise you ten. That must be why they imprison family members. When the time comes to replace them they roll out the son or daughter they've had years to indoctrinate. Pretty effective plan."

I shook my head. "Not really. It only works if the son or daughter is in the community earning the respect of the people. Legacies don't continue without deeds to back them up."

Aasha was trying to play it cool. "Do you think that's what they're doing with your dad right now, reeducating him? See and raise twenty-five."

Sara and Boldrini folded. Aasha had overplayed her hand.

Looking over at Sophie, I could tell the conversation was getting to her. "I don't know. When the rest of the galaxy gets its act together and puts an end to the Erethizon invasion, I hope we find our father alive and himself."

The cyborg looked dubious, but let the conversation drop.

***

We jumped to Sagitta without further incident. I wasn't surprised to find an Erethizon destroyer sitting outside of the system when we arrived.

Sara was less than thrilled. "Are they watching us, or gathering intelligence on the system?"

Jenna scowled. "I could be optimistic and say that they're here gathering intel. Sagitta is likely the next system they'll hit after Aspen. Sagitta is heavy industry. They have a larger fleet than Yale or Aspen to protect them. They may try to take out Norma first."

She cocked her head. "But?"

"But given our luck, I'm betting they're here for us too."

The captain had summed it up well: they were here to keep an eye on us.

After two and a half days in the system, we retracted our reflectors. We extended them in friendly systems so we'd show up on long-range scans. Without them, our absorbent paint made us effectively disappear to all but visual scans. Short-range scans were more detailed and could still pick us out.

With the reflectors retracted, we changed course. A day later we fired up the R-drive and started making our way to Aspen.

***

We arrived a couple of days out of the Aspen system and gave ourselves a big push with the gravity drives to get us moving. Once in-system, we used thrusters to change course.

When we were fifteen AUs out, our passive scans picked up the Erethizon fleet.

"Three battle groups." Sara was looking at her scans. "That's going to play hell with our exit vector."

CHAPTER 29: ASPEN

The captain shrugged. "Nothing we haven't dealt with before. Keep an eye on their movements and we'll find a hole we can use."

She turned to me. "Mark, what's the political situation down there?"

"I visited Aspen before the blockade."

"Great," said Jenna, "'cause I ain't been here before. Give me the skinny."

"Aspen is a socialist republic. They have a representative government. Instead of senators and representatives, their elected officials are called custodians. They have almost no political corruption and the culture is built on the idea that everyone works for the good of the community. That being said, the people are mostly of Arabic descent. While women are highly respected in their culture, they are not allowed to hold public office or receive an advanced education. They are expected to be covered from head to toe at all times. We won't offend anyone if the female crew members wear combat armor with the faceplates down. Don't be surprised if our contacts invite you to have tea before getting down to business. If you want to do business here again, don't refuse the offer."

She regarded me like I'd just told her sharks were cute and cuddly. "Tea?"

"Tea. It'll be bitter. Even though 90 percent of this planet is covered with water, they still have a lot of desert traditions."

***

We coasted in using thrusters to slow our approach and came to a relative stop at a distance of two million kilometers from the planet. We waited and watched the Erethizon blockade formation with passive scans.

In scanning the planet, something odd soon became apparent. There should have been nine major floating cities. After a couple days of observation, we only counted seven.

"We should be able to come in through here." Sara pointed out an area in the southern hemisphere after half a day of observation. We were in the conference room with Aasha and the captain, trying to come up with a plan to get past the blockade.

The captain shook her head. "I think a southern polar insertion would work better."

I rubbed the coin in my pocket as I studied the representation of the planet on the viewscreen and nodded. "I think Ms. Chew is right. They had a couple of starfighters positioned over the pole when we left Yale. I bet they're doing the same thing here. If it were me, I'd have upped the ante and put five of them out there. If they're hiding in the planet's magnetic field, they'd be right on top of us before we ever knew they were there."

The captain shrugged. "I don't think they'd up the number of fighters, but I wouldn't put it past them to have someone waiting for us. We could come in at more of an angle and a few degrees north."

I considered it but rejected the idea. "They'd still see us. Timing it to come in here, on Ms. Chew's coordinates, while these two battle groups are on opposite sides of the planet makes more sense."

Jenna pointed. "And these one-meter satellites?"

Sara magnified the image. "Erethizon communication satellites."

She studied them. "A bit low. They would be more effective in a higher orbit."

I bobbed my head in the direction of the image. "They're spy satellites doing double duty as communications. Back on Yale, we destroyed hundreds of them. They'd have new ones up in a couple of days, but we could get a lot done in a couple of days."

Aasha raised an eyebrow in my direction. "If they're spy

satellites, won't they see us coming? Call in fighters to intercept us before we reach the safety of the planet shield?"

Standing up, I walked to the image. I pointed out the imaging arrays. "They're oriented to look at the planet surface. They won't see us until we're already past them. We'll be inside the planet shield before they can reach us."

Sara cocked her head, looking at the image. "If they're spy satellites, why aren't they stealthy? Also, why are there a lot more here than there were at Yale?"

"They aren't stealthy because the Porcu-bears aren't good at stealthy." I waggled my eyebrows at her. "And on Yale, we cleared them out before you got there." I zoomed out to look at the full planet again. "Aspen hasn't been as successful in getting rid of them."

Aasha pointed toward an area on the northern hemisphere near the north pole. "So why aren't we coming in here, where there aren't as many satellites?"

Sara and I answered in unison, "That's our way out."

In the end, the captain went with our plan.

***

"Easy does it, Wally." The captain admonished while watching the blue marble of Aspen get closer and closer. Wally decreased our speed again.

She called over her shoulder, but her eyes never left the forward display. "Any sign we've been noticed, Ms. Chew?"

"No, ma'am."

The next few minutes passed by in tense silence. I reviewed the position of every piece of junk orbiting the planet in our general vicinity. It wasn't long before I found what I was looking for. "Captain, what do you say to running over a rat on the way in?"

"No. Wally, you can come in within a hundred kilometers of one of those satellites, but don't run it over. I don't want anything scratching the paint."

She was joking about the paint. Our shields could easily take an impact with a flying hunk of metal less than a meter in size, but she was right. We shouldn't stress the shields. We might need them later.

We were sneaking in right underneath one of those eyes in the sky when it spun around and launched itself towards us.

I just had time to think "What the?" before an explosion rocked the ship.

The captain barked, "Tactical, report!"

Sara didn't hesitate. "Ma'am, the satellite nearest us fired maneuvering thrusters and collided with us. It detonated on impact with our shields. Five more are heading our way. Shields are down 20 percent."

"What the hell, Mark?"

I shook my head. "It's a new one on me, ma'am. They appear to have upgraded their spy satellites to also function as mines."

"Wally, best speed. Get us under that shield. *Leo*, notify planetary control. We'll require our rabbit hole a little sooner than we'd anticipated."

The AI and Wally answered, "Aye, aye, ma'am."

Wally poured on the speed and our shields flared as we impacted the planet's atmosphere. I glanced over at the tactical map and swore under my breath. We weren't going to make it. Two mines would hit us in about thirty seconds. If we survived that, the remaining three mines would converge on us. It would be over before we could get under the planet shield.

I could tell by the look in Jenna's eyes that she could see it too. There was never a note of panic in her voice, but she did utter a stern, "Wally."

"I see it, ma'am. Hang on, everyone!"

Wally turned the ship on its head and used the vertical thrusters to decrease our angle of descent. We were coming in almost perpendicular to the planet surface. Riveted to the tactical display, I saw the shield power creep downward as friction with the atmosphere ate away at our strength. I braced myself as best I could.

BOOM! I was jerked left as one of the mines hit our port side.

"Shields at 50 percent." Sara was trying to remain calm, but there was an edge to her voice everyone could hear.

BOOM! Another mine impacted our keel and I felt weightless for just a moment.

"20 percent." As she said it I saw the shields fall below nineteen. We were losing shield strength at the rate of a percent a second.

The three remaining mines closed in. I held my breath as I

watched the shield strength drop to 15 percent... 10 percent... 5 percent...

At that moment, I prayed. There are no atheists in foxholes.

CHAPTER 30: BELOW SEA LEVEL

I heard a distant explosion and the display turned to static. It came back almost immediately.

From the overhead speakers, a soft female voice intoned: "Welcome to Aspen, *Leonard Fox*. So pleased you could join us. Please decrease to port speed and proceed to your prearranged meeting."

I let out the breath I'd been holding. We'd made it. Wally had increased the angle and speed enough to get us below the shield in time and it had intercepted the mines. Wally fired breaking thrusters and I watched our speed on the tactical display decrease. The shield strength continued to lower but at a slower rate as our helmsman gave us a better angle of descent and our speed slowed. Still, we had a lot of speed to bleed off. I watched it go to 2, then 1 percent, before flickering back and forth between 1 and 0 percent.

After a couple of minutes, the shield strength started climbing again.

"Helm, bring us about 88.2 degrees port and down 3 degrees."

I shot a questioning look at the captain. Wally hazarded a "Ma'am?"

The captain arched an eyebrow at him and he straightened, eyes forward.

"88.2 degrees port and down 3 degrees, aye ma'am."

The captain smiled. "Sorry. Change of plan. Our new rendezvous point is 39.7392 north and 104.9847 west."

Sara converted the coordinates to our map of the planet surface and displayed it on the main screen. It put us in an expanse of open water with nothing around for several hundred square kilometers. This wasn't too surprising, given that 90 percent of the planet was covered in water, but I was at a loss for what we would do when we got there. The ship would float like an anchor—which is to say, it wouldn't. We would be fine inside, but the ship couldn't be submerged in any environment denser than air at four times Earth sea level. It would prevent the engines from firing. Liquid water on almost any Terran habitable planet would greatly exceed that. I knew that the captain would be aware of this, so I said nothing. I couldn't help but wonder what she was up to.

"Bridge, this is Aasha. Should I get my men ready for transport to the drop points?"

The captain answered. "Negative. Please have your marines get ready for unloading operations, but do not break them up into fire teams."

"Aye, aye, ma'am."

***

After months of deep space, hearing the sound of air whistling across the outer hull of the ship felt odd. The sound of the engines was always there, but in space, with millions of kilometers of nothing outside the ship, a new constant sound was unheard of.

We arrived at the coordinates in the middle of the vast northern ocean and began to hover above the water. Wally looked over his shoulder. "We're here, ma'am."

The captain smiled. "Good. *Leo*, please send a coded message using encryption protocol Gamma. The message is to say 'we're here.'"

For a few minutes, nothing happened.

From the main viewscreen on the bridge, I watched the endless rolling swells of this water planet, wondering what was going to happen next. Perhaps we'd receive new coordinates?

What I didn't expect was for the water a hundred meters in every direction around the *Leo* to come to life as if it were boiling.

The bubbling waters reached a fevered pitch and then a flat metallic plane appeared from out of the water beneath the ship. It was bluish gray and extended three meters above the waterline. There were obvious grooves along the surface where the armor plates intersected. If seeing a metal disk five times the size of the ship erupt out of the water wasn't enough, what happened next was astounding. Doors retracted, revealing a landing pad complete with guide lights.

"Set us down gently, Helm."

Wally didn't move. He stared slack-jawed at the monitor.

The captain cleared her throat and tried again. "Wally?"

"Huh?"

She smiled in amusement. "When you get a moment, can you set the ship down? We're burning through a lot of fuel just hovering here."

"Yes... sir! I mean, aye, aye, ma'am! Right away, ma'am!"

Wally set us down without so much as a bump. Once settled, I had a moment of panic as it looked like the water level was rising and we were sinking. It took a moment for me to realize that the landing pad was retracting into a much larger structure. We sank twenty-five meters. It felt like we were being swallowed by a giant sea monster.

We stopped sinking and the overhead doors slid shut. Seawater dripped from the edges of the plates until they closed together. The clank of the doors shutting could be heard echoing through the large chamber even through the ship's hull. That felt even more odd than the sound of air across the hull.

Once the hatch closed it was pitch black for a couple of seconds before floodlights lit the chamber. A masculine voice issued from the bridge speakers. "Greetings friends. I am Custodian A'hid. Welcome aboard the Khidi. If your officers would meet us at the forward lock, it will be our pleasure to invite them for tea. We regret that it will not be possible to offer you leave during your stay, so please have your crew stay aboard your ship for the time being."

The captain looked at me. "Tea?"

I shrugged. "Bring sugar. It'll help."

***

The captain, Sara, Sophie, Rowdy, and I met A'hid and his officers at the forward lock. Aasha and Boldrini, being department heads but not officers, were not required to attend. Sara wore combat armor, while Sophie wore a stylish abaya with a hajib in emerald silk with black flowered accents. The captain wore a simple veil over her hair. It conveyed the impression of regal professionalism while still adhering to the local custom. A'hid was visibly impressed. After our meeting, I'd have to ask my sister where she'd gotten it.

I was careful to move slowly and envied Sara in her combat armor. Aspen's gravity is 1.2 Earth normal. I felt heavy and clumsy.

I'd coached the captain on what to expect. When we met the custodian, she greeted him with, "*As-salaam alaikum.*"

A'hid grinned and responded, "*Alaikum al-salaam.* Thank you, Captain Houston." He indicated a door to his right and we walked toward it.

We entered a large hallway and had only gone a few meters when we were guided left into a conference room. While the hallway looked like it belonged on a ship, it was wider than any passage I'd seen on a ship. Whatever this place was, it was enormous.

We entered the conference room. I indicated to Sara and Sophie that they should sit at the end of the table on the left. It was an oval table made out of some sort of black and white marble I had never seen before. The walls were painted a soft bluish green. I motioned for the captain to sit at the head of the table next to A'hid while I sat to his left. A'hid's officers sat to his right. The custodian squinted at me as I gave direction to my shipmates.

As we sat, I whispered in the captain's ear, "Feel free to discuss anything you need to with me. Expect our negotiations to be interrupted several times while he confers with his officers. He might even ask to pause while he talks with his family."

She hung her head. "This is going to take a while, isn't it?"

"A couple of hours. He'll feed us, though."

We settled in and a serving girl set up the tea service. I saw the captain take a sip of the bitter liquid and suppress a grimace. She added sugar and cream.

A'hid smiled beatifically. "What do you think of the *Khidi,* Captain Houston?"

The captain remembered to look the custodian in the eyes when she spoke. "Most impressive. Is it a ship or a base?"

His face lit up. "A ship! Right now we are traveling under the surface of the great northern ocean at seventeen knots. We have several of these submersible platforms. The Erethizon have good sensors and detection gear, but they are not set up to scan underwater. It was no surprise to us that they would come to Aspen sooner or later, so we prepared for them."

She nodded in acknowledgment. "You're lucky that Aspen is mostly water. It will give your people an advantage."

The custodian's smile faded somewhat. "Almaa is our home. We know it better than any barbarian invader. We will use that to our advantage, as my people have for centuries."

"Almaa?"

A'hid grinned. "We cannot change what the great Terran explorer William Vancleave called this world, but here we call our home world Almaa. It means the great sacred waters which grant us life."

The captain nodded in respect. "I understand this is a military vessel and my people can't have liberty here. However, is there anything I can offer my crew? It's been a long journey and I know they would appreciate the opportunity to trade and mingle with your crew."

His sad expression told us the answer. "Security here is very important to us. Our survival depends on it." A'hid held up a finger and turned to the officer on his right. There was a brief discussion after which the custodian turned his attention back to us.

"I regret that we will be unable to let any of your crew out of the hanger bay. However, let us prepare a feast for you and your crew. There is more than enough room for pillows and tables in the shadow of your mighty vessel. We welcome the opportunity to share food, drink, and stories between your family and ours."

We negotiated the details of the feast and the payment for the shipment over the next hour. I coached the captain through a few tricky issues of culture and protocol, but in the end, an agreement was made to the satisfaction of everyone.

***

The crew of the *Khidi* unloaded the cargo in short order. Aasha threw a fit about being kept out of the loop. She was mollified only when we pointed out that it was much less dangerous for her men this way. That had the effect of sending her to her quarters to sulk.

The crew of the *Khidi* set up an amazing feast. Some of our crew found it odd to sit on pillows around low tables, but the Muscat got a real kick out of it. That isn't to say everything went smoothly.

War had to be sent back to the ship after he grabbed a serving girl, but the issue was soon forgotten and entertainment resumed. Another time Pace gave a thumbs-up gesture that was horribly misinterpreted. The matter almost came to blows before cooler heads prevailed.

I caught Sophie and Boldrini whispering to each other toward the end of the banquet. Sophie was leaning into him, her face flushed around her eyes.

"They look good together," Observed Aasha. She sat down next to me. She was wearing light body armor, but she had the face shield up so she could eat.

"They are good together." I took her hand in mine. "But so are we. Fancy a night in later?"

"Oooo," she cooed, "I have to check my guard detail. It'll take me a bit since they're so spread out. Meet at your place?"

"It's a date." She left and I turned my attention back to my sister. I felt content in a way I couldn't describe to see them so happy together. It made me feel a bit melancholy, too. I had a relationship with Aasha, if it could even be called a relationship. Aasha wanted to be with me, but only on her terms. That was fine for now. That thought reminded me of Sara and how isolated she must have felt after letting Dan go. I sought her out in the crowd, only to find her looking at me out of the corner of her eye. She held my gaze for just a moment before returning her attention to the small group of *Khidi* officers gathered around her. I wondered again if she might be the spy in our midst, then shook the thought away. Sara had warmed up to me a lot since Gra'nome.

I noticed Rafe grinning broadly. For a moment I thought he might be on some sort of drug, but when I questioned him about it, he just said our supply of ale was low. He also said he hoped we would make port on Aspen more often. I didn't ask any more questions about it.

All in all, I thought this was going to be the most uneventful delivery we'd made so far. I should have known it was too good to be true.

***

A'hid came to our main airlock the next day. Behind him were two marines carrying a box covered in a cloth between them. The captain, Sara, and I were summoned to the lock to meet him.

I expected him to be the same cordial host we'd interacted with for the past day and a half. One look at his narrowed his eyes told me otherwise. He was serious.

"Captain," he said by way of greeting, "is there someplace we can go and talk in private?"

"Of course, honored custodian. The ship's office is right this way."

We preceded the men down the passage and entered through the hatch into the ship's office. The marines had followed A'hid into the office, the captain asked if we could join them. The man glared at us before nodding.

The office was cramped with the six of us in there. His marines placed the cloth-covered box on the table and stood on either side of their leader. He looked at each of us in turn before removing the cover.

On the table was a nondescript, grey metal box. He waited, searching our faces for something. The captain looked at me. I shrugged and turned to Sara. She offered a confused shake of her head.

A'hid pointed at us. "Do you know what this is?"

All three of us leaned in to see if there was anything special about it. There were several tense moments of awkward silence before I hazarded a guess. "A medium-sized metal box?"

His expression went from angry to contemplative. "You don't know, do you?" It came out as more of a statement than a question.

The captain shrugged. "I'm sorry, A'hid. We don't know what it is. Care to enlighten us?"

Without the slightest hint of emotion, he stated, "It's a bomb."

CHAPTER 31: IT'S A BOMB

Sara jumped back, the captain gasped, and I put my hands up in a placating gesture.

The custodian continued, "It is a six kiloton nuclear device—crude, but effective. It was discovered in our engineering wing last night."

It took a moment for reason to replace the fear I was feeling. "Wait, you think we planted it there?"

"No," he said with conviction. "I am a politician. The three of you are not responsible."

The captain followed the logic. "But you suspect someone on my ship is."

A'hid nodded.

I used my AI to fire off a message to Rowdy. "Custodian, we are most grateful that you brought this to our attention. We will take charge of this bomb and have our engineer disarm it."

"What?" The captain exclaimed. "I don't want that thing on my ship!"

"Captain, we have an armory full of firearms, grenades, and missiles and an engineer who can make something lethal out of chewing gum, baling wire, and engine tape. If they got it up here without it going off, Rowdy will have it pulled apart in ten minutes."

Sara looked at me oddly. "What are you planning, and what's baling wire?"

***

"Helm, what's our status?"

Wally checked his display before replying. "Captain, we've cleared the *Khidi* and we're riding the rail to our exit vector at top speed." The crew had loaded up the return cargo in record time. The water and frozen fish would fetch an excellent price.

"Tactical?"

Ms. Chew responded without hesitation, "Full stealth systems engaged. No indication that we've been noticed."

The captain let out a sigh of relief. "*Leo*, please send a message using code Gamma. 'Thank you for your hospitality. Our chief engineer is still working on the device, but so far has had no luck. We will keep you apprised of our progress.'"

After a moment, *Leo* responded, "Message sent."

"Good."

After a pause, there was a tentative question. "Ma'am?"

"Yes, Wally?"

"Is that why the office is off limits and there are guards posted outside it?"

The captain answered him with an unreadable expression. "There is a sensitive project that our engineer is looking into right now. That project resides in the ship's office. At the moment, I can't tell you any more than that."

I watched Wally out of the corner of my eye. Gotcha. The news would be all over the ship in an hour. I'd been wrong about Rowdy. It took him seven minutes to have the bomb pulled apart and disarmed. The surveillance in that room was tighter than an Aspen snapping clam. We were going to catch the spy when he tried to get rid of the evidence.

***

We lined up on our exit vector and waited for the Erethizon battle group to slip below the horizon. In a few minutes, they no longer had a line of sight on the *Leo*.

The captain took a deep breath, then let it out with a soft but firm, "Go."

Wally eased up the power and we accelerated toward the satellite mines. If we attracted the attention of even one of them, we'd have the fleet on us in no time. It wouldn't be like coming in to the planet, when we'd had a nice big shield to hide under. This was going to be tricky and the consequences of failure were dire.

A gust of wind threatened to throw us off course. The strong blast of air was coming from starboard. I watched the screen as our ideal and expected plots shifted. Wally saw it too and adjusted, but overcorrected.

I tried to caution him, "Helm, pull it to port about eight degrees. This wind will stop a lot sooner than you think and..."

The wind dropped to nothing. Wally jerked the controls in the opposite direction and I thought for a second he was going to overcorrect in the opposite direction. He adjusted and put us back on track. It wasn't fluid and controlled, but it got the job done. We sailed through the hole in the web and waited for one of the satellites to move. They didn't so much as twitch.

I was about to let out the breath I'd been holding when Sara interrupted. "Two ESF32s inbound, bearing seventy mark eighty-two."

Oh crap. The satellites had seen us and called in the cavalry. But then, two fighters wasn't much of a cavalry...

The captain kept a cooler head than I did. "Any indication they've seen us?"

"No, ma'am. If they stay on their current course they'll pass underneath and a bit behind us. About five hundred kilometers."

She shook her head. "Damn that's close."

The next moments passed in tense silence as the two fighters glided ever closer. They weren't close enough to see us unaided while we were in stealth mode. The tactical display highlighted each fighter with a red circle, a short description, and a threat level. It didn't take long for them to pass under us. I breathed a little easier as the patrol continued its trek across the blue expanse below, but didn't relax until they neared the horizon.

"Mr. Martin, please set course zero mark seventy-two. Take us straight up from the plane of the ecliptic. I don't want to spend any more time here than I have to."

***

Four days later there had been no attempts to remove the bomb. We had pulled out of the system's gravity enough to start the next leg of our journey. Wally glanced up from his console at me with a questioning look. I double-checked our position and gave him a smile and a slight nod.

With a bit more confidence, the helmsman called over his shoulder. "Ma'am, we're clear of the system's gravity. R-drive can be engaged at any time."

"Sounds good to me," The captain smiled. "Engineering?"

"Rowdy here, ma'am"

"Fire it up. Let's get the hell out of here. Helm, set course thirty-two mark..."

A huge explosion rocked the ship. Everyone on the bridge was thrown to the right. Gina, who had been on the bridge to relieve Wally, was thrown out of her chair and landed in a heap.

CHAPTER 32: SABOTAGE

The captain yelled over her shoulder, "Tactical!"

Sara shouted, "No one's here, it's just us!"

"Engineering, report!"

The speaker responded with a couple of coughs. It didn't sound like Rowdy. "Randy here. Emergency medical to Engineering. Dad's hurt real bad. There was some sort of overload in the R-drive. We're losing atmo back here."

The captain looked at Gina. "Emergency medical to the bridge."

I noticed a blackened mess in front of the comms station where Gina had been standing. A red warning light blinked on the cracked screen.

I ran for the console and confirmed what I suspected. "Ma'am, we're broadcasting a mayday!"

The captain's eyes got big as saucers. "*Leo*, shut it the hell off!"

"The comms system is malfunctioning. Access is unavailable."

"It isn't accepting any commands," I told her. Not good! Not good! I dropped to the floor and turned the two knobs of the quick release on the maintenance panel. It came loose and I threw it halfway across the bridge. I reached in and yanked out three cards from the circuit board. Only then did I breathe a sigh of relief. "We're dark. Comms are offline."

The captain nodded at the communication boards lying around me. "Quick thinking." Then she turned to Wally. "New course, 80 mark 270. Max thrust. Someone will come out here wondering why there was a distress call, even if it isn't broadcasting anymore."

Looking to my left I saw Jay, our marine medic, checking out Gina. She was a bit groggy, but responded to questions. He told her to relax and called for a stretcher. "You're going to be just fine, Gina. You've got a broken arm and a mild concussion. The doc will have you fixed up in no time." He held her hand tenderly.

She looked in his eyes with warmth and affection. "You going to nurse me back to health?"

He gave her a wolfish grin. "You bet, princess."

I hadn't noticed they were together before. It seemed the normal interdepartmental prejudices between marines and sailors I'd witnessed among other crews weren't present here if Jay and Gina were any indication.

"Thanks for getting up here so fast, Jay."

"Glad I could be here, sir. I was posted outside the ship's office, so it didn't take long to get here."

I closed my eyes. My gut twisted.

The captain caught the exchange and wordlessly motioned for Sara to check out the passage. She turned back to the couple on the floor. "Son, who had the duty with you?"

Jay looked over his shoulder, startled that the captain of the ship had addressed him directly. His voice shook. "Uh, it was Trey, ma'am."

I buried my face in my hands and fell back against the communication console behind me. Trey. Of course, it was Trey, the Muscat medic we'd picked up on Gra'nome. Medical emergencies at both ends of the ship. Our two medics on duty guarding the ship's office at the same time. Of course, they'd be called away for the more pressing emergency. The marines would wait to be relieved, but medics wouldn't wait until it arrived. It was a set up from the beginning. If I hadn't been so depressed, I would have laughed.

A minute later, Sara arrived back on the bridge. She shook her head grimly. The captain motioned me over to the bridge wing and the three of us huddled up.

"The relief is there now, but when I checked inside the office, the package was gone," Sara said.

The captain sighed. "Then let's hope like hell we got the bastard farthog on tape."

CHAPTER 33: LEAVING ASPEN

I shook my head in amazement. "Damn, he's good."

The captain pounded the conference room table in front of her with her fist. "I want him found and I want him strung up on my yardarm."

Racy twisted her head to the side. "What's a yardarm?"

Sara answered her. "It's a reference to sailing ships. It's the part of the mast that holds the sail up."

That was enough for Racy to get the rest of the reference.

We'd just reviewed the tape for the third time. The camera in the passage and the one in the ship's office both went to static two minutes before the explosion. The original duty roster for the marines had Jay paired with Joe Kostelecky. Some unauthorized user had adjusted the roster the day before. The adjustments had been made from a spare console in engineering. The computer terminal itself did not have any record of being used for months.

Remnants of a small charge was found on the comm's input lines. There was also a program to broadcast mayday on a timer.

Lastly, the spy had replaced the liquid nitrogen on the R- drive with liquid hydrogen. The engine spooled up, heated up. Hydrogen mixed with oxygen and bye-bye engine room.

I sighed and buried my face in my hands. "We'll investigate, but I'm betting we won't find any more leads. This guy is just too good and too careful."

"You giving up on me, Mark?" The captain raised an eyebrow in my direction.

"Not a chance. I want this bastard as much as you do."

Sara frowned in concentration. "What do we do now? Our bait is gone. What do we use for our next trap?"

She was right, of course. Just because this plan didn't work, we couldn't give up. I thought about what we knew about our saboteur. "We could leak that we've discovered how the mole is communicating with the Erethizon."

Sara waggled her head back and forth. "No way to make it credible. We need to know more about how they're doing it to get them to bite."

The captain scratched her chin. "Off-ship intelligence? Do we know about a more organized resistance to the Porcu-bears?"

"Maybe," I said, "but we'd need to come up with something believable and store it on the ship's main computer. Our spy is good with computers."

Racy's eyes lowered to the deck. "Does that make me a suspect?" she asked.

I put my hand on hers. "It might, except for two things. You're too obvious, and you would never have endangered your dad.

That satisfied her and she nodded up at me.

"Okay," The captain started, "so what information are we talking about? I'm thinking we store a flash drive in the safe in my quarters. I can rig a mechanical trigger so that it will notify me if the safe is opened. No computers to foul up, just a simple communication device."

There was silence as we all thought about it for a few minutes.

"They'll never believe the Terrans, Muscat, or Dru would offer to help an independent system. What if we suggested that the three remaining systems were pooling resources?" I regarded the others. "Creating a fleet to repel the Erethizon?"

Sara shrugged. "Plausible, but where would they get the credits? Where would they find the manufacturing to pull it off?"

The captain snapped her fingers. "An undiscovered metal world. Some exiled industrialist found it and has been building it up for the past ten years. Now it's ready for production. The mining colony and the new ships are in the same place."

I nodded. "It could work. We were outbid on the supply contract, but we have the nav data to find it and that data is stored in the ship's safe. Brilliant."

The captain slapped the table with her hand. "Good. Sara, you and Mark put it together after the meeting." Her face became more serious. "Racy, how's your dad?"

She lowered her eyes again. "Dr. Martin says he'll be okay. He'll be asleep while the machines work on him for the next three days. When he's awake, Randy and I will be able to talk with him and get his help putting the engines back together. We don't know enough to do it ourselves, and even when he's up, Dr. Martin says he'll be on bed rest for a week."

The captain grunted. "So we're dead in the water until he's out of the can, and even longer before we can get moving again." She chewed on her lower lip. "Sara, post guards on the engine and parts printers. If it were me, I'd sabotage our ability to make repairs. It would keep us close and increase our chances of being captured."

She was right, of course. I mentally kicked myself for not thinking of it right away. A thought occurred to me though. "Rowdy is key to us getting back to port. Post a guard in medical too and take both marine medics off guard duty."

She nodded. "Good thinking. Okay, let's be about it people."

***

It took two weeks to get us underway again. After Rowdy woke up, Sophie kept him sedated so he'd stay in bed. It was odd to see our frenetic engineer immobile and speaking slowly. Not that he didn't try to leave. He did. Several times. Towards the end of his stay, his guard was spending as much time keeping him in Sickbay as they were keeping an eye on visitors.

The crew was jumping at puffer mice. We officers did what we could to get people to work together.

Sara and I created the story to bait and catch our spy. We changed the story a little bit, claiming that we missed picking up our cargo due to repairs. It was more believable. In the six weeks it took us to get back to port, nothing happened. The rumor had spread the length and breadth of the ship, but there wasn't even a hint of suspicious activity.

A week out from *Ocelot* I found myself sparring with Aasha in the gym.

"Has anyone tried to get into the captain's safe?" she asked.

"What?" The question threw off my rhythm and allowed her to sweep my legs out from under me. I crashed to the mat and she pounced on top of me. "What are you talking about?"

"The captain. She has some data or something in her safe. It's all over the ship. Has anyone tried to get it?"

Aasha was not in on the secret. Sara and I had debated for half an hour before finally deciding to keep it between the three deck officers. The fewer who knew the truth, the less likely it was that the plan would leak.

"You're gettin' it every other night. Why are you worried about someone else's safe?"

"Don't change the subject." She ground herself into me. "Or else."

"I give. I don't know what you've heard, but there is no data and I have no idea what Houston keeps in the safe."

She bit my lower lip playfully. "Don't give me that. It was an obvious ploy."

I kissed her nose and hugged her close. "Believe what you want. She might have something she hasn't told me about. Our captain plays it close to the vest sometimes, but if there's something going on, I'm not part of it."

She gave me a sidelong glance. "I can never tell when you're lying to me."

"Part of my charm. I can sing, too."

She pulled my shirt over my face and kissed my chest. "Okay, scoundrel."

"What, those implants don't read my heart rate or something and tell you I'm lying?"

"They don't work like that, flyboy."

"Hmmmm. How do they work?"

Aasha kissed me through the shirt over my face. "Faster reflexes, I'm stronger, I can see and hear better. I've got software that lets me aim through my gun sights. Combat stuff."

"Do Rowdy or Sophie help you with maintenance?"

"I splurged when I got the implants installed and bought the self-maintenance package. You never know when you'll be stuck somewhere without a mechanic. I've got a bunch of minibots inside that take care of it."

I pulled my shirt back down and flipped her over. Now I was lying on top of her. "So that's how you do that thing."

"Flattery will get you everywhere." She bit her lip. "But I can't feel as well as I could with flesh and bone. Feels like the AI runs them more than it should. I feel, I don't know... less human, I guess. This helps though. You make me feel human again, Mark."

I gave her my best smile and got up on my knees. "You cover it well." I checked the clock on the wall. "Meet me at my place around 2100 hours? I need to see a man about a horse."

She gave me a funny look. "Yeah, I'll bring that lacy thing you like."

"Rowr! Something to look forward to."

I left the gym and snaked through the passageways. I passed by marine berthing and stopped short. War 'n Pace were crouched next to Aasha's bunk on the far side of the room. I was heading for the mess hall, but decided to see what trouble they'd found.

As I approached, I tapped a "come here" request to Aasha on my wrist AI. I noticed a cluster of cleaning rats around their feet. Pace was sprinkling a bunch of the food pellets in her bed. The rats were crawling under her sheets and in her pillow to get it.

I cleared my throat and they turned around.

"Hey, flyboy," War said through a forced smile. "This isn't what it looks like."

"And what does it look like?" I asked.

Pace searched the ceiling for an answer. "Um. Like we put the rat food here. But, uh. We didn't."

War looked around the room. "It, ah... it was Jay. We just got here, you see, and found it like this."

I scratched my chin and made a show of considering it. "Then how do you know it was Jay?"

Behind me, Aasha bellowed. "War 'n Pace, your ass is mine!"

I didn't stick around for the festivities. I needed to get to the mess hall before the shift change. I found Rafe coming off duty. "Mr. Sanzio, a moment of your time if you please."

He waggled his eyebrows. "What can I do for you, sir?"

"I need some items procured in the next port. Everyone says you're the guy for items that are hard to find."

The grin on his face spoke volumes about the pride he had in his skill. "What did you have in mind, sir?"

Producing a list from my pocket, I handed it to him.

He sucked air between his teeth and looked less confident. "Uh, sir? The AI implants won't be cheap. And the pinch grenades? I have no idea where I'd even find them."

I found his eyes with mine. "I have great faith in your abilities. I know you won't disappoint me."

He swallowed hard and gave me a weak smile. "Aye, aye, sir."

Continuing up the passage, I heard him mutter, "Where the scrut..."

CHAPTER 34: BACK IN *OCELOT*

We docked at *Ocelot* two weeks later. The rest of the trip was uneventful—by which I mean the entire crew was jumping at shadows and second-guessing every interaction. Nothing broke, no one got hurt, and everyone thought everyone else was a traitor.

We'd just reentered normal space, but we hadn't docked yet. The captain, Sara, and I were in the conference room just off the bridge. I'd compiled a bunch of news clips and we'd finished watching them.

"What do you think?" I asked.

Jenna let out an exhausted breath. "I think we're screwed. Damn it. Sometimes I hate being right. The Dru have decided the ocean is too dangerous and have retreated back to the pond."

"We expected that." I gave a one-shouldered shrug. "At least the Terrans and the Muscat are still talking to each other, even if just barely. The Dru have made a few for research and medical purposes. It turns out there's a genetic variance. Some Dru can't tune their thoughts and hear everyone all the time. They used to slowly go crazy, now they can treat it."

Sara sipped her tea. "I wonder if the Erethizon have it yet."

I shook my head. "They don't."

"You sound sure." Sara eyed me skeptically.

"I am. The Dru wouldn't dare give them one. The Muscat factory reports several attempts to steal the tech or purchase it through shell companies. They're having their own people install every device. The Terran factory is being just as careful."

"Who has the Terran contract?" asked Jenna.

I bit my lip and looked down. "Um, that would be Songbird Mining and Manufacturing in Eureka. A friend of mine runs it." I could see the gears turning as the captain processed that and then narrowed her eyes at me. She must have figured out that I had another motive to visit that system earlier.

Sara came to my rescue. "On the bright side, the resistance movement on your planet is still strong."

"Yes," I acknowledged, "they're keeping up the fight. That, in turn, is keeping Porcu-bear ships near Yale, and not causing additional trouble for Aspen, Freya, and Saggita."

"Okay, that just leaves our snake in the grass. Any ideas who's passin' notes in class?" Jenna looked at each of us in turn.

"Well," I offered, "I'm ashamed to admit it, but at first I thought it was Sara. I don't think that now, of course."

"Me?" Sara jerked her head back. "Why?"

I put my hands up in a gesture of repentance. "Well, it was when we first came aboard. You were angry for good reason. Then I saw you coming out of Werga Components on *Ocelot*."

"Oh. We get our parts for galley equipment there." Sara lowered her voice, "We also buy the latest Erethizon military codes from them. Not all Porcu-bears support the Theocracy." She scratched her head. "What do you all think of Jay or Aasha as the spy?"

The captain frowned. "Unlikely. Aasha was on Virgo when the Porcu-bears invaded. Her whole family except for her and her sister were killed. That's when she got all the metal finery. We picked up Jay when a drop went bad on Mitas's Star. Pirates tried to steal our cargo. It could be him, but I doubt it."

"War 'n Pace?" I asked.

The captain gazed at me levelly.

"Yeah," I rolled my eyes, "sophomoric pranks, sure. Spy masterminds, not enough brain cells."

Sara laughed. We threw around a few more names but didn't come to any conclusions.

***

I drew the first port side watch. There were a thousand and one administrative tasks necessary to keep the ship running. I was sitting in the ship's office reviewing logs when I glanced up just in time to see Trent zip through the doorway. "Hey, sergeant. What can I help you with?"

Scampering next to me, he left just enough room to bow formally. "Sir, it's time we reviewed your security while you're in port."

"What?"

Trent continued, "While you're aboard the *Leo*, one of us is to accompany you at all times. When you're ashore there will be two of us. Please schedule your shore leave with as much notice as possible so I can arrange for two of my men to be with you. Please don't ask them to carry anything for you. It will impair their situational awareness."

I blinked as I tried to process what he was saying. "Wait a moment, Trent. You want me to have a guard detail? What on Terra for?"

"The situation demands it. I wanted to do it while we were underway, but Raw'scadi convinced me that you were safe enough on board. No assassin would be able to escape while we were underway. But we're in port now."

It didn't surprise me that he'd spoken to Racy, but the rest... I shook my head in disbelief. "Assassinate *me*?"

He placed a hand on my thigh. "Yes, sir. The traitor cannot be allowed to harm the Gran'osida. You must be protected at all costs. The queen would never forgive me if you came to harm."

Drawing a slow, deep breath, I bit my lip. Trent took this seriously. "Sergeant, aside from you and the other Muscat on board, no one knows I'm the Gran'osida."

He dipped his head in understanding. "But many more know that you're a prince, Your Highness."

That set me back on my heels, and all thoughts of the ridiculousness of the situation evaporated. While attending to my duties on the ship and worrying about the traitor, I had almost been able to forget about my newfound royalty. If I was lucky, only the senior officers on the ship knew that secret. But it was unlikely. The Erethizon certainly knew.

"You raise a valid point, sergeant. Have you given any thought to the princess's security?"

He nodded. "Yes sir, and I'll be speaking with Dr. Martin next."

It made sense. From Trent's point of view, I was the one his queen had charged him to protect. His concern for me would extend to my sister. We were family after all, and among the Muscat the pack was paramount.

We spent the better part of an hour going over the details. I objected to a lot of what he proposed as being too restrictive, but it slowly became clear that he had made those suggestions fully expecting me to reject them. As we haggled over how often I could leave the ship and when, I had no doubt I'd ended up agreeing to exactly what he thought was best. Note to self: Trent would do well at poker.

***

A few hours later, Sara relieved me for watch and I hurried to the mess hall. Rafe was starting to clean up so I hurried to get a plate of food.

I was almost done when Boldrini walked in from the passageway, followed by my sister and the Muscat medic, Trey. They looked like they were going out for a night on the station.

"Everything under control, Rafe?

"Yes sir, Mr. B. Everything's shipshape and Bristol fashion," he said with a lopsided grin.

"Good, good," he said with a full belly laugh. "Sophie and I are going ashore for a meal I don't have to cook myself. Do you think you can handle breakfast mess on your own?"

"Breakfast mess, after the first night of shore leave? We'll be lucky to get five people. I've got it covered, chef," he saluted with a spatula.

Sophie sauntered up to me in a blue cocktail dress that made me blush.

"Wow, sis. Where did you find that?"

She twirled around and batted her eyes. "I'm after big game tonight."

"He's a lucky guy." I jerked my head toward Trey. "I see Trent got to you, too."

She sighed and sat down across from me. "Yes, it seems like overkill, but Trent made some good points. I agreed to let him give me one bodyguard when I'm off-ship."

You're lucky," I snorted, "he's making me take two. I did manage to convince him that we were safe enough on board that we don't need someone with us all the time. Where are you off to?"

Sophie smiled with appreciation. "Grant's, over on R2. Where are you taking Aasha?"

"Haven't worked that out yet, but Grant's would be a good choice." I peeked around to her armed shadow. "What about you, Trey?"

He gave me a smile that showed way too many teeth. "Don't worry, sir. The reservation is for two tables. I've worked it out with the hostess. I have a table next to theirs with a good view of the door."

"Hey, Mark." Boldrini joined us. "Are you ready, princess? Our reservations are in half an hour."

I half expected her to roll her eyes at the pet name, but she batted her eyes and kissed him on the cheek. Then, waggling her eyebrows, "Yes, and I'm very hungry."

He blushed a little. "Lead the way, Trey."

"Have a good night," I called after them. They made such a good couple. It filled my heart with joy to see my sister happy, especially given everything she'd lost when we fled Yale.

***

"I need stuff, Trent. Weapons. Armor." My glare didn't have any effect on my small bodyguard as we stood inside the lock. I had been unsuccessful in sneaking off the ship without my escort. Gina was manning the airlock and watched our argument with interest.

"Then let me or Tracy get some of that stuff for you," Trent scowled back.

"Because I won't know until I get them if they're right for me."

He closed his eyes and took a deep breath. "Sir, there will be a lot of people on the shopping promenade. It will be hard to keep you safe."

I threw my hands up. "No one will be expecting me. How can someone ambush me or lay a trap for me if even I don't know where I'm going?"

"Someone is out there, just waiting for you to step off this ship. They want to kill you or kidnap you."

Crossing my arms, I looked down on him. "You don't know that."

"Neither do you."

Pinching the bridge of my nose, "Look, I'll be happy to take any precautions you like, but I can't get by with the marine hand-me-downs. They don't fit right. I need my own gear."

He stared at me hard for a minute.

"Please," I said, "I'm going stir crazy."

"Fine," he spat, "but you're not going unarmed, and our first stop will be Second Skin on R1."

"Don't you already have body armor?"

"They make human-sized equipment too, sir."

I shook my head. "I'm not going to walk around the station in powered armor."

"We're not getting you a mechanized suit. You need new clothes and light armor, right? Then part of that new wardrobe will be nano-weave."

***

An hour later we were in Second Skin. Trent and his daughter Tracy stood on either side of me in light armor. The proprietor tilted his head at the three of us. A mousy looking Muscat, he introduced himself as Iret'vaning.

"You can call me Irving." He bowed. "Who do I have the pleasure of serving today?"

Trent stepped in front of me. *"Ter'ris nada?"*

Irving looked around the store and shrugged. *"Rashi."*

The salesman went to the front of the store and closed and locked the double doors. "So a Terran and two Muscat walk into a store. It sounds like the beginning of a bad joke. My suits can't protect you from bad humor," he said with a smile.

I chuckled briefly. "My friends believe I will be suffering the slings and arrows of outrageous fortune. They suggested I come here to bear arms against a sea of troubles."

His eyes brightened in recognition. *"Hamlet,* Act Three. Shall we see what in my shop will help you bear the whips and scorns of time?" He waved in the direction of a display case. Inside were six sets of Muscat combat armor and two human-sized suits. The smaller sets of armor progressed from simple to intimidating. The larger ones were pretty basic.

Trent shook his head. "We aren't looking for armor. We'd like to see what you have in nano-weave."

Irving didn't bat an eye. "I don't sell that kind of stuff. It's expensive to make and requires specialized equipment you can't find out here."

The sergeant and Tracy shared a look, then Trent gave the salesman a half smile. He switched to Muscat. "Iret'shona says differently."

Irving responded in kind. "No, she doesn't. If you'd met her you'd know that."

The fact that I was following this at all pleased me. To be fair, listening to the language was easier than speaking it.

Tracy smirked at him. "Shoni did say that. She also says you'll never find a mate if you keep putting too much ref in your skrit'caresh."

"Yaf!" he exclaimed with obvious excitement. "How is Shoni?"

"She's good. Rotated out of the queen's guard. She and Fero are expecting another couple of babies soon."

"How soon? Do I have time to make it back for the birth?"

Tracy shook her head. "No, you would have had to leave a week ago."

"Too bad." Irving let out a long breath, "and in regards to the nano-weave, it can't be done. Sorry."

Tracy nodded in understanding and turned to me. "Sorry to have wasted your time honored Gran'osida. Perhaps another armorer can accommodate our needs."

The salesman's eyes narrowed. "You're not claiming this man is Jean Claude Richeax. He looks nothing like him."

"No. This is Mark Martin. He saved the prince's life on Gra'nome."

The edges of Irving's mouth curved down. "Really?" He plainly didn't believe her.

Trent regarded him without humor. "Really." He pulled out a tablet and turned it to face the skeptic.

The armorer touched the biometric tape at the bottom of the pad. It chirped a confirmation of his identity and lit up with an image that at this angle only he could see.

Eyes wide, the salesman's jaw dropped. Turning to me he bowed low. "I'm am so sorry, Gran'osida, but in this port of thieves and conmen, I can't be too careful. I can most certainly make you nano-weave clothing. As I'm sure you're aware, it is prohibited technology. Other races are not allowed to possess it.

The equipment to make it isn't here. I can take your measurements and have it here in four hours."

I'd never heard of nano-weave before, but it must be pretty impressive stuff if the Muscat were so secretive about it. "Four hours?"

"Three! Three hours! I swear that's as fast as it can be done."

"Master Irving," I began, "quality over quickness. Four hours is fine. Let's get the measurements so you can get started."

He gestured for me to stand on a spot on the floor next to a mirror. Just as in a high-end tailor shop, I saw a red line travel up behind the glass in the mirror. My measurements taken, Irving and I discussed style and fit until we reached an agreement.

He summoned a servant from the back room and gave him some instructions.

The shopkeeper bowed. "Will there be anything else?"

I was about to say no when Trent jumped in. "Yes. Do you have any light combat armor in his size?"

Irving put his fingers to his lips and studied me. "Yes. I have a plasteel suit that should fit the Gran'osida well. Mr. Martin, are you picky about the colors? I have one in black with red trim."

Plasteel was lightweight ablative material. It wasn't good against plasma rifles, but should be fine against most projectile or beam weapons. "That color scheme seems a bit dramatic, but otherwise it sounds fine."

"I apologize. Appearing dangerous is important to a lot of my clients, especially the ones who can afford plasteel. I can manufacture green, gold, purple, brown, or grey if you give me a day."

Trent rubbed the top of his nose in thought. "Can we borrow the suit you have until the nano-weave is complete and then come back tomorrow?" Turning to me, "Mr. Martin, I'd like your armor to match ours, with the gold crest of the royal house on the left shoulder."

Walking around with the Muscat royal crest didn't strike me as a good idea. "I understand the intimidation and respect the crest might cause, but wouldn't it be better not to advertise?"

Trent looked up and right with a frown of concentration. "You may be right." His eyes riveted on Irving. "What about ops patches to go over the crest? That way we can blank them."

"Of course, would you like some right now? They're popular in these parts."

In a few moments I was decked out in my borrowed armor and Trent and Tracy had patches over their royal crests. We said goodbye to Irving and went to find lunch. Walking through the station's hallways, I was expecting us to attract a lot of attention. I needn't have worried. While there were a lot of sailors and stationers dressed in civilian clothes or ship suits, there were enough marines in light armor that we didn't even rate a second glance. I guess I hadn't noticed them before. The only thing that made us stand out was that we were a mixed-race group. Most of the soldiers and sailors on leave were Terran, but there were a few Muscat.

We took the lift down two levels. The doors opened, but we found our way off the lift blocked by three kids who rushed on. One of them, a little girl, mashed both the buttons for closing the doors and stopping the elevator at the same time. Tracy and Trent drew their weapons on the kids.

"Wait." I looked at the girl who had mashed the buttons. Her eyes were wide as saucers and her knees knocking together.

"Holly?"

"M-m-mr. Martin. P-p-pith." She swallowed hard.

"Trent, Tracy, this is Holly. She's a friend of mine. She's only dangerous to personal items you want to keep. Holly, why don't you introduce us to your friends?"

Holly relaxed when my guards lowered their weapons. "This is Snip and Reedy. We won't steal from you, honest! Pithy said you were off-limits."

I knelt down to her level and gave her a smile. "And I believe you. You came in here in quite a rush. Is someone chasing you?"

"No. Pithy said you'd be here and she neededtoseeyourightnow."

I nodded. Everything that had happened since my previous encounter with Pythia made me certain that if she wanted to see me, it was definitely important. "Guys, we need to make a stop on the way. It shouldn't take long. If history is any prediction of the future, it will be well worth the time."

***

We took the lift down three levels to the lower hallway. The lighting panels still hadn't been repaired. Armed, armored, and in force, we didn't have the same problem of uninvited followers as last time. The halls emptied ahead of us and doors closed. I wasn't sure this was an improvement.

Two guards—different guards from the last time I was here—stood outside of Pythia's chamber, but held the door open as we approached. The waiting room was empty except for Sandy, who looked relieved to see us.

"Oh, thank goodness you're okay. Come right in." I realized that was the first time I'd heard her speak. Her voice was a rich alto that I hadn't expected from the powerfully built woman. In fact, she seemed altogether more worried and welcoming than I expected from Ms. Guns-and-Knives.

Pythia was pacing back and forth, running a hand along the stage that held her chair. Her milky eyes turned in our direction as we entered.

"Sandy?"

"They're here."

She was wearing a sundress with unicorns on it this time, but her blank eyes were wider than I remembered. "Are they okay? Did Holly get to them in time?"

"Yes, honey," said the kinder, gentler version of Ms. Guns and Knives. "They don't appear to be hurt."

I was a bit shocked by the change in her guard. With brash confidence stripped away, she seemed almost human.

"Mark?"

"I'm right here, Pithy."

At the sound of my voice, she launched herself across the room. Her aim wasn't true, but I caught her in a hug. I'd completely forgotten about the electric shock. I hadn't spent much time with kids. Hugging the young oracle felt right, though. I was overcome with an intense desire to protect her.

I winced a little as I felt the full force of her static charge. "I'm here. I'm okay."

Tears were streaming down her face. "I'm so sorry. I'm so sorry. I can't stop it."

"It's okay. Whatever comes along we'll deal with it. Just tell me what you can." In armor, I didn't have tissue or anything to wipe away the tears, and this made me feel oddly powerless to help the weeping child in my arms.

"The bear is here. On the station. He's got little bears he's sending out. He wants you."

"I'll go back to the *Leo*."

"You can't," she pleaded. "It's worse if you do. You have to finish what you were going to do today. Also, you have to go with the old lady to see Reggie."

"Okay, I will."

"Trent and Tracy, are they here?"

Trent twisted an ear oddly. "We're here."

She turned to his voice. "Keep him safe. Promise me you'll keep him safe."

"We will. We promise."

Pythia nodded. "Okay. He needs to live to see the bear zombies. Everything becomes clearer when he sees them. You'll meet the big bear when you see them. Hell will break free. When that happens you must remember to do something. It's very important."

"Okay, what do I need to remember?"

She wrapped her arms around my neck and pulled her wet cheek to mine. She whispered in my ear. "Duck."

"Duck?"

She nodded into my cheek, then pulled back so I could see her face. "A lot of people are going to get hurt. When I try to find a way where fewer people get hurt, it's worse. If you make it, you're going to find something for me. I'm not sure what it is, only that you'll know it when you see it."

"Okay, I'll keep an eye out for whatever it is. Is there anything else you need me to do for you or Holly?"

She sniffed and nodded. "Sandwiches. I'm fine, but Holly hasn't eaten today. When you go to lunch please get her some sandwiches. When you leave the restaurant, carry them in your left hand."

She was trying to take care of her friends. What was this sweet girl doing with cold-hearted Anubis? "I will."

"And let me know when you get back to the Lion. Send a message to Sandy."

Over her shoulder, I saw Sandy nod and hold up an ID chip. "Will do."

"Okay." Pythia took a ragged breath. "You need to go now. You've got important stuff to do, but don't forget to let me know you're okay."

"Take care, Pithy," I said as I followed Sandy out.

***

Back in the throng, we made our way to a highly rated, nearby steakhouse. We tried to look everywhere at once on the way there. Pythia's predictions had set us all on edge, but we didn't see anything suspicious.

My bodyguards requested a corner booth so they could see both the door and the kitchen. I tried to concentrate on my food, but the oracle had given me a lot to think about. Who were the bear zombies? What did I need to find for her?

Dinner eaten, I ordered some sandwiches with a couple of sides each to go. I paid the tab and Trent led us out into the mall.

I looked around for Holly and her friends, but they were nowhere to be seen. I noticed I was holding the sandwiches with my right hand and switched them to my left.

We hadn't gone twenty feet when Trent drew his pistol and body slammed me into the bulkhead. Time slowed down as some poor girl who had been standing behind us crumpled to the floor. Tracy was firing at a man fifty feet up and on our right. There was something about the man's eyes: empty, vacant.

Rounds slammed into him, tearing bits of flesh and grimy clothing away from his body, and yet he didn't seem to notice. His unfocused gaze moved toward me. The shiny blaster in his grip contrasted with his wild hair, five-day beard, and grimy clothes. In slow motion, I reached for my pistol. I wasn't moving fast enough. Shots hit the wall behind me on the right. He pulled the trigger over and over; each shot a few inches closer to ending it all. He squeezed the trigger again. I could see right down the barrel.

CHAPTER 35: ASSASSINATION

The man's head exploded in a fine spray of red. I felt the heat of the blaster bolt singe my right ear as the energy missed and expended itself in the bulkhead behind me. Tracy put three more shots into his chest.

Time sped back up and I yanked Trent to his feet. Finally freeing my pistol, I took in the chaos. People were screaming and scattering, but no one else was pointing a weapon.

The woman who had been walking behind me was stone dead. No one came forward to check on her. If she'd been walking with anyone, they were long gone. I studied the hallway behind us, then turned my attention forward again. A few moments of stillness, then we walked briskly and warily back to the ship.

I found Holly around the first corner. She was shaking like a rattle bug. I hugged her close. "It's going to be okay. Here are some sandwiches. Find somewhere safe to eat them."

She grabbed them and ran.

I sent a message through the station intranet. "Sandy, please tell Pythia that we're okay."

The answer came back almost right away. "We're glad to hear it. Be careful. It isn't over."

Station security showed up at the lock about an hour after we got back to the ship. Actually, to call them "station security" would be generous. They were thugs—big and burly, and they glowered at Wally in the airlock.

He let out a sigh of relief as I approached. "Thanks, Wally," I told him. Then to the guards, "What can I do for you?"

The shorter of the two stabbed me with his eyes. "Were you down on level 3 at 1330 hours station time?"

Stroking my chin in thought, I answered, "Yes. Yes, I think I was there at that time."

"Were you in the company of two tree rats?"

Putting on my poker face, I controlled my outrage at the slur. "I was with two of my ship's company. They're Muscat."

He rolled his eyes and imitated my voice in a singsong. "Well, then this belongs to you." He tapped something on his tablet and my wrist AI chimed.

To my surprise, they turned around and left. As I thought about the weird meeting, I pulled up the message. It was a grainy picture of the firefight taken by a security camera, accompanied by a bill. They had billed me 3,000 credits for the disposal of two bodies and repair of the damaged bulkheads. If it wasn't paid in two days, the charge would be added to the ship's docking fees.

That was it. There were no criminal charges to answer to. No one would wonder what had happened to make some nameless soul attack someone he'd never met. No one would ask why some innocent bystander had died. The station security—Anubis's thugs—were only concerned about his bottom line.

Feeling sick, I paid the bill and messaged my sister.

Have a moment to talk? It's been a bad day.

She responded after only a couple of minutes.

In Medical. Wrapping a sprain. Should be done in five. Stop by?

I dropped down to Sickbay and bobbed my head at Pace, who was just leaving with a bandaged.

"Hey, sis."

"Hey, dorkface. What's on your mind?"

I jerked my head toward the door. "What's up with Pace?"

She rolled her eyes. "What he said, or what he actually did?"

"Both?"

"He said he got a sprain while working out in the gym, but I suspect it was aggressive self excitement." She mimed an up and down motion with her hand. "What did you come down here for?"

"Oh. My." I snorted a laugh, then with more seriousness gave her the rundown of my afternoon.

She shrugged. "Okay, so what's got you all worked up? Besides the almost getting murdered part, I mean."

"The senselessness of it all."

Sophie shrugged. "It's a pirate base. Life is cheap and everyone is looking to make a profit. I don't think it really cost them 3,000 credits to get rid of a body and repair a bulkhead. How would *you* run a bunch of lawless hooligans?"

"Well, you could..." The response died as I opened my mouth. What would I do? Enforce the rule of law? These people were, by definition, criminals and brigands. Real-life pirates. Anubis ran a syndicate. Each ship was its own gang that worked with the base. It was foolish to think things worked any other way.

How would I run things? I turned the idea over in my head. Could you run a smuggler's den by respect, rather than force and fear? For that matter, how would I run my own ship?

Sophie waved her hand in front of my eyes. "Marky? Hello?"

Blinking, I returned my attention to the room and realized several moments had passed. "Sorry. Distracted by... possibilities."

"Possibilities for..." She prompted.

"Not fully formed," I said, still staring at nothing.

"Marky "

"I'll tell you about it later."

***

I was still mulling things over when the captain knocked on my door. "Suit up. It's time to go see the big dog."

"Aye, aye, ma'am." I beat feet down to the armory to suit up. My new nano-weave armor had been delivered.

It looked good. Shiny, new, and black, it wouldn't impress a veteran marine, but it did wonders for my self-esteem.

In the forward lock, I was expecting to see the captain and Sara. The captain was there, but in Sara's place, I found Trent and Tracy.

Of course, I thought to myself. No offense to Sara, but I felt better with my bodyguards by my side, especially as they'd just saved my life. We were soon tromping down the halls toward Anubis's offices. I kept an eye out for anything suspicious, but nothing was out of the ordinary. It was strange that I felt better once we got to the antechamber and we only had to keep an eye on one disreputable thug.

Like last time, we were kept waiting for about forty-five minutes.

When they finally let us in, Anubis was behind his desk and one of his security guards was pointing. "You see. There he is here and again here. He's our guy."

"A shame," said Anubis. "He was a good middleman. Please send Aziz around to dispose of the trash. Tell him to make it public. We need to send a message with this one. No one makes smuggling deals on *Ocelot* unless we get our cut."

The guard nodded and exited.

"Well, Captain Houston, ready to reach for the stars again?"

"You know I am. What have you got for me, old dog?"

Anubis tapped a few keys on the console. "I have two jobs suited for your ship and crew. We have a load of Shine going to Mitas's Star and medical supplies going to Freya."

"Freya," she answered without preamble.

He arched an eyebrow in her direction. "Mitas will pay three times as much."

"The way I see it, the choice is between sneaking illegal drugs past the Confederation or sneaking legal drugs into a war zone. Freya will pay plenty enough to bandage their troops."

He waved a hand. "Suit yourself. I'll send over the details."

Another guard waited to show us out. Anubis stopped us when we reached the door. "Mark. Did you get the notice I sent you?"

I looked him in the eye, trying to get the depth of the man. Nothing. He seemed dead inside. "Yeah, Reggie. I got the bill. It's already paid."

"Oh good," he said, like it was the most pleasant thing he'd heard all day. "Bon voyage."

***

Back on the ship, Rafe found me getting out of the armor.

"Here you go, sir. The AIs are 10,000 credits each."

That was too expensive. "Why so much?"

He shrugged. "A couple of reasons. First, we're in the middle of fricking nowhere. Second, these are brand new Falkenburg EX12s."

Top of the line. Damn, he was good. "Okay, done. What about the grenade?"

He handed me the marble-sized weapon. "Ten credits. They're more popular here than I thought and I was able to get a good deal

213

on it. Pirates use them for boarding actions. Not everyone can afford good armor. This will shut down any but the latest models."

"Great Rafe, you're a life saver." I instructed my AI to transfer the credits.

CHAPTER 36: PLANNING

The cargo was loaded and we were on our way in a couple of days.

I should have felt better that we were underway. Instead, I felt exhausted. Thoughts chased themselves around inside my head. Anytime I was not on watch, I thought about what it would take to take a disorganized bunch of miscreants and make them into a resistance movement. I'd been spending so much time getting used to the crew and surviving one scrape after another, I had missed the big picture.

Yale. Home. My dad. That's what mattered.

Jay and I were in Cargo Bay Two. Sometimes things shifted or came loose in transit. Aasha had asked Jay to check on it every week. Inspecting each of the four holds took forever, so Jay had asked me to help him out.

"Do you think it's a waste of time to check all these straps and latches?" asked Jay.

I chuckled. "No. I was delivering a bunch of heavy mechs over an ocean once. The wind came up and jostled us a bit. Turns out, one of the mechs wasn't tied down properly. Next thing I know, my cargo master is yelling and my transport is nosing down and to starboard. There was a rolling crash I can't begin to describe. The cabin door busts open, and I'm spending some quality time with part of a crate."

Jay's eyes were wide. "Whoa."

"The bulkhead stopped the cargo from exiting through the

cockpit. I righted the transport and completed the mission. That loose container killed two crew members and injured the cargo master. It nearly doomed us all." I smiled at Jay. "So yeah, I think it's important. No wind out here, but we get shot at."

"I'll be extra careful then." A crate caught his attention and his head tilted as he studied it. "What the..."

I joined him. "Something?"

"There's a small box strapped to this container. It's not part of the shipment."

The thought struck me that it might be a bomb or something put there by our spy. "Is it attached to the crate?"

"No, it's loose." He pulled it out and grabbed the lid.

"Don't..." Too late, he'd already unsealed it a centimeter. If it had been trapped, it would have already gone off.

"What?" He asked.

I took a deep breath and let it out. "Nothing. What's inside?"

The box had a dozen vials of Easy with droppers. "Oh my." I said, "Unless I'm mistaken, that's the latest date rape drug. The captain would string up anyone she found with this."

"Not before she keelhauled them first in a leaky space suit." Jay pursed his lips, "There's gotta be about $4,000 credits worth."

Just then we heard two people come into the cargo hold. They weren't trying to be quiet. It wasn't hard to figure out who they were.

War 'n Pace stepped around the corner and froze.

"Oh shit," said Pace Jones.

I smiled. "Gentlemen. I'm going to do you a favor. I'm not going to tell the captain I found this."

Dave Warren's lips twitched up nervously. "Uh, thanks, sir?"

"Don't thank me yet." I held up the box, "This is going out the airlock."

"Fuck," they said in unison.

***

I dropped by engineering and found Rowdy and Randy's legs sticking out from under a piece of equipment. Racy was sitting on a table not far away, working on her tablet.

"*Crava monk crid,*" Rowdy said, sticking his hand out.

I walked across the room and handed him a wrench from the

pile of tools nearby.

"*Daka.*"

"You're welcome," I replied.

"Mark?" came the muffled question.

"Finish what you're doing, Rowdy," I said, crossing to look over Racy's shoulder. "I want to talk to you, but it isn't urgent."

Rowdy grunted a response.

The code on Racy's tablet wasn't anything I recognized. "What is that?"

She didn't stop typing as she shrugged. "AI code."

"Your personal AI?"

"No," she said, shaking her head. "It's a copy of *Leo*. I'm smartening him up a bit."

"To..." I prompted.

"To be better at questioning her orders."

"Um." I wasn't sure how to broach the topic. Giving an AI too much of the ability to make its own decisions might be a bad idea. "Racy, I don't think we should be letting *Leo* choose which of our orders he wants to follow."

She waved a hand. "Not everywhere or anyone. He won't be able to countermand orders given on the bridge or in engineering. He'll also have to follow orders given by the four senior officers. Oh, and me of course." She gave me a toothy, canine grin.

That made me feel better. I wasn't worried about Jenna or Rowdy. Sara could be difficult, but it came from a genuine desire to protect the ship. "Have you told the captain?"

Her big brown eyes looked up at me with feigned innocence. "I'll get around to it." She returned her attention to the code. "I'll have *Leo* log each command order he follows, who gave it, and where. I'll also ask him to keep track of any orders he didn't follow."

"You think someone is using *Leo*'s AI to cover their tracks," I said.

She waggled her head from side to side. "Or has a purpose-built AI helping them out. It wouldn't be too hard to hide. You could fit one inside of something the size of a small suitcase. It'd be heavy, though."

That got my brain moving. "I could pull up everyone's mass records." Then another thought occurred to me. "Maybe not. I bet all the crew do private trade and the marines have lots of heavy equipment. If they're as smart as this guy appears to be, it wouldn't even be under his personal mass allotment. He'd have booked it to the ship, engineering, or some other place where it's harder to track."

"So we keep track of access and ask *Leo* to flag anything that looks suspicious." Racy eyed a piece of code on the screen.

"How do you tell a machine to look for something suspicious? Isn't that a pretty big intuitive leap?"

Racy pointed at some characters on the screen. "That's the hard part, pointing *Leo* in the right direction. AIs are like idiot savants. They crunch numbers and learn patterns better than most beings, but nuances escape them. How do we define someone who just wants some privacy as being different from someone out for mischief?"

"Tell *Leo* to watch Rafe." I snorted, "That boy is always up to something." He'd gotten me exactly what I'd asked for: two AI implants and a pinch grenade.

Rowdy approached from the reactor, wiping his hands on an oily rag. "What can I help you with Raw'osida?"

I was momentarily speechless as I translated his meaning. "Rowdy, did you just call me your brother?"

The three of them looked at me solemnly. The side of Rowdy's mouth curled up. "I did. What did you come to speak to me about?"

"Well, Rowdy Martin," I said, returning the honor, "I wanted to ask you if you'd help me lay another trap for our saboteur."

"What did you have in mind?" His expression became more feral as he exposed his sharp teeth in a grin.

"I have something that will disrupt hardened electronics within a small, confined area. A pinch grenade."

All the fidgetiness I associated with Muscat came to a halt and Rowdy became laser focused. "Destroy or disable?"

"Disable. I don't just want the guy responsible. I want the one pulling the strings. I want to tear apart their gear and find out where it came from. I want someone to question when we catch the bastard." I slapped the table for emphasis.

"Destroying things is easier, but I get your point. How big an area?" His eyes were in motion and I could almost feel the determined energy rolling off him.

"About three meters. The device is small. I want to put it in my old wrist AI casing. I have a new one. Can it be done?"

He chewed on his bottom lip. "You'll want it to look like it's working. I'll need a few hours."

"Sounds good."

***

Running up the ladder to officer country, I had the feeling I had just missed someone in the corridor. I heard footsteps receding at the other end of the passage, but no one was there.

I entered my quarters and sat at my desk. Reaching to turn on my console, I noticed there was a small dent near the base. When I touched it, it moved.

I got a cold feeling in the pit of my stomach. How long had it been there? "*Leo?*"

"Yes, Lieutenant Martin?" The AI's calm voice issued from a speaker next to the door.

"Please ask Racy to come to my quarters."

"Of course. Notifying Raw'scadi of your request."

Racking my brain, I tried to think of what, if any, of my thoughts or plans I'd recorded on the console.

Racy knocked on the doorframe as she came in and stood next to my leg. "What's up, Mark?"

"That," I said, pointing to the dent.

"The bump in the casing? What about it?" She bent to inspect it. Like me, she touched the nub and it moved. "Oh."

She used her wrist AI to analyze the bump. "It's a thumb slaver. Hackers use them to take over computers. I'll need to scan your console to see if it's done more than just copy all of your files."

"Remote access?"

She tapped her tablet a couple more times. "Looks like. Broadcast transmission. No telling where on the ship it could be." Another couple of taps. "Let's see how clever they are. I'm going to copy their codes. See if we can counterhack."

There was a soft pop, and then the smell of burnt electronics. Where there was a bump, now there was a scorch mark on the casing.

"Well, scrut! Sorry, Mark."

"Not your fault, Racy. Any way to tell what they got?"

She shook her head. "What do you keep here?"

I thought about it for a few minutes before answering. "Ship's logs, astrogation information, and readiness reports mostly. Useful information to anyone trying to find us and determine how much military force it would take over the ship, but nothing planet shattering. Most of the crew could reason that out for themselves without much effort." Another thought struck me. Notes. I'd made a lot of notes about motivations, manpower, and resources. Was there anything in there about my long-term plans? Yes, but since it was all a bit vague in my head, it would be vague there too.

"Mark?" Racy tugged on my pant leg.

"Sorry. There were some notes about different planets, ships, and command structures. Notes about what systems do what, produce what. That sort of thing." I wasn't ready to trust anyone with my half-baked plan. Yet. "What can we do to prevent this in the future?"

Her nose twitched like it did when she was thinking very hard about something. "We can set it up so that the console alerts your personal AI every time someone asks for information. If we do that, I'd like to add some features to it to smarten it up a bit."

I trusted Racy, but when you give an AI the ability to make independent decisions, there is always a risk. "Okay, but give me the chance to say yes or no for each skill."

She gave me a wolfish smile. "What? You don't trust me?"

"You tell the captain you were messing with *Leo*'s AI?"

"Touché."

"When it comes to systems and security, I trust you completely," I said, "but the personal AI will live in my head. I just want to be well informed."

"Okay. I'll let you pick and choose, but I'm going to suggest that you give it some autonomy to protect you. You know why Muscat combat armor is the best, right?"

"Self-healing nano-fibers, 50,000 target tracking, and multi-level threat processing?"

"That helps," she conceded, "but it's because machines think faster than flesh and blood beings. Muscat marines know to trust their equipment. The soldiers don't second guess the combat AI in the middle of a firefight."

"You ever hear of the Second Mars Massacre?"

She gave me an odd look. "No. Mars is one of the Terran colonies right?"

"Right. The Martians were technophiles. In the early days of Terran exploration, they relied heavily on AIs. There were a lot of machines that kept them alive on newly terraformed worlds," I said. "No one knows what started it. The AI that ran the life support and construction equipment turned on them. Every man, woman, and child was killed. The first two search and rescue teams were slaughtered before they figured out it was the AI that was the problem."

"Oh." Her hand went to her mouth. "How many people died?"

"Twenty thousand. It shocked and horrified a generation of Terran explorers. Any advanced civilization needs AIs to function. Humans developed a policy of limiting what decisions an AI could make on its own. It's the reason why the AI that runs the ship can't fire the weapons."

"But your computers talk to each other," Racy pointed out. "Are you afraid they'll gang up on you or something?"

"No." I shook my head. "We also build in limited purview. The weapons AI only thinks about defending the ship. The operations AI only thinks about running light, heat, and water. That sort of thing."

"That's why the *Leo*'s ops AI is so dumb about internal threats. It was never designed to talk to the weapons, engineering, and navigation computers except on a limited basis."

"Huh." I thought. "I guess I never considered that a weakness." I picked the coin out of my pocket and started rubbing it.

Racy nodded in satisfaction. "That explains a lot and gives me a starting point. By the way, what's with the coin?"

I looked down at the bit of metal in my hand. "That's a long story."

"Tell me," she prompted.

I took a deep breath. "With modern tech, Terrans can live a long time. My great-grandfather, the one who used to be king, I knew him when I was a kid. On my twelfth birthday, he sits me down and shows me this coin." I held it up for her to see. "He asks me, 'You know what I miss most about being king?'

"'What?' I asked.

"'The people,' he said, 'I love our people. They are the most creative and caring men and women in all of creation. Yale produces the best singers, actors, engineers, and scientists in the known universe. It was my job to protect them. I loved that job.

Your mother was one of those scientists. She was a fine woman. Your father was lucky to have her.

"'The Monarchy is gone.' He tells me, 'We're a Republic now, but you want to know what?' He touched me on the nose, 'Monarchies never die. Even after I was no longer king, I cared for my people. My son, your grandfather, he loved them as much as I do. Your father, too. Yale is special, and it needs good people to protect it.

"'You,' he says, 'were born to do great things. To protect your people from harm.' He opened my hand and put this coin into it. 'One day it will be your turn to be the shield our people need. I know that when that day comes, you will have the strength, the wisdom, to do what needs to be done. Can you do that for me?'

"And I told him I would." I let Racy hold the coin. She saw the image of my great-grandfather and flipped it over and saw the sun on the back. "He told me I would be the leader our people needed. The burning sun that would guide them."

She handed it back to me.

"Anyway," I put the coin back in my pocket, "I rub the coin whenever I get nervous or scared. I rub it to get the wisdom of my father and great-grandfather, and all the kings before him. I want it to rub off on me, and help me make the right decisions.

Racy stood close to me and put her hands on mine. "I'll help you. You're my family now. Your responsibilities are mine too. I'll start with this." She pointed to the computer. "I'll have a patch for your console by the end of the watch."

***

Two days later, I was getting ready for my watch. I had just gotten up and was padding my way to the head when someone grabbed me from behind.

They put something over my head and pressed me against the bulkhead. A second person pulled my arms behind my back.

I tried to yell, but the first sound earned me an elbow to the skull. I saw stars as I was half dragged, half carried down the corridor.

Stomping, I tried to catch one of their feet. I must have made contact. There was a yelp and my head was slammed into the wall again.

I jerked from side to side, trying to hit one of their heads with mine.

One more shove sent me sprawling.

CHAPTER 37: STICKS

Sticks. I was tangled in a bunch of sticks.

I pulled the bag from my head and rubbed my sore arms while I looked around myself. I found myself in the broom closet next to the head. There was only a little light coming from under the closed door. I reached for the light panel.

Nothing happened. I hit it again, and still, there was no light. Grabbing the handle, I pushed the door. The handle didn't budge and neither did the door.

"You sons of bitches." Speaking brought something sticky and salty into my mouth. Great, I was bleeding too. I grabbed my wrist AI, intending to use it for light and to call for help, only to find that it had been removed.

I pounded my head on the door. "Well played." Installing the internal AI was a much higher priority now.

I sat in the darkness and silence of the broom closet and waited. Someone would be along soon, and I'd get help.

About twenty minutes later I heard soft footsteps in the corridor.

"Hey!" I yelled and pounded on the door. "Can someone get me out of here?"

"Mark?" I heard Randy's voice say. "What are you doing in the broom closet?"

"Someone stuffed me in here on the way to the head. Can you get the door open?"

"Yeah, give me a minute." I heard him try the handle. "They've jammed the handle. It'll take just a moment. I have your AI. It was lying on the floor across the passage."

"Thanks."

Ten seconds later there was a loud snap and the door opened. Randy stood less than a foot away, examining me.

"You've got a bump on your head and a small cut on your lip," he observed. "I'd ask who it was, but I think I know the answer."

"Yeah," I confirmed. "It must have been War 'n Pace. I think I got a piece of one of their feet. Check to see if one of them is limping."

"And if they are?" Randy prompted.

"With a little help from you and Racy, I think our ship is going to get a visit from little green aliens."

***

As I arrived on the bridge for my shift, Ms. Chew glanced at me. "What happened to you?"

"A disagreement with a broom closet," I responded. "The closet won, but I gave as good as I got."

"Okay," she drew out the last syllable. "You ready to stand watch?"

"Yeah."

"The ship is on course and on target, Mr. Martin. You may have the watch."

"I relieve you, Ms. Chew. I have the watch," I intoned.

I saw Wally relieve Natalia, and we settled down to business.

About half an hour later there was a chirp from my AI. The message was from Randy.

Pace got his foot wrapped in medical. Your sister said he grinned a lot for someone who had dropped a crate on himself.

I typed a quick response. *Operation little green men is a go.*

Got it.

A few minutes later, my AI chirped again.

"You're a popular man tonight, sir," Wally mused from the helm.

"I could do with a little less attention, Mr. Walachek." I looked at the AI to find a message from the captain. She was scheduling a strategy session for the next day.

***

"Okay, people," the captain began. "First, does anyone know who reprogrammed the marine berthing showers?"

Everyone looked at each other and shrugged.

The captain continued. "Someone rigged the showers to spray a copper oxide solution. It's only affected Dave Warren and Pace Jones so far. The green color won't wash off though, so those showers are off limits until Randy has a chance to fix them."

"Next order of business. We have bandages for delivery to Freya."

In truth, it was medical scanners, medi-nano, artificial blood, and the like, but we got the point.

"We'll pop the bubble about a light hour outside of the system." The captain pointed to the screen. "The Hedgehogs haven't had time to bring much here, and Freya has more than a dozen cruisers and battleships. The expectation is that we'll find a few Erethizon ships near the gate and near the planet. Nothing we can't pussyfoot around."

"They have a space station," said Sara. "Is that where we're going to deliver?"

"That's the plan." The captain brought up a representation of the system on the conference room wall. "After we get the lay of the land. We go in full stealth. Once we're within ten thousand klicks of the station, pop goes the weasel, and we scare the hell out of the locals. Ask for a slip, drop off the owwie kisses, pick up our load of frozen Hildis steaks, gemstones, and Violet Monkeys, and be on our way."

"Violet Monkeys?" asked Sophie. "We're carrying drugs back to *Ocelot*?"

"The dried flowers. Not processed. I'm sure I don't need to remind you that Violet Monkeys can be made into more than just aphrodisiacs."

Sophie narrowed her eyes at the captain but didn't pursue it.

"Well," said Aasha, "Let's not get them mixed up. We don't need oversexed, genetically modified pigs with big stones running around the ship."

"What?" I offered. "Your marines don't want the competition?"

Aasha stuck her tongue out at me.

***

"Okay, Mark. What do you see?" My sister had just woken me up from a medically induced sleep.

"Medical bay, Racy, and some girl who's putting on weight now that she's snogging the cook."

"I have needles and I will use them." My sister scowled at me with mock fierceness. "Okay Racy, fire it up."

The diagnostics showed in the bottom right of my vision. "It's doing the startup routine. Self-checks. Okay, it says it's ready."

"Mark, send me a test message," asked Racy.

Not one to walk when I could run, I thought clicked and sent her the words to one of the songs she liked. "How's that?"

"Good." She grinned. "What's our current distance from Freya?"

"0.82 parsecs." The *Leo*'s AI supplied my personal AI with the data.

"Next question," said Racy. "What is the square root of 458,962?"

"677.4673. Okay, that's cool." My mind could now do its own math or ask the personal AI to do it for me.

"Last one. What's the solar mass of Freya's primary?"

"1.8," I answered.

"What did you ask him?" asked Sophie.

It was then that I realized Racy had asked the last question in Muscat, and I had answered in the same language. "Oh, that's stellar. Does it translate Erethizon and Dru too?"

"Yes," she answered with a grin.

"Okay you two, scoot. I need to get Jay down here," said Sophie.

"What for?"

"To install mine, too. I can't wait to download medical texts without having to read every line."

***

I nodded to Boldrini as I got into the mess line. Rafe was serving.

"Sir, I thought you were getting that thing replaced?" Rafe was pointing to the AI unit on my arm.

I shrugged. "I haven't had time. I'll get around to it. It isn't a priority. If I upgrade now, I'll have to reload a ton of files and teach it to predict my commands." I shook my head. "The cargo drops need my attention now. I'll fix it after the mission."

Aasha slipped into line behind me and punched me in the arm. "What are you afraid of, a little work?"

I grinned at her. "Only so many hours in the day. I suppose I could get it installed, but I'd have to forego our... workouts."

She bit her lip and wiggled suggestively. "You'd better wait. I want you in good shape for Freya."

"And I'm not in good shape now?"

"Guys!" Rafe exclaimed, "I got people to feed. Take it to a table." He pointed his chin in the direction of the engineering crew. Rowdy, Racy, and Randy waved us over.

Walking over to the table, I wondered why I hadn't told Aasha the truth. We'd been seeing each other for months. I'd replaced the AI days ago. The one on my arm looked like it was working, displays and all. The fact that it was a booby trap that would explode on command had unnerved me a little, but Rowdy insisted that it was completely safe.

I bumped Aasha's hip playfully with my own as we walked to the table. She smiled in response and gave me a wink. It wasn't important. Maybe I'd tell her later.

***

We came out of our R-drive bubble a little short of our one light hour target.

"Mr. Martin, what does the system look like?"

"Just a moment, Captain," I said as the data started flowing in. "Oh, you've got to be freaking kidding me."

"Mr. Martin?"

"We've got Porcu-bears in-system, Captain," translated Sara. "I believe what has Mr. Martin so riled up is the three Erethizon destroyers outside of the system about forty light minutes from us."

"More data coming in," I continued. The AI identified more of the system in a steadily growing radius. "The system gate still appears to be contested. The Freyans have two battleships and a couple of cruisers staring down a cruiser and two frigates."

A few minutes later the inner system resolved itself on the display. "And the hits keep coming. The Freyans have two battleships and three cruisers for planet defense. The Porcu-bears have two more cruisers. What I don't see is a space station. There's a debris cloud where it should be."

CHAPTER 38: BETRAYAL

"Well," said Jenna, "this cargo won't deliver itself. Full stealth. Set course for planetary intercept."

I started the calculations. "So, we deliver planet-side?"

"Looks like."

Wally echoed my thoughts. "I hope it goes better than Yale."

"Incoming message from the Erethizon blockade, Captain. General broadcast, repeating automatically. They don't know we're here. Message is as follows: 'This is Commander Grova. *Leonard Fox*, please cease your terrorist actions and turn over our rightful property.'"

***

With stealth engaged, we had no trouble sneaking past the picket. What was troubling, however, was that Grova knew where to park to be in the best position to catch us. It was an unpleasant reminder that we had a spy on board and I still had no idea who it could be.

Days later, we were light minutes out from Freya.

"*Leo*," said the captain, "bounce a communication laser off the lead battleship in the Freyan formation. Give them our location so we can talk."

"Link established." The AI responded a moment later. "Response lag is one minute fifty seconds. Transponder indicates the battleship is the *Loki*."

"Attention *Loki*. This is Captain Jennifer Houston of the freighter *Leonard Fox*. We have your medical supplies, but it looks like the hedgehogs have crashed the shindig. How would you like to handle the delivery?"

"*Leonard Fox*, this is Captain Sven Borgar of the *Loki*. We are very happy to hear from you. Please transmit your ident code."

"*Leo*, if you would be so kind."

"Of course, Captain," the AI responded. "Identification code sent."

Jenna grunted. "Racy's been messing with the AI again. It's acting more like crew and less like a computer."

"That would be a safe assumption, ma'am," I offered.

"Thanks, *Leonard Fox*," Borgar's voice crackled through. "Providing meeting location now."

The planetary nav beacons showed up on my screen and I nodded to the captain.

"Thanks, *Loki*. Safe voyage."

"Ma'am," I asked, "why are we meeting them so far off the beaten path?"

"Just bein' safe. The Hedgehogs like to pretend to be merchant freighters. They send 'em down with troops or a few fighters. Detonate drives or a whole rack of missiles on bases. Anything to get a few soldiers to buy the farm."

"Clever. Where do you want to set down?" I brought up a map on the display. "Here in this depression? It's pretty close to the three delivery spots."

"No. Too obvious and I bet that depression was caused by a Hedgehog crust buster. No sense tempting lighting to strike twice. Here." She pointed to a cliff.

"That's gotta be a park or something." I traced a nearby road. "It's also less than two miles from a town. Not a big town, but still."

"Exactly what we need," said the captain. "We can send in a squad of marines to borrow some transports. Boldrini, Rowdy, and your sister can go in for supplies. When the mission is done we can let the boys and girls have some R&R before we head out. What do you think, Sara?"

"About 25,000 people. They should have a couple of supermarkets, a clinic, an electronics depot, and a dozen bars." She nodded. "Yes, ma'am. That should be fine."

"All right, Wally." I pointed at a large clearing with picnic tables off to one side. "Set us down here, as close to that rock face as you're comfortable with."

***

Wally set us down about six meters from the cliff, an amazing feat. There were large trees on one side of the ship and a rock overhang on the other. The captain was right: it was a good hiding spot.

The marines had begged, borrowed, or stolen three transports in short order. Other marines in powered armor were loading them with the cargo. The captain had called a meeting in the main conference room.

"All right people. It's payday, but we have to earn it. That means three delivery teams."

She called up a slide on the screen. "Team one will be with Ms. Chew. Harrison, you and your squad are with her." The next slide was a map with a red line marking the route. "You're going to this warehouse district in New Keflavik."

The captain pulled up the next slide. "Jay will lead team two. Trent, your squad is with him."

"Ma'am," interrupted Jay, "I've never run a drop before. Shouldn't you or Mr. Martin be running it?"

"Jay," said the captain, "you've been with me on nine drops. You've seen me do it plenty. I'm sending Trent's squad with you. You've seen them drill, you know what they're capable of. You can do it."

"If you say so, ma'am." Jay didn't look convinced.

"You're going to a strip mall in Selfoss. You'll take the highway most of the way."

"That brings us to team three." The team popped up on the screen and I closed my eyes, knowing what was coming next.

"Ma'am," Trent began, "if the second mate is making a drop, I respectfully suggest that my team would be the best one to be his back up." His tone was respectful, but I could see his jaw clench and the fur rise on the back of his neck. He was gearing up for a fight.

"Have you ever delivered contraband, Trent?" asked the captain.

"No, ma'am, but..."

"But nothing. I'm sending Mr. Martin in with Ms. Gudka. He needs to learn how it's done and Aasha has run more than a dozen operations like this. And before you suggest it, no I'm not going to split your squad. The whole point is to keep the people used to working together, in the same herd."

Trent's mouth snapped shut. His eyes burned, but he accepted his orders without further comment.

The tense silence stretched out for a moment more before the captain pulled up the last slide. "You're going to a reclamation plant in Hella. Any questions?"

No one said anything.

"Good." She continued, "Rowdy, Dr. Martin, Boldrini, I want each of you to head into town and pick up any supplies we need. Divide up the last squad, but I want two marines on board at all times."

"I'll stay," said Boldrini. "I need to check what's available and run up menus. I won't know what to put in the larder until that's done."

The captain grunted in response. "Okay, cowpokes. Lets round 'em up and head 'em out."

***

The other two trucks had left and my squad was finishing loading ours. It was about a hundred yards from the ship to the parking lot where the transport was and they were bringing the last of the medical supplies.

The AI in my head pinged, followed by the voice of the *Leo*'s AI. "Mr. Martin, I've discovered something odd in the message traffic."

"Have you contacted Racy about it?"

"Ms. Raw'scadi and Mr. Raw'noriede, are not within secure communication range. Ms. Raw'scadi left explicit instructions to contact you if she was unavailable."

I bit my lip. "Okay, transfer it to me. I'll review it while we're on our mission."

"Of course, Mr. Martin."

Aasha walked up, grinning at me. "Talking to yourself?"

"I hear it's only a problem if you're surprised by the answers."

"Ha! Don't worry, flyboy." She bumped her hip with mine. "I'll take good care of you. We're ready whenever you are."

We boarded the ground transport and were soon rumbling down the road. It occurred to me that I didn't know any of my marine squad, except Aasha. I knew them by face, but not any of their names. If Aasha trusted them, it was good enough for me. I put it out of my mind.

On the way, I reviewed what the *Leo* had sent me. It appeared to be something about the message traffic to and from the ship each time we made port. The AI had discovered odd sounds in some messages it couldn't identify.

I started reviewing the messages and tried to pick it out. The AI was right: there was some additional noise in the lower bands. I was still puzzling over what that might mean when we reached the reclamation plant.

You couldn't have picked a creepier place to meet. There were a few lights around the yard, scattered and dim. Piles of junked aircars, construction supports, and appliances hulked everywhere, technology at the end of its useful life, now only metal to be reclaimed.

We pulled up to a cleared area in the middle of the junkyard. Sure enough, I could just make out soldiers here and there in the shadows, leaning against the refuse.

We stopped the transport and climbed out. My marines, under Aasha's direction, spread out and joined the local men at the perimeter. I approached the guy leaning against the other transport. He looked like he must be in charge.

It was dark, so it wasn't until I got up close that I realized something was wrong. Half his face had been blown away.

I started to yell a warning to my men when I felt the barrel of a rifle against the back of my neck.

"See?" Aasha hissed. "I told you I'd take good care of you, flyboy."

CHAPTER 39: IT ENDS

I didn't move. Instead, I mentally clicked the emergency signal on my implant, for all the good it would do. We were four hours away from the ship and another two from either of the other teams. It would all be over before any help came. I thought about going for my pistol, but every scenario I thought of ended with me dead.

"Don't even think about it, flyboy. You couldn't even on your best day. Avery, please relieve the second mate of his weapon and his wrist AI."

Avery took my pistol and unclasped my wristband. Aasha forced me down to my knees. Around me, Porcu-bear soldiers in powered armor joined the marines of Aasha's unit. Aasha didn't know about my new AI implants, but I didn't know how that was going to help me now.

"Hands laced behind your head. Good boy."

"Voice modulator. You coded your messages for all to hear in the outgoing message traffic. Damn, if I had only discovered it earlier."

"Well done," Aasha said from behind me. "You get high marks for figuring that out. Now sit still until Grova gets here for you."

"Grova is on-planet for me? I'm flattered."

"You should be. He's high up in the secret police. He must have big plans for you and your sister."

Seething, I tried to come up with some way to buy time. The only thing I could think of was to keep Aasha talking.

"All this time I was looking for one spy, when I should have been looking for six." I shook my head ruefully.

"Not exactly. It will all become clear when you reach Enlightenment."

"Which will be soon." Grova emerged from behind a pile of aircars. He addressed Aasha in Erethizon. My AI translated for me: "You have the daughter?"

Aasha responded in flawless Porcu-bear. "Yes. I sent four of your operatives to intercept her group. The two men with her will be no match."

My sister. They would get her, too.

"Good. How did you get rid of the tree rats?"

"The captain is gullible," she said. "I convinced her it would be better if they were in the second team."

I felt sick. If only we had known. If only we had suspected.

"Success," he said. "And for your mission as well. After you sabotage the shield generators on this planet, it will be time to station you on a new Terran freighter. Is everything ready?"

Aasha had been late getting back from her delivery on Yale. She had been the one who sabotaged the shields. My heart sank. It was happening again—to another world, another people.

"Yes, sir. I have the trigger here. It will override the safeties and dump all the fuel into the reactor. It will go critical. They'll never know what hit them."

That was it. Checkmate. They were going to wait until everyone got back and blow up the ship. Everyone I'd met since leaving home. My friends. The captain, Racy, Rowdy, Wally. All dead. Their lives would end as their home became a dirty bomb. The size of the explosion would depend on how much radioactive fuel was left. Nothing within a mile would survive.

Grova switched back to Terran. "On your feet, Mr. Martin. Time for you to join your family."

"My family, my planet, will never serve the Theocracy, Grova," I said it with conviction, but I knew the Erethizon were good at breaking people.

Grova's bearlike eyes narrowed over his snout. He showed me his teeth and his fetid breath washed over me. "You won't have a choice. You belong to the One True Way now. We own you, body and soul." He hauled me roughly to my feet.

I was still frantically thinking of a way out. He didn't know I had an implant either. I couldn't think of a way it could help, but there must be something. Could I use it to hang on to my sanity during torture and brainwashing? No, they'd discover it and rip it out of my skull.

I closed my eyes and stood still. It wasn't much, but I wasn't going to go quietly.

Grova grabbed me by the neck with one hand. His hands were so large that his fingers met over my Adam's apple. My vision tunneled as I grabbed at his hand with mine. Stupid. My right hand hit the quills on the back of his, and I felt them sink into my flesh. I would have cried out if he hadn't been choking the life out of me.

My brain starved for air. I was going to pass out. The last thing I would see would be the message at the bottom of my vision: *We are here.*

***

The hand let up just enough for me to gulp a lungful of air.

"I'd prefer not to carry you to the transport, Mr. Martin, but it would only be a minor inconvenience. Please don't do that again."

We are here. We are here.

"Grova. My wrist AI. There's something on it you should see."

"What?"

What's on it? What will make him want to take a look? I sent a text message back. *When hell breaks loose.*

The hand clutching my neck didn't let up. "Information about the exile fleet. The resistance. I discovered something about them before we left *Ocelot*. Let my sister go, and I'll show it to you."

"Aasha?"

Behind me, I heard, "Maybe. He spent time with Anubis. He's a crafty son of a monkey."

"Bring me his wrist computer."

Grova set me down and turned me to face him. "How do I access it?"

"It's password protected," I said.

"What's the password, Terran?"

I squeezed my eyes closed and ducked my head. It had seemed appropriate to use Pythia's words as the passcode. "When hell breaks loose." Then the wrist computer—which wasn't a wrist computer at all—exploded.

***

Duck.

Pythia's words came back to me and I hit the deck.

Someone hit my head hard on the way down and I blacked out for a moment. It must not have been long because the crack of rifle fire and the ringing in my ears brought me back. Who was shooting? I put my hand to my head where it hurt and felt the skin split there.

Blood, but I wasn't dead. Move!

Next to me, Grova lay on the ground unmoving. I grabbed his sidearm, an ELP10 laser pistol. Simple to use: two firing studs pressed at the same time.

I was in battle. Had to find cover. It was a reclamation yard. Cover was everywhere if I could reach it. The transport the Freyans had used was closest and I dove for it.

Sitrep. The fire was coming from the way we'd come into the yard. There were two Porcu-bears and three Terrans returning fire from a pile of rusted I-beams on the other side. Aasha was one of them. She had a good defensive position, but I was on her flank. I could get one good shot before they'd be able to force me under cover.

Aasha. The way she'd played me. She played everyone and destroyed everything. Aasha, who had turned on her own species. I'd take her out.

I took careful aim and saw her whip her rifle in my direction. She'd seen me. She was faster than me. I'd lost my chance.

Invisible light bored into her head. Her finger on the trigger. Her rifle on full auto aiming at me. If she was going to get me, I was taking her with me.

But she didn't. She missed. I ducked under cover. Rounds slammed into the transport.

I waited for my next chance, but an eternity later, thirty seconds real time. It was over.

The shooting stopped and I poked my head out. The four remaining defenders were dead.

"Mark?"

"Over here, Trent."

Trent, Trey, and Trippy trotted up to me.

"Tracy on overwatch?" I asked.

"Yes, sir. Over that way."

"Sophie. They set up an ambush for her."

"No, sir." Trent shook his head. "The clinic didn't have what she needed. Dr. Martin went into the dispensary. Next town over. The locals rounded them up."

Trey, the medic, was trying to pull me down so he could get at my head.

I waved him down. "Just a minute. Aasha sabotaged the ship. She got some sort of trigger on her."

"Let's check her out." He turned to his men. "Trippy, you and Trey check these guys out. Make sure no one's playing hesha, pretending to be dead."

I pointed. "Trey, that's Commander Grova. If he's dead, he's dead, but he's worth a lot to us if he's alive."

"Yes, sir!" He ran in that direction, while Trent and I approached Aasha's last stand with weapons ready.

Her rifle was still in her hand so I put my foot on it. Aasha's artificial eyes were a blacked mess where the laser had destroyed them. She looked like her body had been dragged through a meteor shower, with bits of it missing everywhere.

"I don't think she's getting back up again." Said Trent.

"She's a combat augment. They're built to survive. Check out the arm behind her back. She had some sort of trigger device, and we need to find it."

Trent put his boot on her neck and pulled her arm free. There was a cylinder in her hand. I watched in horror as her thumb moved and pressed the button on top.

The sky lit up in the west. I turned and my AI identified where the *Leo* used to be. The same place as the mushroom-shaped cloud was now.

Her mouth spat out words from her wrecked body. "You'll never go home."

Trent and I shot her in the head.

CHAPTER 40: EPILOGUE

"How's it healing?"

My hand went to the cut that ran from above my left eye to the crown of my skull. "Sophie says it will heal without scarring, but I'm not sure I believe her. What do you think, Sara?" I gestured around the spartan room that contained only a desk and three chairs.

She frowned. "I think it's a maglev station."

We had found the abandoned station in Hella. "Think of it as a docked ship."

"I'm trying, but it's still a maglev station."

"We'll fix that. What I need to know is if you still want to fly with me."

She eyed me for a long moment before answering. "Do you have the credits to purchase a ship? And do you really think you can get a master's license?"

"Yes. I can download the data for the exam. I've got enough experience. My contacts on Eureka have been rounding up all of the Yale assets located off-planet. Merchant contracts, mining colonies, bank accounts, all of it. Admiral Norbert said he'd put in a good word for me. Turning over Grova made him happy. If I pass the written test, we should be good. I've been studying since *Ocelot*."

Sara looked me up and down before putting a hand on my shoulder. "Yes, I'll join you."

I offered her my hand. "Welcome aboard."

She gave it a firm shake.

"Well, Captain, we have a bunch of curious crew in the café. By now the rumor mill has them more informed than we are. They should hear what's going on from us." She gestured to the door and we moved out of the room I'd claimed as my office and into the hall.

I raised an eyebrow at her. "Don't you mean the mess?"

"It's a maglev station. I mean café."

***

It was loud in there, but the clamor died down as if by magic when Sara and I walked through the door. A dozen long tables filled the room, boxes of food and large drink bottles stacked at the far end of one of the tables.

Walking up the aisle, I spotted Trent and Jay keeping things organized. "Jay, can you save me a couple of slices of the finach cheese and sun lizard pizza? I'll be hungry after addressing the crew."

"No problem, sir."

The café had been set up for live music with a small stage off to one side. I mounted the stage but chose to stand beside the makeshift podium. Sara stood just behind me and to the left.

"Okay, let's put some rumors to rest." All eyes were on me. "First, you may or may not have heard that Aasha was working for the Porcu-bears."

There was an uproar. Several of the marines shouted at once, War 'n Pace foremost among them.

I made a patting motion with my hands and they subsided. "Trust me. No one was more shocked than me when she put a rifle to my head and told me she was turning me over to the Erethizon. If not for Trent and his team disobeying orders and arriving to save my ass, I'd be on a ship bound for a prison planet right now. As it was, Trent finished his drop in record time and stole an aircar to join me. He left Jay with only Trevor for back up.

"His quick thinking took out the Porcu-bear squad sent to capture me and the traitors with Aasha. We captured the Erethizon officer, Commander Grova, and turned him over to the local authorities.

"Unfortunately, Aasha had booby-trapped the *Leo*. When her

plan came apart, she blew up our ship."

Dead silence. I let it hang there for a moment before I continued. "The captain, Wally, Gina, Natalia, Lavesh, Randy, Boldrini, Rafe, Greg, and Hank were on board when it blew. Sara and I are arranging a memorial service for them in a few days." I found my sister in the crowd. The sadness I felt was mirrored in her face. Rowdy and Racy embraced, looking as bereft as I'd ever seen a Muscat.

"Had Aasha's plan worked, everyone except for her and her traitors would have been on board. She then intended to leave the system with the Porcu-bears, where she'd be assigned to another ship. Kill another crew."

"I'm sure the question on everyone's mind is: what do we do from here? A lot of things are up in the air, but I can tell you this: I am arranging for the purchase of a new ship. I intend to be the captain. Sara has agreed to serve with me. I won't presume to speak for any of you, but I would consider it an honor if you would serve with me too."

The End

.

ABOUT THE AUTHOR

TH Leatherman is a writer from Firestone, Colorado. He enjoys science fiction, fantasy, wine making, and the Rocky Mountain lifestyle. When not busy writing his next book, he can be found hiking with his wife and two sons, or walking his rescued dogs. He graduated Summa Cum Laude from Regis University with a degree in Business Management and a minor in Psychology.

Connect with Mr. Leatherman

Check out his blog and links to other books
https://thleatherman.com/

https://www.facebook.com/TH-Leatherman

@thleatherman on Twitter

Can't get enough stories by TH Leatherman? New chapters of exclusive stories are posted every other week on his Patreon page.
https://www.patreon.com/THLeatherman

Check out TH Leatherman's YouTube Channel for weekly videos. Author interviews, book reviews, and tips for writers.
https://www.youtube.com/channel/UCpB5ygo4EBYzt3V8X XyyrHQ

Reviews!

Authors (especially me) love reviews. Good, bad, or indifferent tell me what you think. You can do it easily on Amazon and Goodreads, but anywhere book lovers congregate is appreciated.

THE BURNING SON